The NOVEMBER CRiMiNALS

The NOVEMBER CRIMINALS

a novel

SAM MUNSON

DOUBLEDAY ■ NEW YORK LONDON TORONTO SYDNEY AUCKLAND

DD

DOUBLEDAY

This book is a work of fiction. Names, characters, businesses, organizations, places, events, and incidents either are the product of the author's imagination or are used fictitiously. Any resemblance to actual persons, living or dead, events, or locales is entirely coincidental.

Copyright © 2010 by Sam Munson

All rights reserved. Published in the United States by Doubleday, a division of Random House, Inc., New York, and in Canada by Random House of Canada Limited, Toronto.

www.doubleday.com

DOUBLEDAY and the DD colophon are registered trademarks of Random House, Inc.

LIBRARY OF CONGRESS CATALOGING-IN-PUBLICATION DATA
Munson, Sam.
The November criminals : a novel / by Sam Munson. — 1st ed.
p. cm.
I. Title.
PS3613.U6936N68 2010
813'.6—dc22
2009016750

ISBN 978-0-385-53227-3

PRINTED IN THE UNITED STATES OF AMERICA

1 2 3 4 5 6 7 8 9 10

FIRST EDITION

For Rebecca

There is no negator who is not famished for some catastrophic yes.

—E. M. CIORAN, *The Trouble with Being Born*

The NOVEMBER CRiMiNALS

I.

You've asked me to explain what my best and worst qualities are. So let me begin by saying that it's hard, ladies and gentlemen, for me to consider myself a bad person. I mean, I experience *qualms*, sometimes more serious and sometimes less. Everyone, even a real champion of immorality, sees himself as good. Or as working for the good, no matter if his actions— looked at one by one—are transparently self-serving, murderous, etc. Kind of a strong argument against the value of terms like *good* or *bad*. People feel this way even now, in 1999, when we're all supposed to be repenting and wailing and gnashing our teeth. But you can't go through life without making any distinctions. And selling small-to-medium amounts of weed to safe, calm rich kids (which I spent much of my spare time these past four years doing) is not a behavior *worth* agonizing over. That would make it seem too important, you know? I don't even need the money.

Nonetheless—judged by my actions—I *am* a bad person. Let's get that clear, so you don't have any misconceptions. For more than one-fifth of my life to date, I was a drug dealer, albeit a minor one, and a client of more successful, higher-volume drug dealers, who are in turn clients of bigger firms, and so on and so on until infinity. Grim, right? Human, but grim. I owned a digital pharmacy scale. An expensive black safe, which at the peak of my prosperity contained $12,380 in four shoe boxes, the cash organized in bundles by denomination. (How lame is that!) A gun, although that was a later acquisition. A suspicious supply of Biggie-brand plastic bags. A pager. All the sordid, dead-giveaway equipment.

I am eighteen years and five days old. I live in a tree-heavy upper-middle-class neighborhood in Washington, D.C., with my father, who makes clay pots. He also teaches classes at our city's semi-renowned art academy, the Cochrane Institute. Classes about how to make clay pots. My name is Addison Schacht, if you can believe it: my dead mother's dead father was named Addison. Because I am an unknown quantity, I am unpopular, even now, my last year, in my class at John F. Kennedy Senior High School. How unknown, you ask? I could not, under pain of death, tell you where a single member of my class wants to attend college, that's how little I have to do with them. I have no extracurricular activities beyond the study of Latin and the collection of offensive jokes about the Holocaust. I live on X Street, on the Xth floor, I weigh X pounds. What do you want? An index of my soul? My dick measurements? I could give them; I'm not *ashamed* or anything. But would they help you understand? This whole involved and stupefying story has been gnawing away at me, though. Which is why I'm writing it. To like *unburden* myself. I've wasted enough time. And I'm not unintelligent; don't think that. On every practice test I took, my scores were identical to what I ended up getting on the real SAT: 770 verbal and 650 math. This is from three sets of results. How's *that* for precision? On my battery of Advanced Placement tests, I scored three fives and two fours. I've got nothing else. Except for one silver and one gold medal on the National Latin Exam. Latin literature is devoid of most human feeling, but I'm still proud of my medals: my teachers have been a goddamn embarrassment.

Selling weed did not figure in my list of permanent plans when I started four years ago, right after I arrived at Kennedy. Just a little, at first. But it was easy, and more challenging than my classwork. It also gave me a foothold in the school's *ecology*, which I wouldn't otherwise have discovered. I didn't think overmuch about it. People wanted it, they came to expect I could provide it, and then I found myself the proprietor of a small but flourishing business. I promised myself that I'd stop when I graduated. Just for practical reasons. And I *did* manage to stop doing it, even before my target date. This was not out of volition. Circumstance played its usual forceful role, in the form of a classmate of mine named Kevin Broadus.

Kevin was this quiet, stocky kid, a marching-band geek. I didn't really know him, except to nod at between classes. And because he was one of the handful of black kids in the Gifted and Talented Program, I was just sort of *aware* of him. At least until our junior year, when, about five months before the brutal events occurred that got his name in the papers, Kevin did something that I found . . . *admirable* is maybe the best word. Or not admirable, because it's presumptuous to admire someone you don't speak to on a regular basis. But uncompromising. It happened in February. Ms. Prather, our English teacher last year, was going on and on in this artificial way about what's called "black history." February, as I'm sure you know, is Black History Month, an occasion of much wariness and nervous self-congratulation among the teachers in the Gifted and Talented Program here at Kennedy. We learn, every year, the same tired story, like a long round in a game: the founders were hypocrites, the Three-Fifths Compromise was bad, the *Dred Scott* decision was bad, Frederick Douglass good, Booker T. Washington bad, Tuskegee Experiment bad, Tuskegee Airmen good, Langston Hughes good, jazz good, and we're all still racists today. Thanks for playing! It's like this compressed version of American history, one that fails to do justice to all the complex nonsense that people get up to in political life, and also fails completely to convey any real sense of how awful life must have been (and in a lot of ways still is) in America for slaves and their descendants. It's like a gesture. I don't know how else to describe it.

So: we were talking about Music and Its Relation to African American Literature. And Ms. Prather was in the spitty middle of her oration about how great it was that African American litera- ture was not *constrained* in the way the other literature of its time was, how it was *filled with a new and vital energy, a rhythmic current.* A lot of the kids in my class nodded along, some of them actually convinced. And after she had reached her crescendo, waving her hands and making her voice throb, after she had her little like orgasm or whatever, she stopped and looked at Kevin and said, "But let's ask our resident musician. Don't you agree, Mr. Broadus?" I wish I could communicate the hideous empty quiet that followed her remark. Everyone craned around in their wooden chair-desk combo sets to stare at Kevin, who gazed at his hands. The afternoon sun slanted down and blanked out his glasses. And he said, "Not particularly." That's all. Ms. Prather stood with her hands lifted and her mouth open. She looked hurt, wobbly-eyed at Kevin's betrayal. The silence persisted. Then Ms. Prather sighed and said, "Well, it's generally *accepted*, Kevin." More silence. Kevin spoke again. "Yeah, but if it's accepted, why did you ask me." Someone spluttered a laugh into cupped hands.

Ms. Prather had literally nothing to say. So she repeated herself. As though Kevin did not exist. And we continued with our lesson. This is the only clear memory I have of Kevin speaking in class. Again, I don't want to presume and call it admirable. But it demonstrated real brassiness of balls, in my opinion. I wanted to congratulate him, but he lost himself among the sighing after-class crowd before I could. It's lucky, I guess: that would have been a kind of presumption, too.

Kennedy is a segregated school, I should mention. Not because black kids are less able or whatever, but because—and I'm *theorizing* here—because my neighborhood and the other neighborhoods that provide it with its white students are filled with the kind of parents who *just love* black people—in the abstract. And Kennedy is majority black, by a considerable margin. And they (the neighborhood parents, I mean) all originally wanted their kids to go to private school, anyway. So all these ex-hippie history and English teachers at Kennedy like twenty years ago set up this little 90 percent white school *inside* Kennedy, the Gifted and Talented Program, and they let in six black kids or so every year to balm their consciences, and set up pantomimes like Black History Month and Diversity Outreach (which is just as horrifyingly inept as its name suggests). Although if they had consciences would they have set up these internal divisions in the first place? But whatever. Kevin stood out because of all these accidents, these circumstances. Through no fault of his own he was visible. He played in the marching band, like I said: baritone saxophone. And he worked after school at Second Mate Stubb's, which is a nationwide chain of coffee shops. Their coffee, their whole scheme, is reliable and mediocre, so the artfucky kids at Kennedy mock Stubb's. Which seems unjust. Reliable mediocrity, I've decided, is the most important thing for the continuation of human existence. We can't get by on Romantic disaster. We would die of exhaustion.

Anyway, it happened at the Stubb's on Wisconsin Avenue, near M Street, where the hump of the avenue dips down toward the soapy-looking grayish water of the Potomac River. Someone came in one night and slaughtered Kevin and the other two people working there. One had a memorable name: Turquoise Tull. She was twenty-three. The other was some guy named Brandon Gambuto. The shooter just laid into them: two shots in the manager, Turquoise, one in the other guy, and twelve in Kevin, according to the salivating article. By this "feature writer" (according to his byline) for the *Post*, Archer B. Sexton. (What kind of a name is that? Its components are interchangeable, and therefore it's nonhuman.) You know the kind of thing I mean: "Kevin Broadus was a model student at Kennedy High School. Turquoise Tull was a hardworking single mother. Brandon Gambuto was an aspiring musician. All of them died last week in what some are calling the most sensational murders in recent memory." "These brutal killings have stunned a peaceful Northwest neighborhood." "Lieutenant James Huang, in charge of the task force leading the investigation, offered assurances that the metropolitan police force is doing everything it can. But residents of the Second Precinct, Huang's area of jurisdiction, remain unsettled." Sexton discussed the copious maplike bloodstains, the lack of any robbery, the tribulations of the police. This happened the July before my senior year, this year. We were beaten over the head with the story for the worst, most blinding months of the summer, in the cruel heat and wetness for which our city is famous. For a while people were talking about *gang retaliation*. I mean, that's what *I* thought at first, gangs or drugs. You had to figure that all the extra bullets in Kevin *meant* something. But he seemed—and I say this, as I said, without having known him well or at all—too passive to be involved in anything that would require retribution. The local reporters droned on and on about it, but they gave up their gang theory after a day or two and then talked about *senseless tragedy*.

Really? Just think about it: you're some boring kid working a boring job, because your parents pressure you to, in a boring neighborhood. The heat and swampiness of summers here are repetitive and soul-numbing. The bored mothers, college students, and antique store owners who patronize that particular Stubb's gaze at you with supercilious anger as they wait for their orders. Your sad-ass manager (who's made a career out of this, which horrifies you) calls you out for errors sometimes. But she also praises you, which is in its own way worse, the pledge of some defeating mediocrity she recognizes in you and sees as kin to her own. So this goes on for a month or two, no relief in sight. It's not torture but it's a chafe against the restlessness that you feel now, the sense that you can encompass anything.

And then one night someone comes in—someone who looks, in theory, no different from anyone else—and shoots you. A man of average height and build, wearing dark clothes, so any blood won't show, loose clothes, so the gun remains invisible. Older than Kevin. White, in my mental viewer, although that's statistically improbable in D.C. He walks with a calmness in his eyes. Calling it emptiness would be stupid. He *ipso facto* has enough inner strength to plan and realize three murders, which is—if I can put it like this—more than most people ever accomplish. His hands refuse to shake. He looks around; there's no one else in the store; he lifts his gaze up to the employees, one by one. The ordinariness of his face is incomprehensible and horrifying, as is

19

his normal brown hair, its color borrowed from some actual person I know. As every physical facet of him is borrowed. And then, radiating his normality, he takes out the gun. What if he kills you second? What if the first shot just maims you, knocks you down? What if the sun hadn't set? Can you imagine that? Dying on the floor of a Stubb's with the last of a summer sunset in your eyes? At seventeen? Just when you've first tasted autonomy? I mean, I've only been having sex for about two years, and I can tell you without hesitation: losing that would hurt just as much as losing life itself. Also driving. I'm not a huge fan of it, but it's necessary in my line of work, and other people *love* driving. And college? The prospect of green quads and unlimited drinking and fucking? Or telling off Ms. Prather, the way Kevin did? *That's* the sweetness of autonomy.

Tragedy isn't the word for it, in my opinion. I have no doubt that it crushed his parents—although it's also impossible for me to understand their loss; I can *think* about it but I have no way to *grasp* it—but the real loss would be to you. To you! It's your life! There's something selfish about our idea of tragedy, since it depends on other people watching. I guess it's been that way since ancient times, though, at least according to Mr. Vanderleun, the twelfth-grade English teacher, who talks about tragic irony at least three times a week, and without any apparent awareness of the colossal waste of his own life. *Senseless tragedy.* Accurate, yeah, but you could describe the majority of human existence as senseless tragedy, or even existence in general, if you're a true idealist. Kevin's mother never went on the local news, and his father just once. Mr. Broadus, tall, bespectacled, with a slight stoop, was *begging* for the guy who did it to come forward. Though he must have known there was no chance of this happening. When public television finally got its act together, *Capitol Ideas* (perhaps the world's most boring program) invited Archer B. Sexton, who is humpy and bald and pomegranate-flushed, onto their taupe set to talk about the case. He was identified as a feature writer/urban historian, in demure white letters hovering beneath the knot of his crimson tie. He basically repeated the points in his article, with a lot of unibrow wriggles, which look hilarious on a totally bald guy. Like a pinned caterpillar, struggling.

Senseless or not, the murders eventually breathed out the last of their public thrill. All the Samaritans lost interest. There was this hideous memorial set up in front of the Stubb's. Mounds and mounds of cheap, stiff-looking blue and yellow flowers, irises and ragged daisies, still mingled with the baby's breath florists cram into their bouquets. And you know what kind of people leave flowers at public memorials, anyway. The anonymous, lonely, and deranged, in search of some free-floating emotion, some imaginary connection to the dead. Kevin sort of faded from the scene. Yes, there was slight, lingering unease among my classmates. But it had nothing to do with him and everything to do with them, if you see what I mean: it was contemplative, self-directed. As we had been encouraged to be all our lives, from four years old onward, to look for our own metaphysical condition in others. This effacing process continued until Kevin was only memorable as a disruption in the peaceful flow of events.

Then came the third day of school. We had a scratchy announcement about Kevin, about the murders, on the PA. It sounded like the speaker—Dr. Karlstadt, our principal and my world history teacher—was addressing us from fucking Tartarus, harsh, muted, and vague. "Attention, Kennedy students. Attention, Kennedy students. As some of you may already know, the Kennedy community suffered a loss this summer. Kevin." Pause.

The mike cut off then, I assume so that Dr. Karlstadt could check her pronunciation. "Kevin *Broadus*, a rising senior. Our thoughts are with him and with his family." Pause. I knew what was coming next. "Here are this morning's announcements. The women's restroom on the third floor is out of order." And Dr. Karlstadt continued, in her even voice, detailing the day's service failures and after-school practice schedules for various intramural organizations.

There was an assembly the day after this announcement, as though to reassure us that we never had to think about Kevin again. The choir opened with "Bridge Over Troubled Water." We have an excellent choir, restrained violence in their voices. Their name is the Singing Tigers (the tiger is Kennedy's mascot), which is a name that I thought was awful until I realized it was, in a bizarre way, amazing. Dr. Karlstadt gave a speech. The microphone kept keening with feedback, and then she'd bang on it with two fingertips, stroking her gull-colored special-occasion scarf with the other hand. "We gather here today to say good-bye to a valued member of the Kennedy community. He'll be missed by his teachers for his diligence. He'll be missed by the band, which is now short one excellent saxophone player." On and on in that vein, for however much time she and the other administrators had blocked out. Then the choir, in gold-and-amethyst robes (Kennedy's colors), sang "Mary Don't You Weep" to close things out, swaying in time and clapping their hands, making a communal leaden thud, the beat of a huge hollow drum. *Sic transit*, right? Even the unremarkable deserve pomps and works. The thing I remember most clearly, though? Alex Faustner, maybe the number one cunt in my grade, sitting next to me and *complaining* about how "all this"—she meant singing "Mary Don't You Weep"—violated her First Amendment rights. She says things like that. She announced this as we were filing out. I wanted to tell her to shut the fuck up. But she wandered away with her murmuring friends before I could speak. In addition to being a huge cunt, Alex is—I'm sure you're *astonished* to hear this—one hundred percent, rest-of-society-agrees beautiful, long dark hair, slender, a low rich voice.

So there it was. Our duty was done. The tombstone inscribed. However you want to put it. And nothing else would ever have happened to me—I mean nothing out of the ordinary—if I hadn't gotten high and gone to the Bench with a friend of mine that afternoon. Not a friend. An *associate*. Just someone I associated with because one associates with people. Out of habit, right? And not to *talk things over*. That's what most people my age waste their time doing, talking away all their energy and intention. It's hard not to, because everything is so undecided, you believe you can transform into anything, overcome anything. No one can look at all that potential and not sink into terror or at least be tempted into lethargy by the apparently luxurious quantity of time before you. *What a pretentious asshole*, you're thinking. It doesn't matter. I *know* I'm right.

This *associate* was called Digger Zeleny. Not on her birth certificate, but that's the nickname she and everyone else uses. (Real name: Phoebe.) We'd known each other since the beginning of our time at Kennedy. She was a frequent, reasonable customer of mine, and an acknowledger of my in-class sarcasm, as I was of hers. Her nickname is weird, I know, but she's even gotten our teachers to use it. I asked her about it, right after we met, and she refused to tell me. This was four years ago. But a week later, when I sold her weed for the first time, and we ended up smoking some of it together, she came clean. When she was a kid, she had a sandbox in her backyard, where she spent most of her time digging. Not making castles or fake pies and hamburgers or anything, just digging and filling the hole, and then digging some more, and mumbling to herself the whole time, *Dig-dig-diggety-dig*. She continued this practice when she started kindergarten, and some genius in her class started calling her Digger. To make fun of her. So she bashed him in the face with her plastic shovel, and then with her bucket, and afterward refused to answer anyone who *didn't* address her as Digger. She took *proprietorship* of the insult. She's that hardheaded. Her parents had to take her, she told me, to a psychologist to get her to revert to Phoebe. But she defeated him too, and Digger she stayed. "I never liked Phoebe anyway, that much," she muttered through a mouthful of smoke. "I *suspect* I was named after that guy's sister in *Catcher in the Rye*. I started suspecting when I had to read it, I mean. So fuck *that*."

We cut out right after the assembly—there's a little-known exit in the corridor that curves between our main chancel-like building, which is always filled with this horrible brown light, and the auditorium—and headed over to the Bench, which is a cedar bench set in a small deer park on the expansive property of a private school down the street from Kennedy, Brent Academy, named after our city's first and least corrupt mayor, Robert Brent. We discussed a lot of initial trivia, and then I just let her talk, so I could avoid the real subject. She was telling me something about her mother, who's a doctor, an in-depth fumbler in other people's machinery, not some dermatologist or something. Her mother hates me. Understandable. Even though she doesn't know the full extent of my relations with her daughter. We were stoned, a bit thick-lipped but still *compos mentis*. I sat there and watched her tweaking her hair and shoving the glasses back up onto the bump, that little Mediterranean bump, on the bridge of her nose. A path of scalp stood out, a demarcator, in Digger's dark hair, a dumb dead white line. Shadows curtained the grass at our feet, which was still lush, and crept up over our ankles—a heavy cloud was passing. And then we were in the September light again. I was so high my head ached, a beating numbness above the roof of my mouth. Weed is the consummate drug for adolescents, because it induces that weak-shit sense of potential I was just talking about. This cloud swooped over us and cut off the light, and the sudden shift jarred me: here's the light, here's the darkness. Nobody wants to go into the darkness, to cross that line, right there, over by the clump of pines, that rooftop, whatever. The *physical specifics* don't matter. Nobody wants it, it's not at *all* what is wanted, but you can't help *looking* at it, at the dividing line, and wanting to cross it *anyway*. The whole time Digger was telling me this story about her mother fishing a forceps out of someone that another surgeon had left in.

"And you can't tell anybody. It would be proof of malpractice anyway. And it was this old black lady. So it makes the hospital super-vulnerable, legally."

"What like just passed over us?" I mumbled.

"Dude, a cloud? What are you talking about? You are *fucked up*." She chortled, and then I was off into the trees, to get out of the light and into the shadow, which cooled my hot forehead. My limbs hurt now, a dull body-wide ache. From the thicket I heard her call out my name twice, and then give up. It took a few minutes to recover my composure. I was still hideously stoned, though, in that phase of weak hilarity.

"Dude, Kevin Broadus. I mean, what do you even *do* with that," I told Digger, still leaning against a tree.

"Are you all right?" she trilled.

"Do you think they'll find the guy?"

"What guy?"

"The guy who killed him. I don't know. Whoever. The *guy*."

"Dude, were you even friends with him?"

I huffed out a long breath. Grinding my shoulder against the comforting wrinkles of the bark.

"No, it's fine, it's just like it doesn't matter. Your story like kind of fucked me up, I guess."

She squinted at me, saying, "You are all *over* the place, dude." And then returned to her narration. Dr. Zeleny—I'd met her a few awkward times, as I snuck down from Digger's room—was as tiny as Digger. Tinier, maybe. The first time we met, she was wearing a short-sleeved periwinkle Oxford, which revealed her muscle-clotted forearms. The thought of her sawing open someone's chest cavity, the blinding operation lights glancing off her fine-modeled avian head, terrified me as much as it made inevitable sense. The single occasion we'd *spoken* she'd thrust out an arm for a shake, her corded wrist manacled in a matte-silver Gestapo captain's watch. Digger looks nothing like her, except that they're both short. I gave up trying to explain to her about Kevin. I had nothing to explain, really, just a gaggle of stoned, moronic, unrefusable thoughts. So I listened to her talk about the hospital problems some more. My jaw clenched, along with my fists. I wanted to hit someone. For my own stupidity, I guess. But there was no one to hit, so I shook Digger's hand and walked to my car.

I went to sleep when I got home, for an hour or two. In the car, I'd listened to the gargling radio, but I couldn't stand it after one song, so I rolled down the window and listened to the wind inhabiting my neighborhood. The house was dark when I walked in—not dark but dim, as it is when my father is in his studio. He shuts off every light. And pulls the shades. This always mystified me, but it's easier just to open them than to inquire or argue. But that night I stumbled through the dim house shivering, and slept

14

with my heavy shoes still on. Have you ever noticed how heavy shoes are if you fall asleep in them? Like they contained reminders of gravity, of your bound state, right? An hour or two of sleep, and then my father woke me up. He had turned on the light in my room, which I had relocated to the basement in seventh grade. It's comforting and windowless there. Secure. He had turned on the lights and bent over me, and his hilarious ponytail had slipped over his shoulder and was painting the air under his chin. "My Greek urn," he mumbled, "exploded." "I don't know what to say," I answered. The whole intrusion had the stagy, rushing tone of a dream. "It *exploded*. What's the fucking *point* of all this?" My father cannot react to inconveniences without finality, without mentally removing himself from the landscape of life. This makes it easier (I think?) for him to suffer no reaction at all to *major* problems or catastrophes. So call it an adaptation, maybe. I knew where he was going with his speech, anyway: *Sometimes I think, Addison, I just fantasize sometimes about throwing myself under a bus.* His usual rhetorical capstone.

He also *always* uses my full name, in consequence of which I have never developed a nickname, in consequence of which everyone *else*, from Dr. Karlstadt on down, calls me Addison. He finished his speech about suicide, and I gave him a look of . . . what? Sympathy? Consolation? He accepted it and patted my shoulder, the clay still staining his nails and the faint webs of wrinkles on the skin between his fingers. My father's hands, I should note, are huge, the paws of some clumsy, lugubrious animal. I was drenched in sweat. I felt as though I'd been swimming for hours against a nameless and powerful tide. Just from one afternoon of school. We overestimate our fortitude. After my father left me, I tried to do my calculus. No luck. I tried to translate some of the *Aeneid*. No luck. I lay back down, dressed and iron-quiet, and struggled into sleep an hour before sunrise. He was already burning pots when I woke up and checked the backyard, where the kiln is. I could see eyes and leaves of fire lashing out from its ash-colored bricks. Almost feel the sucking heat, in fact.

I made some coffee—which tasted, as usual, like earth—and I drove to Kennedy, early as fuck, and smoked some cigarettes at the Flagpole. This is the flagpole in front of our school. The flag is at permanent half-mast: the crank has rusted and no one can or will replace it. There's a big vacant concrete court between you and school when you sit there. Smokers have used it as a meeting place for as long as I've been at Kennedy. I got through half a pack, watching the light, looking for shadows, which don't exist at that hour in the fall. All the asphalt looked blue. This, I came to believe later, was the day when it began. When the whole process started that left me freed of my part-time occupation. And maybe even in possession of knowledge I lacked. But you'll have to judge that for yourself.

CONTRARY TO WHAT you might have assumed, Digger
Zeleny is not my girlfriend. This is her own idea. Hers *and* mine.
She doesn't *want* a boyfriend. And I don't want a girlfriend,
preferring instead a life of free-ranging (albeit imaginary) con-
cubinage. A lot of people think we're dating. I've been asked that
several times, by my father and others. We're not. We're, as I said,
associates. Not even friends. People who share a set of parameters
in their approach to life. She is *not* my girlfriend. I would fight
you for saying so. *She* would fight you for saying so. It's important
you understand that, during everything that follows.

She'd seen me at the Flagpole and taken my arm, telling me
I looked weird. She never sounds faux concerned, only observa-
tional. I mumbled something about needing more coffee, which
she refused to accept—"Bullshit!" she fluted—and started
marching me to the Tip-Top Diner. This is where Kennedy
students go to avoid school. We have an eternal and inviolable
agreement with the owner, whose name is not known. We
behave ourselves, and he pretends we're legitimate adults. The
Tip-Top Diner, as its name implies, has terrible, addictive food.
It's just a tiled shack, the grout pond-black, the row of fuchsia-

cushioned stools defeated by legions of asses. There's a pay phone, which has served at least two generations of dealers as an office: "Call 6883!" runs our refrain. It spells MUTE, NOTE, and nothing else meaningful. This is covered by the arrangement, too, as long as no commerce happens on the premises. The place was filled with that sad morning emptiness, the hooked column of stools and the short row of booths vacant except for a catarrhal man walled off from his pancakes by a newspaper and a sleeping junkie with an immobile tear lodged in the corner of one eye.

Digger had chosen, her transparent blue eyes hardened with shut-mouth delight, the booth between these two champs. I couldn't decide where to start talking when we sat down. "You're going to make me *ask*," she muttered. So I did something moronic. I told her the truth.

"I'm kind of a mess, I guess. I sort of couldn't sleep."

"So," she asked, "what do you want me to do about it, man?" A cough from the pancake eater: earth being shifted, a grave being scraped.

"I don't know. I can't even really say," I said.

"That's bullshit, man. You were standing there with that look on your face."

"I didn't have a *look*. That's not correct."

"It is correct. Unfortunately." She grinned and poked my shoulder.

"*How* is that correct?" I pursued. "I mean, I *get* it if you have trouble under*stand*ing me, but it's totally unfair to say I had a *look*." I was grinning now, too, through the haze of my tiredness.

"You are such a *jack*ass." Digger's laugh chimed through the absurd thunder of the newspaper reader's cough. "You were making your little-boy face. You get it all the time. And you think nobody notices. But they do. So don't jester around." I sucked at my scorching coffee and started talking. She's hard to deny, ladies and gentlemen.

I said what, you ask? That some more serious region of life had intruded yesterday? That Kevin Broadus something something memento mori something something? I can't remember exactly, because I was in a rush to get it out. But it was along the lines of: *It's not fair that Kevin's dead, and I don't even know why I think it's unfair, and I couldn't sleep last night because of it, and and and.* Has this ever happened to you? You realize that something has disturbed you only when you say it out loud? I hadn't even known I'd been *thinking* about Kevin until that retarded assembly. Digger took it in with her unfracturable slight smile. "And it's just like," I panted, "he took some other *element* with him. From *me.* I mean, why do I give a fuck? Maybe because nobody really cares but they all just *fake* it. I mean, with Alex bitching about the *First Amendment.*"

She hockeyed a butter capsule between her hands, the foil glinting. "So their fake care is worse than your *heroic* emergence from indifference? Come on, man. That's even more bullshit. And you're making the face again now."

I took another scalding gulp and blurted out, "No, man, I don't mean that. I mean, how can you feel fucking *guilty* about not *knowing* someone you didn't even *know*? I don't even know why but I want to know. It's been three *months.*" Another grinding cough. The junkie's pearly tear careened down his dusty face.

"What do you want to *know*?" Digger answered. To my utter lack of surprise, I found that I could say nothing. Her meal came, though, just then, always an event for her, and that balked further discussion.

· · ·

31

At ten o'clock in the morning food horrifies me. Not Digger. She'd ordered the Tip-Top Deluxe, which is an obese hamburger capped by an amnio-slippery fried egg. She's one of those compact, petite people who eats as though she were pregnant and three to four times her corporeal size. And gains no weight. Something invisible makes demands of her energy, I guess, keeping her metabolism jacked up to some inhuman speed. I like to think that this is why, in every season, she carries a slight odor of wood smoke, of burning. The burger, bleeding yolk and shining grease, obscured the lower half of her face.

"How can you *eat* that?" I asked in awe.

"Because it's fucking *delicious*," she grunted, her mouth full.

A truck rumbled up the street, the same truck—I swear—twice. It was a Rex Rentals truck, a well-known local moving company, which uses a servile, staring maroon dog as its mascot. This happens to me a lot. I mean, I look up from whatever I'm doing and some trivial action in the theater around me is being repeated. Fucked-up, right? "What you want to know," she said, having demolished the burger, "well, you could ask *around*. Not about the *shooting*, you morbid jackass. But Kevin. You're just *pretending* to be unsympathetic, anyway." And she drained with a gusty slurp the last of her grape soda.

"Wouldn't people think it's weird?" I asked. "I think they would, right? Some random guy asking questions."

Probing the glass with her straw, she answered me. "No one could think you're any weirder than they already do." This was, I am sure, correct. I mean, I must have done an okay job of faking normalcy, or else my business would have suffered, because there's only so much sketchiness—I'm talking about emotional unpredictability here—that people will tolerate in a guy who's selling them a bag of weed. People consider me odd, though. I can see that look in their eyes, that puzzled look. Digger and I walked after she'd finished eating. She had just cut her hair, and the wind kicked it in oblong strands across her forehead, her dark hair, which she cropped herself, out of stubbornness. I couldn't tell you about her clothes on many other days, but I remember that morning she was wearing all black, which she always started wearing around this time of year with eagerness, and she had a heavy silver chain around her throat. This her mother had given her. She told me once it was from Chile, in a tone that demanded my nod of wise amazement.

She even had the tenacity and kindness to finish our argument. About my little-boy face, I mean. She waited until the old couple dog-following us up the street in the busy wind was out of earshot, though, to explain my misunderstanding further.

"I wasn't trying to *insult* you," she opened with. I stumped along, wrong-footing it to match her motions.

"No, I *know*. I admit it. I *was* doing it. Making that face." I knew exactly which face she meant, too: I'd caught myself making it once, while mooning around the house, caught a glimpse of my pout and half-lidded eyes in our age-dim hallway mirror.

"See? See how easy it is? So why deny it? You just make more work for yourself. Because I'm right like ninety percent of the time."

"You're *wrong* like ninety percent of the time," I sang, and in the black sea of a velvet-backed empty shopwindow we watched the old couple pause and drown.

"You just can't *stand* that I'm right," she said, and sped ahead. I caught up to her at a parking meter whose glass forehead had been smashed in. At this point going to school would have been idiotic. We shared a look of sudden complicity, which shocked me, as it always did. I mean that she was so willing to let me fuck her.

Digger is *not* my girlfriend. She doesn't *want* to be. We're just *making use* of each other, as she puts it. *You* wouldn't think she was hot, and she is not. But she *is* remarkable-looking. A blade-thin nose and pale, fragile-seeming skin, which looks even paler next to her jet hair. She has this constant *stare*, and her eyes are transparent blue. I'm not saying this out of any sense of possession. I'm just being objective here. I could go on and on about her and about fucking her. And you're expecting me to: *I wouldn't know better at my age.* Just to frustrate your expectations, though, I'm going to tell you all the incidental details of that late morning, without any of the salacious stuff. (1) In our eagerness, we knocked over the rubber plant that stands guard in her townhouse's front hallway, which spilled a spray of clean-looking soil on the paws of a white porcelain dog-lion (her parents have a matched set). (2) I tripped three times on the stairs, once on each flight. (3) The handles to the windows in Digger's bedroom are made of bronze, heavy real bronze, and they spin and cantilever the windows open. (4) She did not remove her necklace. (5) We could hear traffic filtering up from the street. (6) We both spoke to each other the whole time. As usual. (7) The answering machine took three calls: one from her mother, responding to her own voice, one from a garbled and soft-voiced man looking for her mother, and one that was a smear of hissy dead air. (8) Judging from the traffic sounds, someone rammed someone else's car, and human cries mingled with the other noise. Afterward the flames of sunlight, through the opened windows, licked at the white ceiling.

. . .

"Why are you even *interested* in this guy." Digger coughed. We were passing her bulbous, vermilion-streaked glass pipe (which always weirded me out with its suggestion of some indistinct human organ) back and forth in the orange light. To that I had no response. I couldn't tell her, *Because of that cloud we saw, man.* Which would have been true, in a sense. But I didn't speak. Relief stabbed through me. I should have told her. She would have figured out, probably, the falseness of my position, which I did not realize until . . . well, more or less until I started trying to answer *your* question, ladies and gentlemen. And she would have talked me down, and all the confused nonsense that followed from our conversation might have been avoided. She's good at talking me down.

"It's just like a project, right?" I asked. Digger was now sitting, still naked, against the wall, her after-weed cigarette dangling out the window, her arm stretched. From her bed, I could see the tender plate of muscle shift beneath her right breast.

"A project? Since when do you do *projects*?"

"Alex *Faustner* does all kinds of projects."

"That's a retarded statement."

"What is it then," I replied as I sat down and rooted through her bag for a smoke, "if not a project?" She pulled in her hand and barked it against the window frame.

"It's *just* peculiarity. And that's all right with me. You don't have to justify it to me."

"*Jus*tify it, justify it to *you*," I sang (my singing voice is horrible), snapping my fingers in time, and then got up and looked down into the street for the accident or signs of the accident, but perpetrator and victim were gone; just the usual stream of honking cars remained, trying to make their way around a construction crew. Who, I could tell even from four stories up, were fat, were joke exchangers, and would work with infinite slowness and carelessness. They had orange helmets and orange vests and moved like an uncertain basketball team around the sandy pit they'd dug in the street.

"How long have those construction guys *been* there?" I asked Digger.

"For*ev*er," she replied, and let go of her smoke. It tumbled and bounced against the stone front of her house, spitting amber-red sparks.

I didn't take any of the numerous pages—they start coming in around this time, late afternoon/early evening—summoning me to work. Sometimes I made people wait. Selling drugs is the single market of exchange in which the customer is always wrong. And making people wait stops them from thinking you're a lackey, which is necessary. Otherwise the customers wouldn't value your product. On the other hand, take it too far and you get a reputation as unreliable. Your business dries up. You're not, after all, selling smack to hardened, hollow-eyed fiends. You're selling weed to rich kids, at once arrogant and frightened. Some of them this makes deferential, some it has no effect on, and some it prompts to show off their own dreamed-up toughness. So keeping people on the hook makes sense, for me, as a business and social proposition. You have to feel it out as you go. You have to set it up to imply that *you're* doing *them* a favor.

Don't think I haven't encountered all kinds of indignant objections to that attitude. I've even made a few myself, in world history. Standing up for Platonic ideas about human rights, equality before the law, do unto others, etc. What a sense of gut-clenching well-being *that* provides. Everyone looks on in bewildered approval: *Addison may be odd, but his heart is in the right place!* Not that I don't hold those beliefs. Everybody does. At least, everyone I've ever met. Maybe generalizing is unfair. But these ideas don't have some kind of *independent meaning.* They're just words; at the small scale nobody *behaves* in accordance with all the high ideals they talk about; everyone acts like animals, domesticated animals maybe, but still animals. So why the fuck not? Why not make your presence felt? Why *not* exercise power if you have it?

My father was sitting in the dark when I got home, waiting for me to ask him what the matter was. He'd cleaned himself up, I saw, as though he had a meeting with his miniature, dark-suited gallery rep, Viktor Something, whom I refer to privately as the Hungarian Pickpocket. Because of his hairline and quick fingers, always kneading air. He would have been a better gallery rep *had* he been a Hungarian pickpocket, I'm sure. As things stood, he was a failed artist helping out my father, another failed artist, or an artist on the way to failing. "Tell me it's *worth* it," my father moaned—his face supported by both his huge leaden hands. The blankness that in the presence of any other person would have been laughter overtook me. It constricted my breathing. But I managed to mumble, "You *know* it is, Dad," before stumbling downstairs.

He's a lot taller than I am—my father, I mean—but narrow. Shoulders, chest, lips, eyes. Narrow except for his walnut-knuckled hands. His forehead bulges, tracing half the curve of a sleigh bell, and his nose would not be out of place among the features of a Roman emperor, though on him it looks starved and weak. The pots he throws are tall, thin, built like him, and—given the frequency with which they break—possess some similar fragility. Although my father is, body-wise, sound as an ox. He never gains weight, needs little sleep and food. I admire him for that. It's one of his few genuine qualities. It's a good thing he has a strong constitution, too, because when he *does* get sick, even with a cold or some minor complaint, a sprained finger, he starts carrying himself as though he were about to be executed the next morning. With the smug, pardoning smile of a saint under torture.

After I was sure he was gone to his meeting with Viktor or whatever, I went outside. Sprigs of stars glittered in the turkey oaks interlaced above our yard. I dragged a patio chair to the shed that houses his kiln, which is made of some indestructible, chintzy-looking material. He built it, or had it built, after my mother died. As though he'd been waiting. Sometimes I go and sit near it, to feel the whisper of heat from it, to watch the air distorted, and to see the transparent rags of flame that slip out from it in a breeze. Sometimes—and this is fucked-up—I fantasize about being inside of it, first protected, just as an observer among the hardening graceful forms there, the brightening colors, forms that sometimes explode under the strain, and then the protection would vanish and I'd be consumed, too quick for pain, for any sensation at all. I was gripping the arms of the patio chair, not a painful grip but with a *certainty*, when my reverie lifted. The air had chilled me, and the hunger for sleep rose through me, like sap in a tree.

This meant, of course, that it was time to read the *Aeneid*. I have been reading it every night before sleep since the end of my junior year, when we studied it in Latin class. I have three copies. One of them is an edition from 1973, "interpreted" by Professor Burton J. Fragment of the English department of Yale University, and it has a floppy paper cover, in teal and rose, a cover that announces how mealymouthed and self-serving the version inside is. I also have two *real* translations. One is a cheap paperback edition of the Dryden translation. I had to tape its spine, I thumbed through it so much. The other one is the best, a hardback in two volumes, from the Loeb Classical Library. They have apple-red paper jackets and blood-colored cloth bindings. The Loeb translation was made in 1926 by a man called E. T. P. Bredon-Howth, from a text of the Latin prepared by Heinrich Balde in 1878. I bought the Fragment translation for my eleventh-grade English class. It was all they had in the bookstore, and the girl working as a cashier gave me a critical, bulgy-eyed look. This was bad. She went to my school, I remembered. And worse, she was good-looking. The Dryden I swiped from a public library I wandered into one afternoon when I was high. The Loeb edition I purchased for eighteen dollars from Don't Shoot the Piano Player, which is this used bookstore right next to the Camelot, a movie theater, in the shadow of its long, harp-shaped marquee. The guy *there* didn't give me any looks. He owns both the theater and the bookstore. This old hippie whose distinguishing features are his nebulous receptive-looking mass of dust-colored hair, and the fact that he drives a gleaming black Rolls-Royce, which is always parked outside Don't Shoot (as people call it). He resembles some second-rate, unkempt butler when he's in the driver's seat.

Why the *Aeneid*? It's exciting but also difficult to understand. The stories in it are kind of incomprehensible. Venus raping Anchises. Aeneas returning from the underworld through the Gate of Ivory, the gate through which Virgil says false dreams arrive in the world. And the way it ends: in a single instant, just like a human life. It all appears at first to be nonsensical, but that's because it belongs to a world that no longer exists. In the centuries between us and Virgil, we kind of lost interest in things that are hard to understand. I'm generalizing, yeah, but am I wrong? It's why, maybe, so much biography gets written now, even of people you've never heard of. Which should be the sole test to see if someone *deserves* a biography: whether a random guy on the street has heard of him. I don't know why this has happened. Everyone, though, seems sort of bricked into his own life. At least, everyone I know, including me. Not in "quiet desperation"—the phrase comes from another terrible author my teachers forced me to read, Henry David Thoreau—but just by the fact of living in the small, boring modern world. And this explains why all my teachers have been so terrible. I mean because they, like Thoreau, see their own selves not as prisons but as subjects of thunderous interest. I don't want to sound harsh, but holy fuck! No one who admires Thoreau should be permitted anywhere near a school.

III.

THE ONE FIT MEMORIAL to the dead is vengeance of some
kind. Against the killer, against some other inevitability, though
that too always fails. By definition. *And what vengeance*, you are
no doubt asking, ladies and gentlemen, *what vengeance do* you
propose—you mouthy coward? The truth is, I had no idea. So,
yes, I'm an emotional hypocrite. Like everyone else. All I had
was this knock-kneed impulse to *find out.* I couldn't ask any of
my classmates, because fuck them. I didn't know them anyway.
Can you *imagine* how Alex Faustner would respond if I asked
her about Kevin? Everyone else is just as bad as her, except for
Digger. And she was my equal in ignorance. So my classmates
were out. Which left my teachers. Who are not, as you may have
gathered from the brief remarks I've made about them, capable
of anything high-spirited. They failed to detect the lie I'd cooked
up to get them to talk. They were *deceived* by a seventeen-year-
old. Isn't that a disqualifying failure? Don't you have to be
savvier than people to instruct them in anything? And it wasn't
even a good lie. It was transparent. I told them—I knew the
phrase would turn their gazes glassy with delight—I told them
I wanted to "do an oral history project." I can't even write this
without laughing. The whole G&T Program has this huge and
inexplicable commitment to oral history. Last year we had to do

this series of *interviews*: hunt up and interrogate a veteran from every war since the Second World.

Mr. Vanderleun I asked first. He has nine fingers in total. He once lectured us about the cause of this loss. When he was a younger man (he's fifty now), he did not want to go to war in Vietnam. So he asked his girlfriend to cut off his right pinkie finger. The story struck me as false, because he didn't specify what instrument the girlfriend used. He just said, "I put my finger down on the block, and *whshhhhhhhht*," making a tight-arced swoop with his other hand. Who wouldn't say what weapon had been used? He got all excited and gleamy-eyed when I told him about my fake idea.

"Kevin was a strong and quiet presence, though blessed with a genuine musicality, a strong rhythm. Aren't you going to take notes? He'll be remembered and missed." That's all he would say. It was basically what Ms. Prather had said last year, when Kevin was still alive.

With Dr. Karlstadt I had not much more luck: "I don't know what you want me to tell you, Addison. I didn't even know you were *friends*." We hadn't been, as I've said. But I still forced some outraged sputters. Which did no good. Dr. Karlstadt waved me out and started rifling through her lunch bag. Their classrooms—Mr. Vanderleun's and Dr. Karlstadt's, I mean—are mirror images of each other, the gray, fireproof, prison-admin door in one corner, right next to the blackboards with the ghosts of other people's handwriting—the most mysterious and saddening thing in the world—faint and visible. Also: she's our history teacher *and* our principal. Isn't that a conflict of interest? Or the sign of special treatment, for her students, I mean? That's how things operate at John F. Kennedy Senior High! As I said: a goddamn embarrassment.

. . .

Digger had no sympathy for my failures.

"What did you expect," she muttered as we were getting high the day Karlstadt shot me down. "They're so into themselves you can't really expect them to care *that* much about anyone else." I told her what Mr. Vanderleun said, knowing it would provoke a spurt of contempt-laced laughter from her. Which it did, which gratified me. Being able to make her laugh, I mean. Even if it was only with *borrowed nonsense*. We were lying—clothed, though— in my bed. My father was out teaching pottery, and the pipes in my house, which are über-old, kept making these weird moans of admonition.

"What about talking to his parents?" I said. Digger vetoed this, on the grounds that it would be better to present them with some conclusive report, not to consult them beforehand: "My mother always says that what you don't know makes no difference to you." I had a vision of Dr. Zeleny at this moment, bloody bone saw in hand, her eyes glistening with butchery above a sterile face mask. And for the second time that week I had to fuck Digger to avoid thinking about something. I'm not trying to be a misogynist here, which I realize *I had to fuck Digger* has overtones of. But she was always up for it, just as much as me, sometimes even more than me. That was a big part of our agreement: that neither of us could refuse. Just to keep things on equal footing. If we were *injured* or whatever, exceptions were possible in theory. In normal situations, though, no refusing. I said before that her complicity always surprised me. I mean, I know *intellectually* it shouldn't have. There was nonetheless this component of *surprise of the internal organs*, of my viscera, every time. I know that's an obscure phrase. But I was high as shit, so maybe it's better to use the ungainly and sententious language of weed smokers. To give you the flavor of it.

. . .

As I'm sure the men among you remember, sex at seventeen or eighteen is kind of strange for guys. Because you have, in the short term, no stamina whatsoever. But you have, in the long term, a huge amount. You can blow your load a whole bunch of times, but it doesn't matter. To you. I can't imagine that it's all that tremendously satisfying for women, who seem to take longer. This is based on my own single-channel experience here, so please forgive any crudity or ignorance in these statements. I'm just trying to get everything down, so that you can form a clear picture. *My best and worst qualities.* Anyway, we had finished and dressed and gone upstairs: Digger gets hungry afterward, and we were looking for food, which in my house is pointless. My father eats almost nothing, and I'm not much of an eater myself. All we could find was a jar of peanuts, in the dark back part of a cabinet, next to a pair of my father's clay-rigid work gloves. Digger had vacuumed down most of them by the time my father returned. This was a Tuesday, which meant he would be drunk.

There's some tradition at the Cochrane Institute of the faculty and students going to this bar called the A and V Lounge after class on Tuesday. I think my father liaises with whatever student he's seeing there. Yes, he dates his students. Don't pretend that you've never heard of that happening at high levels of instruction. He came back alone, which I breathed silent thanks for, because having him bring home a woman while Digger was there . . . I'd have no idea how to deal with that. He walked in with precise steps, surrounded by the sugary afterodor of whiskey. There was a long cardboard tube clenched in his left armpit. What a rolled-up, unframed picture comes in. He doesn't stumble when he drinks. He can even drive, with a murder-eyed evenhandedness. But you can tell, all the same, from the slackness of his face.

"Hello, Phoebe," he sang out as he strode into the bathroom.

My father won't use Digger's nickname. Just, I think, to be an asshole. Or because he thinks it's funny to ignore people's preferences. She's used to it. She refuses to let it bother her.

He was shouting from the bathroom, over the running water. When he rejoined us, droplets glinted in his goatee.

"So what are you two smirking about? You make me ill at ease," he rumbled on.

"Just a little research. For like school," Digger returned. "Just a sort of a *project*."

"Ha!" he crowed, and bowed in self-approval before he yanked the peanut jar away from her. "Young people do nothing but lie, these times." He screwed the top on the jar. That's my dad. Then he was up and shambling around. The dining room is our de facto gallery. For his work, I mean. Most of his stuff either explodes in the kiln or he breaks it himself in fits of gloom, or he crates it away. A whole section of our basement is piled with these crates, on every one of which he has stenciled SCHACHT. In that army block lettering. As though someone was going to swipe his crates. The pots that escape this oblivion—the ones he's suffered the most over, the ones that have provoked his direst outpourings to me—are ranked above the table on shelves he installed, crowding the walls. The walls he painted this sage green, which just makes everything worse. The larger pots, the ollae and amphorae and whatever, stand in mute pomposity on the floor.

"Shit, shit, it's *all* shit," he sang. He was addressing, apparently, a goosenecked red number standing on the massive credenza that hulks at the room's edge. A find of my father's—the credenza, I mean. "Why should it matter? None of it matters." Digger and I stood up to leave, on the point of some simultaneous and limpidly false excuse. He waved us back down. "I'm just going to go hang this, Addison." He waggled the tube, still tucked under his arm. "I'll leave you alone with Phoebe, and you can *continue*." And he turned abruptly to walk out, and his tube knocked a pot— "more of a small *flask*, really," as he once described it—from its place, this swinish iron shelf at eye level next to a window, and his wordless cry of *relieved outrage* obscured the earthen clink of its breakage. "You. Are. A pretty girl," he told Digger as he left. Which is, as I've said, not strictly true, and she knows it. At least, I think she does.

"What's in the tube, Mr. Schacht?" Digger yelled to show she wasn't cowed. (Destined for greatness!)

"Some designs. For exhibition posters. Some designs I was going over with a certain someone." My shame changed all at once into a sudden, moronic happiness: I had my answer. I mean, about what to do about Kevin. That's how life is: it provides these accidental answers. Or seems to. You have to judge by results.

I'd thought Digger would be more into the idea. I explained it to her the next day. That we should put up posters asking for info about Kevin. But her brows contracted in this way that suggested deep hesitance. "I don't know. It seems sort of hackneyed?" We were huddled over our lunchtime cigarettes in one of the few fully hidden corners of Kennedy's field/track/basketball court/lunch area, which is set on two levels of land. Smokers gather by tradition in this corner near the front fence, hidden from the street by bramble and from the eyes of administrators by an overhanging wing of the building, which can't be gotten at from the inside, and whose green doors are bound with a rusty, titanic chain.

"No, man. Look," I argued, "they didn't try this before. And I just think it can't do any damage." I was shouting, I realized, half standing (the overhang of the building got in the way) and shouting. Digger's face was still flattened with skepticism.

"Do you know that you're the only person I know who gets like this? All speechy. Literally the only person. You sound like you're forty." She says this to me a lot. And she's right, and I'm glad to have the chastisement. Because rocketing off on the strength of your rhetoric alone takes you into some of the stupidest possible situations. I kept at it, though, lowering my voice and refusing to abandon my argument. We went through almost a whole pack together, and missed the end-of-lunch-period buzz.

There is a copy machine in the Kennedy offices that students have access to. It has a big sign over it, on eye-hurting pink posterboard. The lettering is purple. BE UNSELFISH, the sign admonishes. With paper and time, et cetera. But it's part of the larger official message hawked by our administration: selfishness is the highest evil. Which means, if you think about it, that all private desires participate in evil. Which means that desire *itself* is in the wrong. The urge to deface that sign is the strongest feeling I have about my school, I think, as an institution. So I had the slip of paper that I surreptitiously made in Latin class. IF YOU HAVE ANY INFORMATION ABOUT KEVIN BROADUS, PLEASE PAGE, and then I put my number, which I won't include here. It would be useless to you. No mention of a reward. I thought that would be presumptuous. No photo. I had none. Just a blank vague plea. I thought it would work. I was *sure* it would work. You understand why Digger was so skeptical.

I'd make a hundred to start, I told myself. And paper them up on weekends, after school, during deliveries. Fucking seamless, right? I was humming with self-satisfaction when I heard the drumming sound of someone sucking mucus back down from their nose into their throat. This could only be Ms. Arango, Dr. Karlstadt's subordinate, whose job it was to maintain the file systems on Kennedy students. Her mucus sound is famous. She's a world-class nose breather. And so ugly. I don't want to sound harsh, but it's objectively true. Her skin is sallow, the color of old newsprint. A rodentine, pushed-forward mouth. A mole crested with three stiff hairs. And this *avid misery* in her eyes, a misery that wants only more and more unhappiness. She gets downright excited by annoyances and problems. And I'm in a position to know. I've had to be processed by Kennedy's disciplinary apparatus nine times, and she is the operator of that process. I have nine disciplinary actions appended to my permanent record. Form 102B4, goldenrod in color. You have to get a parent's signature. But my father, his hair unbound, had instructed me to forge his on the first one, when I was in ninth grade. And that had been standard procedure since. The cause? I told a Holocaust joke to Alex Faustner, who started weeping. Right in biology. Where's the self-respect? So I began my *little tradition* of collecting and repeating jokes of that kind. (*What's the difference between a Jew and a loaf of bread?*) Because she cried. I would have lost interest otherwise. (*A loaf of bread doesn't scream when you put it in the oven.*)

"May I *help* you, Mr. Schacht," Ms. Arango asked, and her mucus rumbled.

"Uh, no, like I think I like have everything under *control* here." I pointed at the copier, which was vronking away and emitting its green hell light. She answered with a snot-fluting sigh. It was widely believed that Mr. Vanderleun was boning Ms. Arango, and students in their dealings with her made subtle references to this fact. I saw them walking or eating together sometimes, and she seemed to find his missing finger fascinating. It *did* make a nauseating show when he combed back his dark, greased hair, which clumped into blades, when he combed it or adjusted it with three fingers and a thumb, the active remnant of his little finger signaling like a stubby antenna. Their affair might have been real. Who knows? Some people find über-weird shit attractive. Her small, neat figure—she has no extra flesh— quivered with some invisible satisfaction.

"Make sure that you don't *overuse* the machine, Mr. Schacht." Behind her, I saw the gray sergeant-like ranks of her file cabinets, which contain the records of all Kennedy students. She stood there, a sentinel, ladies and gentlemen, watching with covetous attention as the copier worked. Like I was taking something from her just by using it. She wore this weary half-smile of acceptance.

So I had to take stronger measures. In the face of this, I *had* to. And stealing Kevin's file from the records office was not a *crime* or anything. It was just sitting there. I came up with the whole plan as Ms. Arango and I faced each other down. There wasn't even any premeditation! If it had been anyone there but Ms. Arango, I doubt I would have done it. If she hadn't put on that martyr's smile, I would have made my stupid copies under the glaring BE UNSELFISH sign and left. But she just *had* to come and stare at me and make that face. And rage gives me ideas. It makes me ingenious and daring. So I started lying, pitching my voice just right, and I knew as soon as her face shifted, the hairs protruding from her mole tick-tocking as the muscles beneath it twitched, that this was going to work. "Uh, Mr. Vanderleun? Like asked me to ask you to come up to his classroom? Four oh three?"

Thought, like a migraine, forced her eyelids lower.

"Did he say why?"

"Toner?" I asked.

What toner is, I still don't know. But its possession and hoarding are contentious subjects among our teachers and administrators. I stared at her, stone-faced. Her eyes glowed with unhappiness, and her hands sought and found each other before she spoke.

"Well, I guess *somebody* has to make sure that the ship doesn't sink!" I swear to God! That's how she talks, in grandiose and banal metaphors. And with these clicky, self-righteous heel taps she trotted out of the office, in her dress that matched the gray of the file cabinets, and I was alone. The file drawers were, of course, unlocked. Not because our administrators trusted us, but because they were negligent. I lifted Kevin's light folder from the BO-BY drawer, which released the tannic scent of decomposing paper. I was too thrilled to open it. So I tucked it under my left arm and my sheaf of posters under my right and ran off, doing an idiot's wobble, knees half locked. Down the echoing brown hall, through the knots of kids sneaking kisses or sly gropes, waiting for class to begin.

When Digger and I met up that afternoon, at the Flagpole, I told her I had something to show her. "The posters?" Her voice was still laden with mistrust. I wanted to keep her in suspense. I promised her I'd say, once we'd smoked. We were driving around in long ovals from her house to Kennedy to my house and back. On our second loop, we saw a man with a sky-blue megaphone haranguing the passersby from the small meadow in the middle of the traffic circle, named for a second-rate general, behind the blind back of the school. We pulled over to listen to him. "Some people want *nothing* to rule over them," he shouted over and over, through his megaphone, into the air. "It's eternity either way you look at it, my friends."

"Are you going to tell me *now*?" Digger sighed, mouthing out a torus of smoke. "Waiting doesn't make any sense." A silence, from me, from the man with the megaphone. Even a miraculous break in the flow of cars.

Then everything lurched back into motion: Digger fumbled the radio on and the shouter spread his arms and yelled straight up into the sky. I could see his Adam's apple bobbing with tremulous effort. He was just putting himself to work at it. Not caring whether he convinced anyone. It was time for me to speak, all signs indicated. I reached into my backpack and removed Kevin's file.

"What's that?" Digger asked. The folder had CONFIDENTIAL stamped on it, in red, and PROPERTY OF KENNEDY ADMINIS-TRATIVE RECORDS. In that army lettering my father uses to indicate *his* private materials. So there was some appropriate awe in Digger's question.

"It's his *file*, man," I whispered to her. I don't know why I whispered this. Because I was high, I guess. She faked a little unease, to hide her eagerness. Why do people do that at all? Fake unease, I mean? We let it lie there for a long moment. Opening it would be *proof* that we were really going to investigate. A Rubi-con. We'd both stopped breathing.

Do I even need to tell you it was a colossal disappointment? Every expected thing is, because it can't withstand the inflating power of the human mind. We went by year. Just for order's sake. First semester, ninth grade. Nineteen-ninety-fucking-six, one of the most style-free years on record. Pre-Algebra: B+. Asian History: B. Band: A. Visual Arts: C. Earth Science he had dead-bang aced, an unmodified A. Kevin had actually *been* in my Earth Science class (by mistake, I assumed, given the aptitude his later science grades suggested; Earth Science is a bullshit class), which I had almost failed—sixty-six average. Mr. Ramses, our teacher, was a charitable man. We skimmed the rest of Kevin's numbers. We could already tell they were going to be boringly normal. The upshot of the whole thing—for me, at least—was that Kevin at the time of his death had been carrying a 3.4 GPA and had a total of zero incident reports of any kind appended to his record.

"Jeez." Digger coughed. "They really thought this kid was in a *gang*? That's so *racist*. He's so *boring*." I had to suppress my surging delight, so I said nothing. My GPA was higher than Kevin's, despite his generally better performance in the sciences. Not to speak ill of the dead or anything. But having a lower GPA than a dead guy would have stung. It would have been a terrible and ignominious failure.

IV.

I DON'T WANT TO BORE YOU with trivial stuff—*Addison Schacht woke up and brushed his teeth. He had a morning hard-on and it was raining*, that kind of nonsense. Or the repetitive stuff: how many times do I need to tell you that I went to calculus? So the next thing that looms up in my memory is the Friday of the college-preparedness assembly. That day turned out to be one of those decisive ones that don't announce themselves. Which I guess all human life is composed of.

The college-preparedness assembly happened ten days after my theft from the records office. The assembly itself turned out to be dull, as I'm sure you are all shocked to hear. But I need to explain something about my line of work, in order for the events *before* the assembly to make any sense to you. Weed sales are not a seasonal business. I mean, if people want drugs, they are going to want them year-round. So there's always this steady base of demand. However, there are certain times when it spikes. Minor spikes around weekends, larger ones before school vacations, and then a long crescendo during summer, which peaks around the third week of July. Then there's a slow descent back to normal, and then we're back in the school year. September, though, is a statistical outlier. It often shows a real drop-off in sales, for me.

A lot of kids decide to "get serious" about school (hilarious!), so they take up the *ascetic practices* that they associate with high achievement. Another instance of the Protestantism infecting our society. But this year, September had been profitable. No one cared about excellence any longer in my class, or maybe the standards of excellence had come to seem trivial to us, faced as we were with the prospect of imminent release.

On account of this I had to get up early, in the colorless dawn, to go and buy more weed. I figured the transaction would take between ninety minutes and two hours. Noel, my supplier, is a weird early riser. Which is convenient. But he considers me a friend (I think). Which always makes our business dealings drag. I should explain about Noel. His father, Eliot Bradley, owns a controlling interest in Envivia, formerly Bradley Pharmaceuticals, formerly Bradley Brothers, formerly Kingman Bradley and Sons, some kind of dry-goods emporium extant in the 1820s, according to my city history textbook, which lists the Bradley family as among the most notable and permanent (white) residents of D.C. Noel has a brother named Paul Preston Bradley, and Noel's own middle name—this is amazing—is Eleuthere. Eleuthere! I got him to tell me this once, when we were making an exchange. And despite his slender, euphonious set of names, he's *huge*: one of those fat guys whose fatness is joyless. With green rings of exertion under his eyes just from breathing and walking around. When he sits his thighs spread to the width of my waist.

He lives on Otis Street, at Tenth Street and Otis. His house is tall and narrow, ash-colored, with decrepit stone pineapple finials jutting from the facade and almost no furniture inside, just a spine-broken leather couch in the living room and a king-size mattress on the concrete floor of his basement. Such houses aren't unusual in his neighborhood. Loose congregations of black guys my age build up outside the convenience stores and identical Chinese restaurants; a few buildings stand blinded with plywood slabs. Smiling and indifferent old people hunch on stoops and porches. But the same heavy blue sky covers it that covers my neighborhood, and the same absurd problems of conscience afflict its residents, I imagine, exacerbated by the grime and poverty maybe, though fundamentally identical, which should prove that squalor isn't ennobling, at least as far as basic inner makeup is concerned. Noel has *chosen* to live there, and contrary to what you think, he doesn't do so on his family money. He'd been bounced from private school to private school, this by his own admission, in D.C., in New England, one in Texas, one in Hawaii. After he was booted out of Chandler, a last-chance kind of prep school in the forests encircling Blue Knock, Vermont, his father disowned him. Old-fashioned as it sounds. I kind of admired Noel for having been disinherited, though I can't say why. His parents divorced right after he returned from the woods. As though they'd been awaiting his homecoming.

How did he get into the wholesale drug business? I have no idea. He never told me who *his* suppliers are. But he took to the work. His fat-guy's friendliness helps, even though it's *overdone*. I was at a party at his house once, right when we first met, which was right after he moved down there, and this old crackhead/junkie/general bum came around, this guy Stokey. This was three years ago. It was a June Saturday. Still balmy, the scent of whole and crushed grass filling my nose and mouth, along with the harsh stinking-sweet smoke from the blunt we were handing around. Noel's backyard has, for some reason, five or six rusted lawn mowers scattered around it. Stokey tripped over one hidden by a thatch of tall grass and weeds, and we in the circle laughed

our various stoned laughs, animal sounds: *grunt-grunt, haw-haw,*
cackles, barks, and hoots. Stokey lumbered toward us, tugging at
the pointed lower corners of the filthy blue corduroy vest he wore,
and called out, "You *best* let me hit that."

So we did, and he stood next to me, and he *stank* of dead
sweat and liquor, of decay. I was the only white guy there, besides
Noel, and that's why Stokey asked me what he asked me. "You
know what D.C. *stand* for? The letters?"

"District of Columbia?" I responded. His mouth was a ruin,
teeth post-shaped and omelette yellow, and his breath vinegary
and choking. He shook his head, as though to get rid of a gnat.

"Then I don't know."

"Drama ci-taaay," Noel warbled out. That was wrong, too.
Stokey—his eyes cleared for an instant, smiling a weird, gentle
smile—croaked out, "Don't. Care."

"Man, dis nigga *always* come up here wissome *non*sense."
Noel cackled, and my terror at his use of THE N-WORD dizzied
me, dried out my mouth. But everyone was already guffawing,
and Stokey handed the blunt to the next guy and crowed a jagged
laugh, and the conversation wandered elsewhere. A natural, right?
Noel certainly dresses the part. In winter and fall, jeans that sit
well below his ass, and billowy T-shirts, white or primary colored,
blazoned with names that mean nothing to me, the hems hanging
almost to his knees. He's too heavy, really, to need a coat. In the
spring and summer he switches from jeans to low-sitting khaki
shorts. These sit so far down that you can see only three inches
of his cellulite-dimpled pale calves above his shoes, filigreed with
greenish veins. A thin strap of beard frames his round chin. He
keeps his hair short, a caplike scrub. All this sounds like it would
look idiotic, but on Noel you half believe it. Still, meeting with
him can be trying, because—as I said—he considers me a friend.

He's always telling me stories, as he breaks off my package, about his recent imaginary sexual conquests.

It was seven a.m. when I arrived. David Cash, who remains the most muscular human being I have ever met, was already waiting on the sofa, wearing a short-sleeved T-shirt, pollen yellow, which hid his sculptural build, but veins and tendons cabled his forearms. He was the one who had introduced me to Noel. A kid from Kennedy. He graduated at the end of my freshman year, from the G&T Program, and entered the world of business. He now presides over all Noel's transactions. I watched him kick a guy's ass once: that same crackhead/junkie/general bum Stokey, who had been hassling us for a beer as we drank on Noel's stoop one night last summer. David struck him without any anger, exerting zero effort, a painter's squint in his eye as he placed his blows. "What up," David observed as I walked in. His voice, not at all as deep as you'd expect from his chest, which is the size of a concert hall, is nonetheless steel-steady. "Come on," chirped Noel, "less *do* dis." I made for the basement door. He gestured me on down, into the usual mineral stink of damp concrete.

Do you know how *weird* it is to be in the bedroom of someone who has nothing else in there other than a bed? No books, no art, not even porn magazines, not even dirty laundry or food cartons or whatever, not even *filth*. Noel's room is like a monk's cell, bare and clean. It's huge, too. One of the biggest single rooms I've ever seen. It runs the whole length and breadth of his house, front to back. Which makes the emptiness even weirder. There're even some subrooms in the back, doored off. And a big drain in the floor. It was once a workshop, I think. Noel's installed sound-proofing, these white baffles, all along the walls and ceiling, which, combined with the concrete floor, make for heavy, cottony, dead acoustics. The air always feels stifling. The only human object there, other than the bed, is a small blackboard hung on a rusty steel hook protruding between two of the baffling sheets. When I asked him, around the time we first met, what the sound-proofing and the blackboard were for, he shouted, "*Dawg*fightin, niggaaaa!" I laughed, but stopped when I saw he was serious. David later confirmed that Noel was telling the truth, although I had never been invited to any of the matches. I didn't know whether to feel relieved or insulted by this.

Noel sleeps with no sheets or comforter. How depressing is that? He has a safe hidden in the box spring the mattress sits on, which in turn rests directly on the floor, right in the cold the concrete sends up in waves. He has to lift the mattress to make any transaction. And I have to help. He won't *ask*, either; he just loses his breath and gets red, then dead-pale, and then I join in. It's in my interest, after all. Which is how it went that morning. "Man, I be *out of shaaaaape*, niggaaaa!" His usual crowed response. As though there could be some misunderstanding about the level of his fitness that required public correction.

Now he thumb-riffled the stack of money I'd brought. He never counted, in front of me, at least. He's indulgent about protocol, as though the worries of a businessman are beneath him: "Shit *sound* right." Does it? To the manner born, I guess. I knew David would feed it through their money counter later. He never·let anything pass with such flippancy. Which undercut the expansiveness of Noel's gesture. That's how it goes with the two of them, though. He handed me my purchase, crammed into a cheap brown canvas tote. Noel puts his weed in a tote 90 percent of the time. They're his signature, or whatever. Although a pretty lame one, in my opinion. I have no idea where he acquires them.

From his mother's charity work, maybe. This one said SIDNEY MEMORIAL HOSPITAL JUVENILE CANCER DRIVE on the side. There was a drawing of a bug-eyed lamb. I waited behind him as he struggled up the stairs. I figured I had less than five minutes to make my excuses before he launched into one of his fantasies. So I tipped David a nod and told Noel that I had to go. He grinned and poked two fingers into my chest. "Nuh-uh, you gotsta give me a ride uptown. I gotsta go see my *moms* and shit." He does this, at odd moments. Reminds you, I mean, that he's kind of one level up from you. But, like I said, why *not* exercise power if you have it? I almost objected: *I'll be late for school.* How would *that* have sounded, putting off a weed wholesaler with that excuse? I'd take the blame anyway, if we got searched or anything. Which he knew, of course. He's one of these amateur-of-the-law guys. He's the one who told me that having three small bags of weed gets you a much worse prison sentence than one large one, because it proves intent to distribute. As we got into my car, he cautioned me, "A smart muhfuh like you ain't need to be *told* what happens if the beast search this shit. So drive real reasonable. Ya heard?"

That fat shithead! You had to admire him. He was wearing this subtle torturer's grin as he warned me. And I knew, I *knew* he was fucking with me, but it worked all the same. (So much for the ameliorative power of the rational mind!) And so we started off, keeping a schoolteacher's pace. Weak sunlight hit everything at the wrong angle. There wasn't much traffic. Noel caught me wiping nervous sweat from my neck: "Shit, dude. Ain't nothing." The brick of weed I had stuffed under my seat. The whole trip, as I kept darting glances around for I don't know what, some manifestation of malign authority, he was unfolding a sexual tale, involved and impossible to believe. "Damn," I interjected at the appropriate times, and even whistled once. I remember nothing of this story except that he kept repeating, "And dat ass! Like a muhfuh shelf! Shit!" After Noel's narrated climax (he spoke with the embarrassing fluency produced by long inner rehearsals) we drove west to Foxhall Road (you can imagine what kind of people live there, just from the name) and then on into Palisades, where his mother lives.

The morning traffic had just started, and I was able to miss the worst of it. Every asshole in the world comes to D.C. in the morning, to work at some government job. It's the only industry we have, and everyone involved in it is miserable. So the traffic is just terrible, physically and spiritually. Noel and I were driving away from the nexus of it. We were okay. *You* know the kind of morning I'm talking about. The air was weightless, like my limbs and head. The pink light exaggerated the innocence of house-fronts and lawns. When I'd parked, he sneezed—as if on purpose, flinging an oystery gob of mucus out to cling to his upper lip. He wiped it off with his hand, then reconsidered. "Shit. You godda muhfuh *Klee*nex?" I pointed at the glove box, which he opened. And into his hummocky lap slid Kevin's school file. Yes, I'd been keeping it in my car. So what! So nothing had come of it yet, so what. It was evidence of an exploit. And exploits are valuable in themselves. Noel has this stupid pennant, anyway. On his wall. From Chandler. It's up over his couch, on the dirty wall, a white-and-red pennant. By far the cleanest thing in his house. No pictures, no posters, nothing but barren, grime-feathered paint—and then that retarded pennant. It's blindingly visible. As though it meant something. As though he played on any of the Chandler teams. Hockey! Cross-country! Lacrosse! Dressage! As though he even gave a shit! Chandler kicked him out for selling porn he stole from the general store in Blue Knock to his classmates. I've never asked him why he keeps the pennant pinned up there. But that's how everyone is. You can't refute it. Everyone holding on to the cheap tokens of their past.

"The fuck is *this* shit?" Noel asked, reading the name on the thumb-grimy index tab. "A'ight, Kevin *Broadus*, shit. I *know* who did *that* boy. You ain't got no tissues, man. And why you *got* this anyway."

I was shocked to notice the calm suffusing me. At his revelation, I mean.

"What do you mean, you like *know*? Like you know who *killed* him?"

"Man, I ain't say I *know*." This apparent self-contradiction stumped me. "And shit, man," he continued, "why you all askin' up in my face?" Sometimes he fumbles his lingo. Such performances are hard to maintain, I guess.

"Dude, I'm not like trying to be *intrusive* or anything." I almost mumbled this. Out of fucking . . . deference. Amazing, right? His audible, moanlike breathing filled my car.

"Intrusive. Shit. Man, ain't you wanna know any more?"

"But like I thought you said you didn't *know*."

"Man, ain't you listen? I ain't say I knew. I say I *heard*. Ya heard?" We go through this a lot, back-and-forths, bickering sessions. He thinks it's how you talk to your friends. He used the same methods with the guys who hung around his house. Although not David, who had kind of a zero-tolerance policy for dialectical nonsense. With the sense of being done a great service, I asked him again what he had *heard*. Phrasing it correctly this time.

So he told me. "This dude Mike, Short Mike. Mike *Lorriner*. He out of, uh, Severn, some redneck shit like that." Severn is a meaningless town somewhere in Maryland, the worst state.

"Short Mike. So like what's his like *deal*," I twittered. Noel inspected his still lightly besnotted hand and cleaned it with a fold of his vast shirt. His clothes are like bales of sailcloth. He's by far the fattest person I've ever spoken to.

"His deal? Muhfuh, you a cop? Why you care? Shit, son. Why you even wanna know?" Another stumper. How to answer this? With a weak-ass piece of obfuscation.

"I knew him. Kevin, I mean. Pretty well, actually." This didn't fly with Noel, who brapped out a laugh.

"You don't know anyone like *him*. Do you expect me to believe that? You hardly ever even come to *my* house, Addison." His accent abated here, for some reason, but he recovered himself. "*Knew* him. Shit. A'ight den, I'll tell you. White people be crazy, though, son." So he explained to me what he knew. That he'd heard from someone that this dude Short Mike had shot Kevin for insulting him at a party, and that he'd shot the others to dispose of witnesses and to make the cops think it was a random killing. "Thass *all* I heard, man. *All* of it."

I didn't believe him, on principle. How can you believe a guy who spends fifteen minutes lying to you about fucking? He'd used the shelf simile about some *other* notional girl's ass before. I remembered the little-boy's gesture he used to indicate it: stroking a new football or something. But I couldn't call him out for lying about Kevin, any more than I could for his other lies. What would have been the point? I mean, *I* was the one toting around some dead kid's permanent record. I was the *weirdo*. Also I had my commercial interests to think of. So smiles and sage nods all around! I shook Noel's hand again, in the complicated, flowing way he demanded: lock, reconfigure, unlock, touch fists. His mother's house loomed huge and cream-colored behind the gate barring the drive from public access. A tall, thin woman (presumably his mother, the former Mrs. Eliot Bradley) was crunching across the gravel in pinpoint black heels, calling out, "Noel? Noel?" She was wearing a smoke-gray suit, and her face had that leathery tan. You know: the color of a boat shoe, maybe a little lighter. Looked about as durable. "Shit, that's my moms. Peace, son." Noel initiated the process of hefting himself out of my car, his cherry-red shirt billowing beautifully. I took off as their gate creaked inward, terrified—for some inexplicable reason—that his tanned and oblivious mother would see me. They were embracing as I drove away, Noel twice as wide as Mrs. Bradley, and their awkward double figure dwindled in my rearview mirror. For all the harshness he's been subjected to by his parents, Noel does not hold them accountable. He speaks of his mother and even his father with genuine—if shy—love and respect. He knows all the particulars of his father's business dealings and his mother's fund-raising efforts. I never once heard him make a single ironic remark about either. Which is kind of astonishing.

V.

THE FIRST NOTABLE THING that happened when I got to school: a fight with Alex Faustner about the correct meaning of the phrase *begs the question*. Which she had misused seven times in a single English class. Mr. Vanderleun backed her up, and we had to go to the dictionary, and then because I was right Mr. Vanderleun got all purple and hush-voiced, and his stump waggled in fury, and by the time the whole thing was over the period had ended. For which I got an invisible wave of gratitude from everybody. Then came the assembly, which we were all looking forward to, because it would eat up another hour of class time. We were seniors, after all. And this was precisely why the admonitions from our teachers started coming. They had noticed a *restlessness*, a lack of *initiative*, a certain *aloofness* on our parts, and they wanted to remind us that, despite being seniors, WE WERE STILL PART OF THE KENNEDY COMMUNITY. It wasn't phrased so explicitly. It never is, at Kennedy. We just got a general sense that our teachers were pissed, but also that they were too . . . what . . . spineless, I guess, to crack down on us. These admonitions against our laziness came compressed into the form of another college-preparedness assembly, which my entire class was forced to attend, a throng of unfamiliar black and brown faces. The G&T kids sat in their own row. It was in the back. No one paid attention to this obvious hideous fact. Our classes were held on the fourth floor, the highest floor, and thus it took us longer to get to the auditorium than anyone else. *That's* why we had our own row, right? Nothing to see *there*.

A whole field of heads swept downward to the stage, where an aluminum stand offered the microphone to nothing. My pager kept vibrating. Digger felt it—she was resting her knee against mine, as she sometimes did in assemblies, and she gave me a knock with her sharp patella, without looking at me, as though to say, *Quite the entrepreneur.* I should mention here that public displays of affection—and this is bizarre, when you consider all the other shenanigans that pass without comment at Kennedy— public displays of affection bring with them downpours and cloudbursts of administrative trouble. So knee-to-knee contact was about all you could get away with. I know for a *fact* that Brent Academy does not have similar rules. You can see the students making out through the fence if you walk by at lunch, sitting or lying on their eternal-looking emerald lawn, goddamn Daisies and Toms (the second book ever assigned at Kennedy that provided me with any pleasure). This assembly took place Friday morning, in the hopes, I suppose, of ruining our weekend by inflaming our wretched consciences. As Dr. Karlstadt explained the nature of our still-meaningful relations to the school—"We are *all* Tigers!" emphasized by a subsequent moment of lull, as though she expected a spontaneous unitary cheer to rise—I ran through the state of my finances over and over in my head, until it was time to leave. Did you know that you can fit, on average, about thirty-four hundred dollars into a standard shoe box? At least when you use the currencies popular among high school students.

· · ·

"What are you smirking about," Digger asked as we trudged up the stairs, lagging behind the pack of our fellow achievers, staring at the flesh-colored marble floor.

"I'm not smirking." She bodychecked me, and I caught a scrap of her scent, her burnt-leaf scent.

"Nope, you were *smirking*." And here she made her idiot face: eyes crossed, crimson tongue limp in the corner of her mouth.

"No, like that was like my thinking face."

"Like your *money* face," she said through a sudden bright smile. And with no further communication the crowd parted and we followed our dividing streams, she into French and me into Latin, and the slablike doors closed and the class-starting noise— you can't call it a bell—buzzed over the PA.

I tried to think about her knee against mine as Ms. Erlacher launched into a furious denunciation of the class's performance on the last test—nice thematic continuance there, you administrative assholes! Although I myself had scored a ninety-seven, I was included in her indictment. But even setting aside Ms. Erlacher's explosion, this was quite a memorable day in Latin class, for me. This was the day Virginia Werfell completely fucked up. Virginia, a girl famous for boning two guys at the same time, just *blanked* when Ms. Erlacher asked her to translate fifteen lines from the start of book two of the *Aeneid*, beginning with *Infandum, regina, iubes renovare dolorem.* This is how Aeneas opens his tale of the sack of Troy, in response to a request from Dido, the queen of Carthage. The line means, "O queen, you command me to know again pain beyond words." *Infandum* is kind of a horrible concept: it indicates something so beyond comprehension it cannot be expressed: *in* (not) + *fandum* (to be spoken). And that's the first word of Aeneas's story! Which is kind of ironic, I guess, because he then goes on about the fall of his city at considerable length. A weird way to begin, right? It suggests that maybe underneath all the talking there really *is* some intractable, inexpressible misery.

Needless to say, not only did Virginia fail to mention any of this, which is *hugely* important stuff in the context of the book, she couldn't even come up with even a basic translation of it. She just stuttered and *uhh*ed and *umm*ed, like some dribbling retard. Ms. Erlacher started looking pissed off. So I stood up, my eyes closed and covered with my left hand, to show I wasn't even using the book, and ran through what Virgil was saying (not neglecting to point out the startling fact that Aeneas calls his city's defense against the Greek assault the *supremum laborem* of Troy, which means both the "worst travail" and the "supreme work") and even went beyond the fifteenth line. Why stop at the appointed boundary, right? I got all the way to the part about the once-magnificent isle of Tenedos now being a dangerous, wasted harbor before Ms. Erlacher started repeating, "Addison. Addison. Addison, I didn't *call* on you. Addison. Addison." She just went on like that, I kept going, and all these nervous titters fluttered around in my private, eyes-covered darkness. I took pity, though, and stopped talking, and uncovered and opened my eyes. Virginia went back to stammering. Class continued. At the end, as I was walking out, someone called, "Addison. Addison. Addison." I couldn't tell if this was meant to mock me or Ms. Erlacher or what. So I did not turn around.

After school let out I went with Digger to the Dump. Technically it's called Trash Facility 10, or so the clattering sign on its chain-link front gate says. But the attendant's shed, a compressed-looking house with green-and-white siding and a fake dormer and everything, never holds any attendant, and you can breeze right through the yawning gate without comment or opposition. It's down by the Potomac, near its eastern border, touching Maryland. It juts out into the water a bit, so there are always cadres of seagulls flinging themselves back and forth above it. You could fish from the edge, if you wanted. There's this retaining wall, gray with birdshit and vivid with graffiti. We never encountered its writers. Going there was our Friday ritual. It had no name, and she'd introduced it, as she'd introduced me to most of the innovative, freeing things I participated in. We would go there to break glass and ceramics and scream. It started as a test of the Dump's isolation. Daring—I guess— whatever authority existed to come and chastise us. No one ever showed up. We have performed this test on one hundred of the past one hundred and four Fridays, by my calculations. Which made the Dump, by far, the most reliable thing in my life. This time, with a breeze kicking from the scummy river, we destroyed a gleaming toilet with rebar rods drawn from the sucking earth. We fenced with them for a while, after the destruction, shouting, *"En garde."* And then lay panting on the hood of her car.

"I had to listen to another one of Noel's *stories* today," I groaned. She was the only person who knew about that side of my commercial arrangements.

"And you want sympathy?"

"No, I'm just like, I don't really know what I can *do*. Right? Get it from some other guy? Right?" I flopped onto my side to look at her face. She was wearing, again, the bright, hard smile she'd flashed after the assembly.

"Don't *complain* to me about that senseless shit. Don't be like obtuse. You're not obtuse. I mean, you're kind of obtuse but not *that* obtuse," she said, voice pitched low and steady. I *taught* her that word, I tell you with regret: *obtuse*. From the past participle of *obtundere*, "to beat something against something else hard and resistant." She was not wrong, however. The rubble of the toilet—an American Standard, the most glorious brand—glittered in the afternoon sun.

You're harboring all kinds of suspicions about my supposed *real feelings* right now, aren't you? Digger and I may not have been *dating*, but I was still concerned for her honor. A concept that also comes in for a lot of ridicule these days. As do most of my beliefs. And maybe I failed in my desire to protect her honor, and I often did stupid things to her myself. Witness the above little conversation. But by and large we stuck to our agreement, which was founded on those principles of honor. We had no emotional involvement. Either of us could leave at any time. Sex is natural and necessary to people our age. And in case you think that Digger or I dictated the terms *unilaterally*, or that it was some kind of tyrant/sycophant relationship: we came up with them together, right after the first time we fucked, which was about two years ago, this soft-aired night in June. We leaned out of her bedroom window smoking cigarettes and arranging the terms. And we've stuck to them ever since. I still don't know *why* Noel bothered her so much, though. Especially in light of our agreement, and in light of the fact that she smokes just as much weed as I do, and it has to come from somewhere, and better it come from someone you know, right? Someone you even have an investment in? We saved the night, though. We got over my explosion of nonsense. Digger, responsibly, took the lead. She's going to be a great woman someday. I mean a senator or what-ever. She can always just *read* you, which is terrifying, but comes in handy for getting out of awkward situations. She knew I would just sit there, not saying anything, forever, if she took no action. So she said, with a sidelong, shy look,

"I *got* one for you. A good one. What's brown and hides in the attic?"

This was the beginning of a joke about the Holocaust. Once you set aside your moral reservations about telling such jokes, another problem confronts you: what is the purpose of the Holocaust joke? It's obscure, yeah. Ninety-seven percent of people will offer you a platitude, something on the order of, *It's a way of managing the tragedy.* Oh, is it? There's no way to manage tragedy, any more than you can manage the law of gravity. It can't be redeemed or transfigured; it persists and persists without rest. Think of a phone book, of the text in a phone book, but it's a list of names, and it goes on and on without end, without even the prospect of an end. And *some* claim it's an expression of Jewish self-hatred. That's at least what the psychological counselor who Ms. Arango forced me to see after my initial run-in with Alex said, in his office thick with the soul-murdering smell of paper and ink. That's nonsense, too. Holocaust jokes are one of my central forms of expression. And only non-Jews consider me a Jew. Though that, once, could get you sent to the camps!

No, the purpose of the Holocaust joke is identical to the purpose of the joke as a larger proposition: the infliction of cruelty on the reason-inundated mind. It's just more *naked* in the case of jokes about the Holocaust. As in everything else, the fuckers responsible for our conventions of thought have mistaken a difference in degree for a difference in kind. That's why I tell them. That's the *cause* of my telling them. A sampling of my greatest hits: *Why was the little Jewish boy sitting on the roof next to the chimney? He was waiting for his parents! What's funnier than ten dead babies in one trash can? Six million Jews dead in the Holocaust! There's no business like Shoah business! Where was the*

highest concentration of Jews during the Holocaust? In the atmo-
sphere! Ketchup is just the Auschwitz of tomatoes! "My grandfather
died in the Holocaust . . ." "Really? I'm sorry to hear that." "Yeah, he
fell off his guard tower!" What's the difference between a ton of coal
and a thousand Jews? Jews burn longer! Have you heard about the
new German microwave? It's got ten seats inside! And, of course,
What's the difference between a Jew and a loaf of bread? The joke
that started it all.

So Digger told me the joke she'd dug up. "What's brown and
hides in the attic?"

"I don't know! What *is* brown and hides in the attic?" This is
the correct ritual response. She paused to collect herself. I held my
breath.

"The diarrhea of Anne Frank." The way she delivered it, in
this coy, quiet voice, a *conciliatory* voice, just *destroyed* me, that
and the fact that we were also pretty stoned, and after I stopped
laughing I told her, "Excellent job." Thus disaster was averted.
She's going to achieve greatness, and this is the proof. Do you
know how easy it is to give in to resentment under these circumstances? *Everybody* does it. Not her, though. She even agreed to
come back to my house then, even with the brick of weed stowed
under the passenger seat. I was still darting paranoid head turns
as I drove. But we made it home unarrested, and I did an invisible
celebratory dance on my way inside. Then it was time to deal with
the pot. I know I promised to spare you the details of my routine,
ladies and gentlemen. But many of you have never witnessed this
procedure. So I thought I would give you a glimpse.

The weed was dense, almost springy to the touch, fragrant.
Furred with faint red hairs. Noel has a very reliable and high-
quality connection. Fibers from the glans-shaped (think of the

head of your dick; *glans* is the Latin word for "acorn," I shit you not) nuggets clung under my nails. Now, I had a customer base to maintain. And in this, as in any small business, you have to have something that distinguishes you from your competitors. The weed Noel sold me was always good, and sometimes even better than good. Good enough to justify my 50 percent markup on it. *Unjust*, you gasp. But that's what the market will bear. And the pussies who buy from me! They have no other real sources, falling as they do in that unclear zone between middle-classness and true wealth. *Actual* rich kids can afford to be decadent, can buy in bulk. Poor or desperate kids buy retail. Good stuff, or shwag whose lack of quality is compensated for by additives: low-grade coke, PCP. Et cetera. Sometimes $H_2C(OH)_2$, or formalin, embalming fluid. Sometimes a well-known and popular insect spray, which causes nausea, vomiting, and eventual blindness. I never had to use these, which helped ensure my good reputation. But clean weed is not sufficient. You have to be *creative*. You have to have an *identity*. This can reside in your personality or person: Noel Bradley. Or in your quiet, confident scariness: David Cash. But I have no personality to speak of, and my physical weakness is pretty apparent. So I had to resort to *cosmetic measures*.

What were they? Orange peels. These, according to the lore of my schoolmates, help to keep the weed moist, which helps to keep it potent. This has always seemed like pure voodoo to me. Don't they have to dry tobacco leaves before you smoke them? And isn't dried sage or whatever, doesn't it have more flavor than its fresh counterpart? At least, you're supposed to use less of it. In cooking, I mean. My father is very insistent on this fact about dried sage, although to my knowledge he's never deployed it in any circumstances. But whatever. Every bag I sold came with a little twist of orange peel. I also made sure to use the type of Biggie bags where the little strip of plastic across the lips of the bag turns green when they're closed. On those weak props was my success founded.

I'd developed this whole little *routine* to deal with packages from Noel. I broke it down into eighths, quarters, half ounces, and ounces. I knew from experience that Biggie-brand baggies weigh between .029 and .032 of an ounce, and so I measured, making adjustments as I went. My method was simple: weigh out; add the famous Addison-identifying scrap of orange peel from the bowl of such scraps I keep in my minifridge; thumb the zip-seal 90 percent closed, leaving a vent; roll up the bag, the air escaping through said vent; complete the seal to its full piss-greenness; secure with a tag of invisible tape. And you're done. The floppy cylinders go back into the safe, to be drawn out, modularly, as needed. I could, at the height of my industrious-ness, bag and seal a pound in under an hour. You develop hor-rible neck cramps; your hands ache. The one unpleasant drudgery I faced in my occupation. I raced myself, to keep it interesting. That day I shaved seven seconds off my previous best.

Digger had stalked upstairs when I started my process. She doesn't like to be around while I do that kind of work. I heard her wander around, opening and slamming cabinets, looking for food. Her steps have a recognizable, martial time signature: 2/2. I shit you not. She clipped downstairs as I finished—she knew how long it took me to deal with a package; she'd been through this with me before—already talking. "I had to go to this thing for my mother, like a surgery-appreciation thing. Did I tell you?"

"No, did she like win the Joseph Mengele Lifetime Achieve-ment Award or something?" I'm a *funny* guy! Digger ignored this, as she pretended to ignore the handfuls of bags I was shoving into my safe. I keep it in my closet, hidden in plain sight. It's not like my father ever inspects my room, anyway. She whipped out her blood-colored pipe, which I packed with some loose weed, making foppish hand gestures. And then we got high. A rhomboid of the day's last sunlight tracked its way across my counterpane.

"What up, Mr. Money," Digger asked. She makes this remark every time I resupply. I *never* have a retort. Digger's voice, if you heard it without seeing her . . . I mean, she's *feminine*. I mean in her character. And also she has gigantic tits, for someone as short and small-framed as she is. But her voice is ambiguous. It can carry real overtones of hurt and anger, just because it's so throat-heavy.

Today, at last, I had something for her. I mean Noel's story about Mike Lorriner. I wouldn't have told her if she hadn't made that *Mr. Money* remark, which is unfair. She knows I haven't spent any of it on myself, or on anything else, other than resupplying. I now had some kind of countercharge to offer, to demonstrate my potency.

"Come on. Noel said that? And you like believe it? Noel said it. *Noel*," she crowed. I told her I did. Believe it, I mean. Just to tweak her. And suddenly I did believe. At least halfway. She—to my shock—stopped scoffing and started challenging me. Why didn't I just tell the cops? What was I going to do about it? I tried to calm her down. But here was this opportunity to satisfy this urge that I'd made a whole speech about, and I was paralyzed! (Her sentiment, not mine.)

"But it's just *Noel*, man," I said.

"Yeah, but it's either true or it's not true, even if Noel says it. And you just said you believed it." Her sudden partisanship of his theory bewildered me. Which shows how little I understand women. And the triteness of the story was suspicious. It made too much sense. Some bulky, black-hating cracker, on the town for the weekend and desperate to prove his credentials, a booze-powered party, shoving, shouts, slurs aplenty, Kevin being heroic and stolid in the face of persecution. Et cetera. But Digger persisted: "At least *check it* out," she said, "at least check it out."

My subsequent decision, if it can be called a decision and not an act of drug-induced lassitude, not a proof of my inability to resist her, could be marked as our fulcrum moment. Yes, something *that* blank-faced and ordinary. Calling Information! Oh, you can convince yourself to do anything. It doesn't even require any real effort. Just a moment of weakness or distraction. According to the 411 lady, there were nine Lorriners living in Maryland with listed numbers. Five of them lived in Baltimore, which Noel's statement that Lorriner was a redneck ruled out. Two lived in Bowie, and though I remembered Noel saying Severn, I took down their info anyway. One was named Jason and one was named Brandon. So no good. One lived in Groton Woods. Her name was Kaneia. But one of the listings, in a town called Brander's Hollow, seemed meaningful. No full name, just an initial: M. Lorriner, 9780 Fork Lute Road: 301-927-1124. "Thanks, just thank you," I gushed. And the operator's fuzzy "You're welcome" sounded charged with delight.

"Well?" Digger asked. "It makes sense," I said. "He's listed in Brander's Hollow. Or M. Lorriner is. *You* know. Brander's Hollow. They have that like Little League world series there? And there was that cross-burning lawsuit?" These statements might have been true. They might have referred to some other, similar town. To this day I don't know. I keep forgetting to look them up. I jabbed the numbers in. The line rang three times. Then someone, a man, answered. With a quack.

Rural flatness is not just a geographical feature. It comes out in the voice, too, and it came out in his. Made him sound young. That much I remember. *No criminal would talk like such a hick*, I reasoned. Right? No aesthetic coherence *there*. Digger was lip-asking something of me, with exaggerated round precision: *Is it him, is it him?* Her mouth looked enormous. I swatted my hand in dismissal, and she punched me in the biceps. Not her strongest blow—and she *can* throw a punch—but enough to distract me, so that I almost lost Lorriner. But I managed to retake control of the situation. I'd give Lorriner a fillip and let him go. No danger there. I'd never felt more secure, my after-weed cigarette bleeding smoke, Digger lying next to me, a victim on the phone. Why *not* exercise power if you have it? And so I spoke.

"Uh, yes, uh, is, uh, is this Mike Lorriner?"

"Who is this?" the man breathed. My lungs tightened.

"I know what you did to Kevin," I mumbled, suppressing a giggle.

"Ix*cyuse* may?" he twanged.

"No, I like *know*, man," I asserted. "And I'm like going to tell the cops. You like can't get away with *that* shit, man." (What?) And then I hung up. Slammed down the receiver. Digger and I laughed ourselves into exhaustion. It took two full minutes, which is an eternity of laughter.

"Oh, my God it was just some like *baseball* hick. You could just like *hear* it. Noel was like wrong. I admit it. You could just hear it. Oh, my gawd," I gasped. I sounded, now that I think about it in retrospect, like Alex Faustner.

"You idiot, man, you idiot, you idiot," Digger kept groaning. And we lay there in the afterhaze of hilarity—provoked by the pointless murder of one of our classmates. That's real empathy, right? The human race is disgusting. You can guess what we did next. At least some of you have been through similar things. It's amazing how mind-clearing a simple physical event like clumsy and enthusiastic sex can be. Does this go away with age? Literature says yes. That's a depressing prospect. What am I going to *do* with myself when I get old? You think eighteen is too young to suffer over your own mortality? *Fuck* you, ladies and gentlemen.

And in the service of ignoring mortality, Digger and I could have gone on for the whole afternoon. We did that sometimes, on weekends, engaged in *marathon* sessions. But the phone started ringing again, just when we'd barely gotten going, and I spasmed my way to the receiver. Digger burrowed her fingertips into the spare flesh of my forearm and muttered, "It's *nothing*, Addison, don't get all absurd." Her voice came from low in her throat. I picked up. I'm not *that* big a coward. It was the same guy, of course: Lorriner. He sounded less breathy, sure of himself.

"Schacht, right?"

My lips went numb with fear. "How do you know my name?" Thoughts of some globe-spanning, anti-Addison conspiracy choked and thrilled me.

"Yew *mother*fucker. Yew can't tell me sheeeit. You forgit about caller ideee?" His vowel dragged and he continued. "Mayn, I am going to like *fuck* yew up. Put yew in the daymn hospital. Put yew in the daymn *grave*yard." Then the dial tone uncoiled, gray-green, infinite. Digger—provoked by my hanging lower jaw—asked me what the fuck was wrong, as she covered her marmoreal tits. "He has caller ID," I muttered. "He knows my name. My last name." Stoned as I was, I had completely failed to reckon with this possibility. "Oh, fuck." She groaned. The rhomboid of sunlight wandered off my bed and fell onto the cold stone floor.

VI.

"IF YOU CAN WAIT just literally one second, Mr. Schacht."
Officer Pontecorvo said this, the phone pressed against her
honey-colored neck. I never learned her first name. She's the
evening desk officer at the Second Precinct, which is where the
cops who look after my sleepy neighborhood have their base of
operations. Officer Pontecorvo was, on the day I went there, just
one member of a color-specked crowd of people in the precinct's
entrance area. They wore suits, they wore coveralls, they wore
glaring print dresses. They filled the pews lining the walls or stood
near the armpit-high desk behind which Officer Pontecorvo
perched like a scribe. She was young, olive-skinned. Kind of hot.
Her dark cap covered massive tresses of darker hair. I stood at her
high desk with a dry mouth, and she flicked her eyes, one swift
up-and-down, as I explained my (stupid) problem. She did that a
lot, you could tell: sum up and dismiss men with a single glance.
She was *nice* about it, though.

The Second Precinct house is, in a word, kind of awesome.
I had walked there from the Tip-Top, where I left Digger and my
car. I use my car for business, so I figure the less the police know
about it, the better. It's distinctive, and you can never tell what's
going to stick in some cop's mind. I think they teach you to notice

stuff like that in the academy. Don't get me wrong, though. Unlike most people my age, and despite my occupation, I have no real problem with cops. They seem to lead a pretty good life. With all the excitement of private technical terms and paraphernalia. And they do provide a vital service, for all of their visible fuckups. There were actual cop cars here. And actual cops. Paunchy cops, thin cops, men and women, strutting around with that hip-shot pride particular to gunwearers. I envied them, to be honest. They conducted themselves without any hesitance. This calmed me. The precinct itself looked like the synagogue (Temple Emunah; wispy-voiced Reform) my father and I attended once every three or four years: blond brick, low and spread out. A lot of windows. I didn't expect that. A milk-pale man with two Bozo-the-Clownish protuberances of gray hair sprawled and slept on a pew, right inside the front door, his blue nylon pants exposing the last eighteen white inches of his shins. That much I remember.

Going to the cops at all had been Digger's idea. She hadn't believed me at first when I told her, still sprawled in the cooling bed, that Lorriner had threatened to kill me. We were both pretty high, and naked. My *hard-on* hadn't even wilted. I had difficulty believing the fact of the call myself. I mean, he was just some hick idiot, right? That's how it looked to me: he was overresponding to my accusation out of fear. I mean, if some stranger called *you* up and accused *you* of murder, what would *you* do? But she insisted and insisted. She got so *angry* when I tried to shrug it off. I think, also, she was kind of pissed about the sex being inter-rupted. Although she would never admit anything like that.

So I agreed to go, "as soon as we come down." A not-terrible idea. I mean, we hadn't done anything *wrong*. But I had an amendment of my own. I didn't want to go in without some cover story. So I proposed telling them that I wanted to do an oral history project about Kevin, the same lie I had offered our teachers. I'd tell them this at first, and then, once I'd gained their confidence, cleverly let slip what I knew about Lorriner. Digger accepted that compromise. We even stopped off at the Tip-Top on the way. I managed to eat one limp slice of toast, and Digger rammed down a Tip-Top Deluxe in under a minute. The grill man, this Stalin-mustached guy, abandoned his suspicious apathy to shoot her an admiring glare. We parted with a single-pump handshake, in token of greater sobrieties and successes to come. "*Should* be back in like an hour," I muttered professionally. Stalin Mustache returned to scraping carbonized fat off the iron horizon of his griddle.

"No, hang on." Officer Pontecorvo was now laughing at the person on the other line, her index finger in the air instructing me to be patient. "Yeah, I got this guy with an unusual request. Addison Schacht, he says his name is. Uh-huh." To me, now, her brow darkening: "You said oral history, right?"

"Yes, that's basically it. I read Lieutenant Huang's name in the paper?"

"I mean, I'm sure he'd like to help you. But I don't know how much he can say." Sweet and assuaging. Her nails, painted white, had little enamel palm trees on them, and I knew she was going to hang up and kick me out. So I started to beg. Subtly. Using this wounded, sort of childish voice. It goes with the face Digger was talking about.

"No, I understand that. I understand that. But if you'll just . . . ma'am, it's like I just *need*—" And here she interrupted.

"Please don't say that. Ma'am. I'm too young."

I licked my lips. She laughed again, at my obvious discomfort, and started explaining over the phone to the lieutenant.

"Yeah, I know it's unusual. Yeah, I know. I *know* about the dinner. Yeah, I'm sorry. He *seems* normal," she told her interlocutor. "Yeah, yeah, in back. I'll send him back. No, I won't. He says it's for school. Right? No, I told him that. No, I told him that already. Okay. Okay. Yes. I owe you a bucket of chicken. All right? And a six-pack. It's agreed." And she hung up. And winked and grinned at me in self-amusement. Her teeth were flawless.

"Go wait in there, down the hall," she said, hooking a thumb. "Where all the desks are. He'll *see* you. Don't worry." *This isn't* actually *happening*, I muttered in my head. That's how foreign even small-scale fake success is to me.

In there was a big bullpen filled with partition-fenced desks. Some bank office, or wherever telemarketers work: that's how it looked. Green baize, photos of children, their tacked-up artwork. Except that it was empty of people. Phones went off and agitated murmurs from the receiving dock filtered back to me. There was a small square filth-specked mirror near the entranceway, and by making dainty leaps and spine contortions, walking toward it and away, I was able to get an image of my whole *gestalt*. I'd put on my holiday suit, lawyer-black, for the occasion, and a tie I'd swiped from my father's closet. Also, for some reason, I was carrying a briefcase with nothing in it, this old narrow-gauge black leather attaché my father discarded when I was eleven, and which seemed to me the height of aesthetic magnificence then. Scars of use dented all its edges, and its vertices had been blunted by handling. I know now that I looked like a gawky, underfed idiot, someone über-insignificant. But I managed to convince myself then I looked pretty *goddamn* impressive. I accomplished this legerdemain in a few seconds and was sitting at one of the desks furiously scratching my balls *sub rosa* when Lieutenant Huang arrived.

• • •

I should, by rights, still carry a real animus toward Huang. He bears no small responsibility for the dramatic subsequent course of my life. Which presented many new and unpleasant complications. Those of you who live in a less absurd city than D.C. will have a hard time granting any credence to what follows. I don't blame you. First of all—and let's be honest—I *sound* like an asshole. I *know* that. I mean, I haven't ever had a *real* job or fathered a child, or even gone to college. I've only fucked one girl. I still believe—though I haven't done much achieving in this department—that you should fuck as many women as possible. Admitting this will negatively influence your decision about me. But I can't help believing it. I also know all these qualities mark me out as someone free of experience. And that my writing leaves a lot to be desired, because it *pretends to be experienced*. How *else* am I supposed to write, though? Despite these vitiating factors, you have to believe me. About my interaction with the cops, I mean. I mention this now because, in retrospect, a little more professionalism on my part that day would have spared everyone involved in this retarded story a number of painful and lasting memories. Though they say life is meaningless without painful memories. Dubious.

I have no problem admitting that Huang makes quite an entrance. A tall man with bulky shoulders carried high and clenched, striding squeakily down the linoleum floor. His close-cut dark hair gleamed like a pelt, scattered with gray. He seemed to be looking over my left shoulder, and his mouth was already open for forceful speech. A golden incisor glinted.

"Are you Addison? I'm James Huang. We're going right over *here*." How could I refuse *that*? We left the telemarketer pen for a long, blazingly lit hall, passing room after room, one echoing with the fuzzed shouts of television, and came out in another large open space. A lecture room. Student desks filled it. You know: hard ceramic-and-aluminum setups, chairs with a swooping tiny desk attached to one side. They're almost impossible to turn around in. There was a dust-patched blackboard, too, on the same wall as the door, which all the desks faced. "Right over here, Addison. Have a seat." Huang remained standing.

"Thanks," I chirped. Huang was already speaking again, though.

"Hey, Baltimore? Baltimore? You wanna sit in? You wanna sit in on this? Addison, this is Sergeant Baltimore. Addison comes to us from Kennedy. He wants to talk to us about the Broadus killing. You were classmates?" he asked me. Another cop hooked himself around the steel jamb of the entrance. He was younger than Huang, rectilinear of build, dark skinned.

"Yes, sir. Class of two thousand. I mean, he would have been class of two thousand. I'm doing a kind of a project?"

They stood there eyeing me from their separate positions, like a vaudeville team. I had no idea what to say. So I didn't say anything. Huang waited before speaking, looking (it seemed) at each separate part of my face, noting each element. I admired his craft.

"Well, Addison, I'd *like* to help you. I know how disturbing it is, something like this. I have a daughter that age. Your age. So I know." Baltimore was flicking through a stack of papers he'd brought with him, his fingers swift and certain. "And I'd *like* to help you with your project." Huang was grinning, flashing me his incisor again. "I'd like to. The thing is, Addison, I assume you got my name from that article? I've gotten a lot of calls because of that. I don't know Arch Sexton. Personally, I don't know him. But

I think he was unfair to us. I think he made us look like we weren't doing our jobs." He worked something out a dental crevice with his tongue. I could see its motions through the skin of his cheek.

"No, sir, I don't think that at *all*." I poured as much saccharine assurance into my voice as I could muster.

"Okay, fine, that's fine. Whatever. I don't want to seem unfriendly," Huang continued. Baltimore stopped shuffling papers, his hands poised and pincered. "I know how upsetting events like this are. But we *are* working. The investigation is ongoing. And because it's ongoing, there's not much I can say to you about it. About Kevin. Do you understand? Legally I can't say anything to you. Does that make sense?" asked Huang.

"I mean, do you guys have like a system for that? For privacy and things like that? Like with priests?" This slipped out, but I actually liked how stupid it sounded, hanging in the still air of the lecture room.

"Do we have like a system? I'm not sure what you're asking. There are procedural *rules* that forbid me to *tell* you anything. It's just a simple matter of protecting the people involved with the investigation. Of protecting their privacy. So I suppose we have a system, yes. But it's not like priest-penitent. Do you know what I mean by that? It's not codified."

I nodded. My *I'm just a dumbass kid* act was working. Huang's speech was couched in a tone of friendly concern, despite the stony clarity of his eyes. As though I were asking him for some confusing but reasonable favor. "You want some coffee?" Huang drummed one heel while he spoke, which made all the metal on his person jangle.

"No, I'm not like the biggest fan of coffee. Although I drink it a lot. That's not like a position of *criticism* or anything."

"Well, in that case," murmured Huang, through his clinkings,

"I think we're pretty much clear here, yes?" Baltimore made an affirmative noise deep in his throat. "So *since* we're clear—I mean about the fact that I can't talk to you, Addison, and I don't mean to sound unfriendly here; I would *not* want you to get that impression—but since we're clear I think we should probably just stop this before it gets into legally murky areas. Do you understand what I mean?"

"Well, it's like sort of like an *involved* situation," I offered, my eyes narrowed in fake confidence. Then I added, "And I wanted to like make you *aware* of it. I wanted to do this project. It's not about the crimes. It's about Kevin. As a personal thing. Just about your opinions. An interview." You know that *voice* you use when you're instructing a bellhop? I had it now.

"An interview." Huang sighed, dropping his heavy lip over the golden incisor. Baltimore rotated himself into the desk next to me, sprawling forward to speak: "We're not trying to hurt your chances in school. But we just *can't* talk to you." Having said this he flicked his (extremely cool-looking, bottle-green with a gray ovoid feather) fedora back from his forehead. I flinched away at the movement and flushed at my own cowardice.

Ladies and gentlemen, you have to hand it to the cops of my city. They had not, in three months, made any visible progress on apprehending Kevin's killer. But they had their script, to deal with questions, and it flowed with such inarguable smoothness. Looked at objectively, I had no rights in this situation. I knew that. I mean, how can you force a cop to do something he doesn't want to? He's the cop; he has the gun, and the whole dreary edifice of the law behind him. It's like in school. You can't get anything done with brute force. You have to be clever. "Now, if you'll just step this way, Addison, Sergeant Baltimore here will show you out. I'm sorry that we can't be more helpful to you." Huang had moved closer to me as he spoke. Not threatening. Just maybe to point out that I was on shaky ground here. He must have been about six-foot-six, and I was sitting. His suit jacket shifted as he moved, enough for me to see the brown leather of his armpit holster. Baltimore grinned in horrible and horrifying intimacy and adjusted with two fingers the crown of his green hat. I could smell their mingled colognes.

Sometimes you have to commit yourself to a next, more atrocious step in order to escape. That was the essence of my plan. Talk my way in, and then really dig myself into the shit. You marry somebody, maybe, to avoid an unpleasant breakup conversation with them. Right? I mean, I don't know from experience, but that doesn't seem *totally* implausible. I didn't think of it this way until much later. I mean that I'd set in motion something I had no hope of controlling. At the time I felt über-slick, like a goddamn spy. I had no intention of going back to Digger empty-handed, which she would blame me for, since I'd explained my plan to her. Some plans you need to keep quiet, because their failure will result in humiliation. Huang and Baltimore stooped like careful vultures over me, smelling of sandalwood and salt. I knew it was time to deploy the second part of my plan. I grinned. I was really about to lay something on them. They both smiled back, taking my grin for a sign of acquiescence.

So I told them what Noel had said. To justify my presence there. Not a lie. But the repetition of what I suspected might be a lie. Where's the harm in that, right? Right into Baltimore's hat and Huang's gleaming grin, right into them, I said, "I think like I may have found this *guy* who has something to do with the Broadus case. Like with an uninvestigated *aspect*. That's kind of why I wanted to do this project. To find out. I thought maybe it could help, too." I used the words *uninvestigated aspect* and *case* for the gloss of insider knowledge they bestowed. This immediately made things much worse than I could have imagined. Or maybe "could have admitted." That's a truer way of putting it.

It *did* make them perk up, at least. Both of them, in perfect sync. I might have just said, "Fuck you." Or called Baltimore THE N-WORD. Or something else unthinkable according to our social conventions. But it stunned them. Just for a second, though. Huang was the first to recover.

"Addison. Uh, I'm going to need you to tell me a bit more about your sources on this. Do you know this guy? Lorriner? Have you seen him?"

"Well, it's more of a like *conjecture*."

"Well, yes, but I still need the name of the person who provided you with this information," Huang purred.

"I can't give you that. He asked me not to. He only told me because I promised to keep him out of it." If Noel found out I had mentioned his name to the cops, he'd have David beat the shit out of me. And worse: he'd cut off my supply.

"Okay, well, then, in that case I'm afraid we're just going to have to treat it as useless. I'm sorry, but we can't just accept speculation. Do you have any idea how many cranks we've gotten? On this case, particularly. I shouldn't even be telling you that. But we have to have some reason to follow up. Is your friend in a position to know? And if so, why would he be?" Huang had his large, bony hands spread out now. Baltimore was looking through his papers again, sitting next to me. I could feel the small wind they kicked up as he riffled them. I had no answer. Huang kept talking.

. . .

"Addison. I have a daughter your age, like I said. And I understand how upsetting things like this can be. But I also know how it is. I mean to be your age. You want to help. You rush into things. You're making a very, very serious accusation here. You're accusing someone of murder. And you won't even tell us the name of the person who passed along this accusation to you. What are we supposed to do with this? Huh?" He was breathing a little harder now. His nostrils had gone pale, and they were contracting and dilating. I was starting to feel sort of afraid now, to be honest. But I had to go on, right? I mean, I'd started this whole thing.

After a slurp of air, I repeated what seemed to me one of my most genius phrases: "I just wanted to offer some insight into what I think has been an uninvestigated aspect of the case."

Baltimore shot out of his seat when I said this: "Come on!" Huang held up a hand. "No, no, don't go. Someone else needs to be here for this. Another pair of eyes. All right?" He addressed me now. "Addison, tonight was supposed to be my first night off in fourteen days. That's how my schedule works, at the moment. I don't get normal weekends. Do you understand what I mean? I'm supposed to be, right now, having a meal with my family. With my daughter. Whom, as I've said, is about your age. Although she does not go to Kennedy. Which I'm beginning to think more and more is probably one of the more responsible decisions I've made."

He was looking at his knuckly hands, twisting his wedding band around his pillar-like ring finger.

"If you have *something*, some kind of description of this guy, some rationale, or if you want to give me more information about your friend, the source, we can move forward. Otherwise, I'm afraid you're going to have to leave. We're going to have to treat this as not worth checking out. *I've* never heard of this Lorriner guy. And you're in fucking *high* school." Baltimore nodded, giving me a bulgy, skeptical eye.

Huang took a showy breath. "I'm sorry. I shouldn't have let my temper show. But Addison, you've got to *help* us here. You say you *want* to help us. Do you have a description? Do you have *something* for us?"

My palm, wet now with the sweat of imminent failure, farted against the attaché handle.

"No, I don't necessarily have a *description* but—"

"But? But? There's no but here, Addison. All right? This is not some negotiation. You seem like a smart kid. But it's time for you to go. Okay? Baltimore can't sit here all night, and I'm not even supposed to *be* here, at the moment. Do you understand that? I have a family, too."

I gripped the handle harder. My sweat was copious, warm and tacky. Like fresh, still-drying blood. Huang looked at me with pissed-off expectancy. "Come on," Baltimore was already drawling. I stood up, yes. But just as a delaying tactic. I had one play left. I would tell them about the death threat. That would move them, I figured. It would have to. I had a vague idea that death threats were illegal. I opened my mouth to speak. And then, ladies and gentlemen, I underwent what at the time I regarded as a major illumination. *I thought of a better story*. I mean, if they didn't care about Lorriner, why would they care about his making a death threat? It was all just some *game* to them. So I changed my story. At the last possible second. I decided to try a more personal tone. As though *I* were the one suffering. *I have a daughter that age*, Huang told me. A point, I thought, of vulnerability. Your family makes you a hostage to circumstance, right? Baltimore clamped his magnificent hat down above his pointy ears. Huang gave me a curt wave good-bye. So I said:

"He was a friend of mine." My throat sort of clenched. My palms were soaked. This *vacuum* coursed through my innards as soon as the lie was out.

"Who? Who are you talking about?" Huang shouted. "This alleged murderer? Who? Who do you mean?"

"Kevin." I'd wanted to put a throb of fake pain into my voice, but it had gone sawdusty. My statement produced a long silence from Huang. I was suddenly too miserable to take any satisfaction in it.

"Addison," said Huang, after several rapid blinks. "Addison, I *understand* why you're here. We *both* do. You want to help. But this is not helping. If anything, it's making the problem worse. Because it confuses the real issues, and it distracts us from doing our job. I know what it's like to lose a friend. I know that you're probably desperate for answers. I hope you never have to go through it again. But the simple fact is that the investigation is ongoing, we're doing everything that we can, and I assure you that we will catch the people who did this. Whoever they are. Have you tried grief counseling? I can give you the card of someone who specializes in that. Okay? I think you should go. I think you should try not to think about it so much. Okay? Is there someone you'd like us to call?"

I had no idea what to say. I'd just told, I was realizing, the single worst lie, morally speaking, the most profane lie I'd ever told in my life. You see why it's so terrible? Why I should have stuck to the death-threat story? You see how bad it is to claim a friend posthumously? Is that even *indexable* on any normal scale of morality? Huang and Baltimore looked at me. With real concern. Which made everything much worse. I'd never felt so morally deformed. Or humiliated. Despite my suit and my empty briefcase, despite the stolen tie, despite my clever, useless plan, I was just some idiot kid to them, whose griefs were to be dealt with through mildness and conciliation, whose lies were to be believed. The anger at being kept from dinner had left Huang's eyes. Baltimore said, "Come on," almost avuncular now. "Is there someone we can call?" Huang repeated. And—out of humiliated exhaustion, or out of my heated and burgeoning sense of guilt—I croaked the digits of my father's phone number. Baltimore took, with a gentle hand, my elbow. The interview was over. I'd been dismissed. The worst part? Walking with shame-shadowed, childish eyes past Officer Pontecorvo, as Huang and Baltimore escorted me, like two court-appointed guardians, back into the precinct house's front area to wait for my father. She got up and stretched, arms overhead, while I was crossing the echoing room. Even through her stiff-lined, graceless uniform, I could see the astounding contours of her tits and ass. A momentous, just-discovered landscape. A reminder from God about my lowly station.

VII.

I HAVE TO INTERRUPT to explain something. I told you my mother was dead. I don't think about her a lot. I was young when she died, and the inexpressible pain that it caused went away over time. I know that sounds inhuman, but it's true. She would have wanted it that way, I think: for me not to be unhappy. And even if I don't think about her all the time, I do *remember* her. She was always happy, or I thought as a child she was always happy, because she was usually smiling. She was a book editor, when she died. At this small publishing house. Black Meadow Press. I never understood the name. It went out of business the year of her death, and when I was a kid I always thought the two things were related. I mean, of course she wasn't *always* happy. No one is, and she and my father used to have terrible arguments, because he's so helpless, I figured out much later.

She was a great cook and a great baker, so that even a kid with no other experience in eating would notice. She was competent too, with her hands. She once put in a new segment of pipe under our sink. Lying on her back, half-hidden in the space under the counter where the pipes are. She let me help her, or pretend to help her. I handed her a vise grip. My father told me that they met at a gallery opening for a friend of his who later went on to become semifamous, a sculptor in wire and untreated animal skins, that they met about a year before I was born. Her family had been in D.C. for generations. Five or six. Her maiden name was Hiller: before she married, she was Katharine Hiller. I'm named after her father, like I said. She had, instead of a diamond on her engagement ring, a cloudy, glimmering stone. An opal chip. I learned the name of the stone from my father.

You don't give a fuck, of course. I'm only mentioning these particulars to help explain the following. When I turned seven, I had a miserable party at which the Eichman brothers, small-eyed, oval-headed twins, ganged up on me in my own backyard and battered my head with two identical white-pine dowels. That's actually their name: *Eichman*. Who wouldn't change their name, if it were Eichman? Someone who takes pride in it, right? Or someone who argues, *Adolf Eichmann had* TWO NS, *you dirty fucking Jew,* SO SHUT YOUR JEW MOUTH! The sticks they hit me with were meant for the piñata my parents had procured to liven up the party. Which failed, predictably, to open. Everyone blamed me for this, I could see by their eyes.

A chocolate cake with marshmallow frosting. That much I remember. My mother had baked it. She stands out, like I said, as an excellent baker in my lucid, fragmentary memories from childhood. The cake was *really* impressive, for homemade. HAPPY BIRTHDAY, ADDISON! With crisp punctuation. The message written in azure frosting. And for some reason, my head still aching from the blows, instead of puffing out the candles I *spit* on them, to the delight and disgust of all the kids gathered around, who emitted a cheery simultaneous groan. My father, I saw when I looked up, was twiddling the bridge of his nose and staring at the floor. I realized in ninth grade that this is his *I'm embarrassed for you and can't look at you* gesture. Which doesn't make the memory any easier. But my mother was trying not to laugh. She'd tied her hair back to do the baking, and it was still up, and a freckle of flour marked her right earlobe.

Two days after this party, I ran stumbling (as usual) through my front door from the schoolbus. As soon as I was inside, the sharp, sweet stench of human feces shot into my nose. I had no idea where it was coming from, but it frightened me. I began yelling for her—for my mother, I mean. With every call that got no response, I felt sicker and sicker, dizzier and dizzier. A sense of things being *unreal*. You remember how nauseating that is, when you're a child. I ran back and forth through the house, down into the basement, out into the yard, then unoccupied by any kiln. I don't know why it took so long for me to check my parents' bedroom, which is on the second floor. I was choking as I ran up the steps. The concussions of my feet sounded dead, flat. When I opened the bedroom door, I saw why everything stank of shit.

Arched over the bed—on her knees, arms spread in mute plea—was my mother. She was wearing a towel and the inside of each thigh was stained brown. I realized I was running in place. Her hair, water-darkened, clung in a thick tendril to her upper back, and the bloody tip of her tongue quivered in the corner of her mouth. "She's sick she's *sick*," I screamed at the 911 dispatcher, when he asked me what my emergency was. My father said that the EMTs found me clinging to her shoulders, and that I lashed one stooping paramedic's knee with the back of my open hand, moaning, "Get *away*, get *away*." We were sitting in the waiting room of Philip Sidney Memorial Hospital when he informed me. My mother died of a brain hemorrhage at the age of thirty-two.

Brain hemorrhages can happen to anyone, at any age, at any time. For no detectable reason.

My father did not shed a single tear over my mother. I'm *not* bringing this up in reproach. I don't know what he went through, because we still haven't talked about it. I came close once. I was eight; it had been about a year. He'd just gotten his silly job at the Cochrane Institute, as a result of which I became—with considerable pride—a part-time latchkey child. "Did you know that I'm a *latchkey* child?" I asked him. He knuckled my head, which was his gesture for affectionate dismissal then, and told me he was busy, and hoped I forgave him. "*I* don't mind," I sang back. We were in our yard, watching the laborers he'd hired build the kiln, laying the specially ordered ceramic bricks, then putting up the joists of a small shed. "Fuck," one of them screamed, and trotted past us, grimacing, down to his truck at the curb. His thumb, hit with a hammer, I think, was empurpled and angry-looking.

That's the closest we ever came to discussing her. And I only ever asked about his involvement with his students once, in a general way, soon after he started seeing the first one: Margit. He justified it by pointing out that he's a *consulting instructor* at the Cochrane. "It's not the same thing as a *professor*," he assured me. More than that I *couldn't ask*. Because I never said anything to him about my mother. Which—if you look at it with strict logic—precluded me from *ever* criticizing him. I let his indiscretions with students pass, making zero comments. He used to bring them by, sometimes, the students I mean, Ingrid, Nadja, Fatima. They were all pretty, in a frightened, foreign way. Or maybe that was just him. He has that effect on people, putting them off without their being able to explain it. I mean, he has that effect on me, too, but I've been getting the suicide speech for five years at this point. Fatima he brought by more than once, six or seven times my junior year. Then a long absence over her vacation. A postcard came from her, which said, WISHING YOU WERE HERE—in all caps—and then something scrawled in cursive. It appeared to be French, which my father pretends to understand. On the front was a photograph of the Leaning Tower of Pisa. Fatima was angled, taller than me. *His* height. With long blue-dark hair and a hawkish profile. Teeth tea-stained with nicotine. A thick open-woodwork bracelet always careening up and down her reedish forearm, hairy as a boy's.

Most guys my age would deny that their fathers wield any *real* authority over them. Or they would claim to admire them as a way of admitting defeat. Mine, however, has never applied any discipline, period. He considers himself to have more important things to do. He believed I'd arrived at an acceptable state of existence without it. That's fair. Even *complimentary* to me, if you look at it right. So why would I resent him for *that*? It makes perfect sense on its own, and it would have worked out that way even if my mother hadn't died. People don't change, you always hear. Yet I can't avoid thinking that, if she were still alive, he would lower himself to the act of disciplining me. I don't know why I think this. It has something to do with my memory of her as a baker, a profoundly serious occupation.

Or at least, maybe he would have better taste in neckties. The one I'd borrowed for my trip to the cops was gaggingly hideous. Three fat blue diagonal stripes on a background of chartreuse. He loves all of them, though, every ugly one. *Cares* about them. In fact, his first words to me in the precinct house were, "Addison, *is* that my tie?" Faux-jolly, hands planted on hips, delivered through bloodless lips. You *know*. How adults sound when they're trying to be *good sports* or whatever? I was waiting near Officer Pontecorvo's desk, and Huang was standing next to me, checking his watch. My father had arrived winded and sheened with sweat. From anxiety. Remember how I said before that he has only a few genuine qualities? Reverential fear of the police is one of them.

"Well, Officer, I'm *glad* we were able to get this all cleared up. And I'm *so* sorry," he cooed to Huang.

"Why are you *sorry*?" Huang asked.

"I'm just. About all this. *You* know."

"Well, there's nothing to be *sorry* about, Mr. Schacht. I just wish we could have been more helpful to Addison." My father squinted in confusion at Huang. "Are you all right, Mr. Schacht? Is there something I can do for you?" Huang's eyes had gone stony and clear again.

"No, no. I wouldn't want to impose. I worry that Addison has. I mean, it's sort of shameful. If you think about it. Wasting your time. It's just." He can end sentences that way, no problem. All aquiver with some subhuman emotion.

"*I* dunno," Huang began, grinding his palms into his eyes. "Everybody makes *mistakes*." He lowered his hands. With his gaze unobstructed, Huang looked mortified now, sorry for my father. And sort of creeped out.

"But still," my father gasped.

"Mr. Shacht, I don't really see a *need* to discuss it." Huang's voice had slackened. So my father jumped back in with, "Well, I'm sure we'll *all* feel better about it in the morning." A slave's grin splitting his face. I worried he might give Huang a bro punch, on the shoulder. "Oh-kaaaay," said Huang. With real caution. His eyes showed a slight gleam of obvious discomfort at my father's bootlicking. I couldn't blame him. I mean, wouldn't you be deeply uncomfortable if some stranger came and started kowtowing to you? For no apparent reason? Luckily, my father had run out of apologetic things to say. So he pawed at Huang's hand and dropped his brow in . . . fucking deference? Amazing, right?

"Addison, you can't just go around talking to the *police* like that," he admonished me in his car. Our progress through the lot and untrafficked streets had been silent, and we didn't speak until the fourth stoplight.

"It's dangerous, for everyone. Why were you there?" he asked, and tousled my hair. "Is everything all right?"

I'd never *actually* wanted to hit him before. Does that make me unusual? I could not believe he had tousled my hair. Or that he was talking to me this way. Although this is how he always acts when he's trying to show concern, which is not often. Using gestures that seem completely fake, and talking the way parents talk in the videos they make you watch in health class, about condoms and drugs and whatnot. I know you're not interested in these details. They can't be meaningful to someone who doesn't know him. I was suddenly so furious that I could barely speak. And he was looking at me in this way he has, quizzical and presumptuous at the same time. Like we're good friends, or something.

He makes that face when he's undergoing a spasm of fatherly sentiment.

"And what did Huang mean when he said he thought what you were doing was good? Are you doing something? Can't you tell me what it is that you're *doing*?"

Who talks like this? Who? I'd just *stood* there in numb obedience while he gushed to Huang, fingering my purloined tie, instead of screaming at him. Why all this muteness in life? And the thing is, despite his fumbling gestures, he didn't even care, really, what had been going on. Because it asked for no public involvement on *his* part. Other than a little obsequiousness to calm the imaginary anger of the police. So I mumbled out a response, my voice sluggish and muddy. If he'd actually given a shit, he would have heard that it was a lie.

"It's for school. I'm just doing a project. Oral history. Okay? It's just a project. About Kevin. I like already *told* you, before. Remember? Last week? Digger told you. When you were—" I almost said *drunk.* "When you came back from class."

"Oh, yes. Right. Right!" That fucking specious assent. He clearly had no idea what I was talking about. Do you see why he's so impossible to deal with? "I see, I see, I see, I see, I see. Well, you should have asked me anyway. It's better not to get too involved with the police. Right? With these things? You see why I'm right? It can be dangerous."

I didn't say anything, and we drove on into the mild darkness. Counterfactuals are useless. About my mother, about neckties, about whatever. I called Digger as soon as we'd gotten home. I had to exchange a terrified hello with her mother, but when Digger came on the line I just started explaining. I left out some irrelevant details, of course, such as my complete and utter sense of humiliation and moral idiocy. I just gave her the basics: they had refused to talk to me; they hadn't gone for my plan. She didn't sound pissed. Just sort of amused. Which made it all right, somehow. You were expecting the *opposite*. That if she laughed it would make me feel *dickless* or something. But I'm not much of an egotist. At least, not in that way. My father was singing in the shower as we spoke. Up and down, bubbling arpeggios. Weird, right? But hey—what's a son *for*, if not to listen? I listened to him hum and gargle his way through some aria, with one ear. Digger's deep voice vibrated in the other. A sudden vertiginous sense of release flowed through me, giddiness, maybe, from having nothing at all to do. I'd tried. And failed. And if the thought of my lies to the cops still nauseated me, it was nothing some weed and an afternoon in bed with Digger would not banish from my mind. You see how easy it is, ladies and gentlemen?

"I'll see you tomorrow?" Digger asked. We had plans. They were showing *The Sorrow and the Pity*—which is this ass-numbingly *boring* documentary about the Holocaust—Saturday afternoon at the Camelot. The Camelot, like I said, is the movie theater right next to Don't Shoot, where I bought my favorite edition of the *Aeneid*. I forgot to mention that it's a combination art film/porno theater. It shows *The Sorrow and the Pity* at least twice a year, and Digger and I always go. To make fun of it, you're thinking. I don't blame you, given everything I told you about my Holocaust jokes. But we don't. I saw a scrap of it on television once, a few years ago. And I couldn't get it out of my head. I thought at first that it was like a public television special or something, but my father told me it was a movie, an actual in-theaters movie, although it came out a long time ago. And it's not action-packed or anything. It's kind of boring, like I said. That's what I *like* about it. It wasn't boring in the trivial way that school or life is boring. It has this more massive boringness. Its boringness *intimidates* you, shuts you up. You can't say anything in response to it. You can't even criticize it, because that would be the same as criticizing history itself. There was also, following the *The Sorrow and the Pity*, a movie called *The Erotic Adventures of Marie-France*. Which Digger and I had joked about sticking around for, but which we both knew we'd chicken out of watching.

"I'll see you tomorrow," I confirmed. My father stopped

singing and the faucets squeaked off. I never heard him leave, because it took me five seconds to fall asleep. A record, in my case.

But in that sliver of consciousness, this memory *ambushed* me. From last year, right near the end of school. It's about Alex Faustner. About the time I made her cry *without* telling a Holocaust joke. Why it should have surged up then, right as I perched at the lip of sleep, who knows. I never think about it otherwise. Anyway, it happened last June. In English class. A hot, fly-buzzing day. Alex was going on and on about the *Aeneid*, which we were reading in English for our world-literature segment (that offensive Burton Fragment translation I mentioned before), about how awful Aeneas's behavior was, how Virgil glorified violence (true, but not in the sense she meant), how Aeneas or Priam or Virgil or the poem itself "prevented dialogue" (what?).

And yes, I admit it: I lost it. Without being called on, and shouting over the objecting chirps Ms. Prather emitted, I launched into a speech, in a choked voice. "No, man, you're missing the whole point. You can't apply *our* virtues here. You can't! They were operating under a whole different set of ideas. You can't *judge* them. You can't judge Virgil. Are *you* planning on writing something that we'll like still be reading in thousands of years? Are you? You have no right! You just don't. Okay?" Or at least, that's what I tried to say. I'm sure it came out as incomprehensible noise, a series of shouts and gargles—I was trying to cram a whole philosophy into twenty seconds. Although that's a good sign for any philosophy, if it *can* be distilled into a sentence or two. I leaped up, tumbling my date-carved chair to the ground with a ringing clatter. My hands moved, chopping and beckoning. Alex smirked in dismissal. Until I came to the crest of my speech and pointed at her, my index finger stiff and aching with anger, shouting in a voice taut with anger, given sudden clarity by it: "You *cretin*. You know NOTHING of what you're talking about." Yes, *cretin*. Yes, emphasis on the NOTHING. Archaic. But it just came out that way, I swear!

Ms. Prather stopped her chirping and looked at me with open hatred. Which I deserved. Then, to my surprise, Alex started crying. Not her usual pleading snivel. But real crying. She apparently gave a shit, ladies and gentlemen, whether I thought she was a cretin. Her delicate, high-boned face collapsed, and her glossed razor-straight dark hair cascaded forward, falling from her tawny neck with deliberate grace, and she stumbled and loped to the slablike door, which she stiff-armed open. I felt no remorse. I was shocked what I said had *any* impact at all. I felt . . . *nothing*. At first. Ms. Prather wasn't saying anything and neither was anyone else. We could all hear Alex's muffled sobs. She was standing right outside the classroom, I could see the top of her gleaming hair through the cross-wired window in the door. I stayed, swaying, for a long three seconds before I walked out, index finger closed in my book, my lead-heavy bag over one shoulder. I still have no idea what the looks my classmates gave me as I passed them meant. But they were *identical*.

There's this paradox that Mr. Vanderleun told us about in the second week of class this year. His eyes showed little pinpoint sparks of self-love when he explained it: *We have no choice but to behave as though we have free will.* Oooooh! Profound! It has all the appearance of some glib, fake-philosophical statement. The sad fact is, though, is that it's true. And how can you distinguish *that* from being free? I mean, wouldn't real freedom have no compulsion involved in it? If you think about it long enough, you see that the paradox is actually pointing you to the idea that we have no freedom whatsoever. If we're *forced* to use free will, what meaning does freedom have?

This is something Virgil understands. I think this is what Alex was objecting to in the *Aeneid*. And if you judge our actions by that principle, I didn't do anything wrong, and she didn't do anything right. We were just two actors behaving in a certain way, because we had no other choice. It makes sense. What else, I mean given all the background conditions of being me, could I have done? What else could she have done? At the time, though, I did not see it this way. All I was concerned with were the faces of my classmates, who had turned to stare at me. Twenty-six adolescents, full of hormones and confused ideas. You'd expect there to be *some* variation in their facial expressions. But they were all staring at me with this mixture of incomprehension and . . . I still haven't found the exact word. But it was *not* disapproval. That much I remember.

VIII.

I DON'T KNOW WHAT other cities are like. But they can't
be as bad as D.C., in one respect: no one gives the slightest fuck
about anyone else here, except concerning that other person's
ability to help them advance in life. Though we also refuse to
appreciate the spectacle of raw power, and we consider having too
much money socially offensive. This is hilarious. Unless you are in
government, and even then involved only in its higher levels, the
social stakes here are minuscule. D.C. is small. Under a million
people. And of that million, about one or two hundred thousand
are involved in the stupid *games* I'm talking about. But there
exists nonetheless a whole class of people here devoted to this
astrology of power, who's-in-who's-out, these failed academics,
with stiff plummy voices. You hear them on public radio and
whatnot, where they get invited to do segments. Or on TV. Every
minute of every day you could listen to this, if you want. People
speculating about the secret workings of power, people you can
tell will never have any, because under their put-on voices you can
hear their doggish panting. I mean that as a metaphor. Sorry if it's
confusing.

I'm a *part* of this culture, though. So I have no real right to
criticize it. I told you about making people wait for their weed,

which I do. I also make it a point to leave my pager at home one day a month. Could be a Tuesday, could be a Sunday, whatever. I make it a point to choose this day according to my whim, with no other rule in mind. I will admit, though, that I violated my principles when I chose that next day, Saturday, to be my out-of-contact day. Maybe I chose it because of Lorriner's phone call and my failure with Huang. Maybe I chose it in spite of these things. They were the cause, though, no doubt about it. I guess everyone fails to live up to their convictions, sometimes. I had no pager when I went to meet Digger in front of the Camelot. I'd picked up my car where I'd left it at the Tip-Top, with a spurt of remembered shame. *The Sorrow and the Pity* got top billing on the marquee, but *The Erotic Adventures of Marie-France* was better advertised inside, by a poster of a nunnish-looking brunette in a *petticoat* or something, eyes lightly crossed, forefinger to her rich lips as though admonishing silence. Our shared knowledge of this woman's imminent appearance on the screen made us more nervous and laugh-prone than normal during our viewing of *The Sorrow and the Pity*. I kept whispering to Digger, "You *know* you want to." I won't lie: I was taking surreptitious whiffs of her scent every time I darted in to speak. She snorted and shoved me away, with practiced agility.

A summary, you ask? Of the movie? Why, yes, that *would* fit here. This process—the description of works of art in writing, I mean—is called *ekphrasis*. *Ekphrasis* is one of the terms you have to know if you're going to study Latin literature. It plays an important role in the *Aeneid*, when Aeneas is looking at a mural of Troy, which was his home city. The mural is in Carthage, where he flees after the fall of Troy, and gets involved with a woman named Dido, who is, to be honest, completely fucking insane, and the whole scene is sort of terrifying. Someone just *staring* at a marvelous image of the wreck of his life. But you're all educated men and women, and have already seen the weighty classics like *The Sorrow and the Pity*. So *ekphrasis* would be a waste of time. I *will* say that *The Sorrow and the Pity* is a two-parter and that they were showing the first part that morning. Digger and I had vague plans to catch part two the following weekend. That has always seemed obscene to me. The division of the movie, whether it was the director's idea to cut it up or the film company's or whatever. I mean, was the Holocaust a mini-series? We ate no popcorn. The popcorn at the Camelot is subpar. It's one of those beat-up old warhorse theaters. Cardboardish carpets. Springs jab your ass when you sit. Dust motes every-where, wheeling through the pale beam from the projector. Et cetera. Some guy in the back was smoking. In a maroon cardigan. His linty hair mounded in two wings. You could just *tell* he was waiting for Marie-France to mince across the screen, flashing her provocative cross-eyed gaze.

So blah blah blah, aristocratic French resistance fighters, some murky explosions, and newsreel footage of mud-clotted tanks driving in a crook-backed file through Poland. We know the movie by heart. There's no reason it should be so gripping: it's objectively boring. After some more grainy images of desolation, part one ended, and Digger and I wandered out into the strong fall daylight, unreality lingering in our skulls. The traffic signals on the street corner near the Camelot fronts are broken, and there's a lot of kids in the neighborhood, so the city has set out these mesh baskets containing bright orange flags, isosceles triangles, that you wave as you cross the street. To warn drivers not to hit you or whatever. A whole troop of kids, a birthday party maybe, were threading their way across Connecticut Avenue in their bulky autumn jackets, waving the flags with weird precision. They weren't moving in that spastic proud-cadet way kids have in lines. They looked like small adults. The kid in last place, for no reason, turned as he stepped off the curb and bellowed joyfully at us. No words. Just one of the pointless screams you let out when you're that age, provoked by general happiness. His jacket was the color of the sky, and it had a legion of white ducks stenciled across the small chest, in geometrical flight. The children wound their way across the broad street and into the yew-hedged park on the opposite side. The poisonous yew berries were glowing in the sunlight on the hedges, with amazing predictability. They must kill so many schoolkids every year, if you think about it. I mean, *I* have a hard time not eating them.

Then there was some residual kidding about going to the porn movie. Digger tried to act indifferent, but she was blushing. Which I don't know how to respond to; it makes me dizzy, if I can use a sentimental-sounding word. So I relented, and stopped pestering her about *The Erotic Adventures of Marie-France.* Although to be honest the thought of watching a porn movie with Digger right next to me gave me a tremendous hard-on. (Is that fucked-up? I'm not trying to conceal anything here.) Given all this, then, and the fact that I had taken the day off from my business activities, there was nothing left to do except to go get high.

For a long time, we rambled around in my car, smoking, with the radio on. Digger would join in the song, start-stop. She even rested her head on my shoulder, which I think was the first time she'd ever done that. It *kind* of violates the terms of the agreement, I guess, but I wasn't going to say anything. Her wood-smoke smell came through above the sweet reek of the weed. She smells like the turn of the year. Like harvests. I can't explain why this is so impor- tant, but it has to be. We still didn't say much about what had happened yesterday. We *did* talk about Kevin, though. I mean, what else were we supposed to do? "Lorriner," I murmured.

"He's probably at a *Klan* meeting," Digger returned.

"We have *nothing* to be afraid of." My car was full of silvery smoke. We had parked, now, near where we started, behind the fenced-in green the flag-waving kids had dispersed into. Their voices came through the still, cold air, and even into my car: faint, disorganized music. A lot of people go there to smoke. A lot of mothers take kids there to play.

"I mean, of *course* they were going to respond that way, Addison. They failed to do their *jobs*. With all that *gang* nonsense. Because Kevin was a *minority*." I did not mention the fact that both Huang and Baltimore were minorities, though she could have figured it out herself. About Huang, I mean. I let her misconstrue the situation. "Look, look," she was saying, and she fished a folded sheaf of paper out of her bag, which is enormous and covered with clicking turquoise beads, each the size of a human eye.

She handed me two items: a glossy photo, a cheerleader in midleap, the image cut off just below her chin; and a fragile newspaper article. The same one I talked about before. You know—by Archer B. Sexton, the man with the interchangeable name? "Look," she said, pointing to a quote. It was from Mr. Vanderleun, whom Sexton had interviewed after the murder: *"Kevin was a strong and quiet presence, though blessed with a certain musicality, a strong rhythm. He'll be remembered and missed."* "Didn't he *say* that to you? When you asked him about it?" He *had* said it. Word for word. I tried, hard, to laugh, but all that came out was a dry cough.

"Fuck, man, that's so transparent. I can't even *say*," I told Digger, and she squeezed my shoulder.

"*That's* why we're doing this," she muttered. As she said that,

I *knew* Lorriner was guilty. A burden vanished. Not a physical burden, though. We were free. We would *find out*. About Kevin. Despite Mr. Vanderleun and his lie. That's a strange word to use. What else can you call repeating some offensive platitude, though? It was a lie when he said it to Sexton, and some kind of hyper-lie when he said it to me. Being young is closely related to being stupid, I admit. But you have to have forgotten your youth entirely to peddle falsehoods that lazy and clumsy.

"Why did you like give me a picture of a cheerleader, though?" I asked.

"No, *look*," she repeated, "the other side. I cut it out of the junior *yearbook*." It was *him*. In the amethyst vest and gold bow tie you have to wear if you're a first chair in the band. (Yes, our band is called the Marching Tigers.) Standing in front of the school with his vertebrate-looking saxophone, a determined and placid calm arranging his stolid face. Light had blanked his round glasses. He had a slight, middle-agey paunch filling the vest. Digger was tapping the photo, making it quiver. "*That's* why." She sighed, and busied herself repacking her vermilion bowl. I smoothed out the Sexton article and flicked the feathery ash off of Kevin's still face, and put the documents with his school files in my glove box.

"I still like can't believe that fucking guy like threatened to *kill* me, though. I mean, how *stupid* is that? Right? Right into the phone?"

"He's *probably* just some *racist*, Addison. So he's *obviously* stupid."

This she delivered in a *tone of voice* . . . It's the single aspect of her voice that puts me off. And she never uses it, or almost never. But when she does it makes her sound like a *kindergarten* teacher. Forgiving. Cadenced. It hides her personality in, I don't know . . . some kind of *social* element, or something? Who knows why anyone does anything, though. I'm not one to criticize. I'd started to look through Kevin's records in moments of boredom in my car, though I thought this was too strange to mention. To carry them around, to go *through* them. It comforted me. Or no: it was like when you have to study for a test, and instead of procrastinating, you do it, and at first it seems so fake, but then you get into it. Into mastering a body of knowledge. Even a constricted one, even Kevin Broadus's student history. Digger never found out about this. Then or later, when it became an even *more* important activity in my life. She would have taken it well, though. The way she took all my stupidity.

With Kevin's photo stashed, we got *into* things. We smoked and smoked, achieving (if that's the word) light-headedness and lethargy. A lot of talk about the departed, yes. But since neither of us knew him, we could only remark on that fact, over and over: *And we didn't even* know *him.* Yes, we sounded like old women or Episcopalians, bloodless and self-delighted. That's all we could manage. My throat closed with fake emotion. Isn't that disgusting? We suppressed all of our natural joyfulness. That was the worst, although I didn't realize it at the time. Grave sadness and set mouths and eloquence dishonor the dead, because life is what honors the dead, its roughness and energy. Or whatever.

Once we were adequately high, once we had talked ourselves into a pleasing moral superiority, it was time to move. We had no plan in mind. But life as an adolescent is so dull that even pointless activity, wandering around for its own sake, enlivens it. The whole setup can be exhausting. And when you add in a pro-level weed-smoking regimen . . . everything gets sort of leaden. I promised I'd *avoid* this. You already *know* what the routines of life are like. As well as I do. Adolescence is enslaved to such routines, which is what makes alternatives to them so promising. Minor escapades of anarchy or sex. College! Promise, after all, requires the threat of its extinction to exist. Otherwise it wouldn't be promise but just another unbearable fact.

So we drove, in long ellipses up and down the boulevards of D.C., which are wide and tree-arcaded, even the unimportant streets, and everything is laid out in accordance with Haussmann's plan, which I don't really know what it is, but it's also how Paris is organized. *Boulevards* radiating outward from a center ringed with large streets, and veining their way in between are the small streets, the ones where people conduct their private lives. They are named according to a confusing recursive convention, so that if a land army ever invades it will have a tough time finding its way around. I mean an eighteenth-century land army. They have spy satellites now to deal with the pathetic ingenuity of the founders. It makes for fun driving. It makes it easy to get just lost enough that it's fun. The light got colder, and Digger went quiet in the way she does before she propositions me.

As soon as we got out of my car, Digger gave a low grunt of surprise. One of the purple curtains that my father chose for our living room (to go with its orange walls) was trailing out through the broken front window, in which there was a jagged, starlike hole. Most of the glass still hung in the pane; you could hear it *creaking* as the muslin curtains snagged on it in the gentle breeze. The curtain was torn in places from the glass, long delicate rents. The whole thing was kind of beautiful. Or I thought so. A collage or something. "Dude?" Digger asked.

"I like have *no* idea like what it is," I returned. She went back to the car. "I'm putting my pipe in here. In the glove compartment. Okay?" She gets paranoid about carrying it in her purse, in moments of stress. Then, with ceremony, to defuse her fear or something, she hooked her arm through mine and we walked inside. Three unusual objects greeted us. Two had fallen from my coffee table, which was now broken and sloped into a V: a thick green glass bottle of champagne, which had emptied itself on the floor, and a smashed white platter of strawberries, the fruit tossed in a neat diminishing arc. "What the fuck," Digger said. The coffee table itself my father had purchased from this antiques place, Azul, where he buys our furniture, which is all, every last piece of it, rickety and uncomfortable, impossible to sit in or use.

The table had splintered down some invisible seam near the middle of the thin plank top, longitudinally, under the weight of a lumpy bundle wrapped in white cloth. Brown twine held it closed. *This* was what had broken the window. "Is this like some fucking *installation*?" Digger continued. She knows about my father's pottery. I guess she figured setups such as this constitute the logical next phase of expression.

"No, he wouldn't waste the *champagne*," I remember saying. I think the bundle was already in my hands. That was the third unusual thing. The bundle, I mean. It was heavy, rigid, a little warm. I yanked at the twine, tied in a sure-handed double gift bow. A brick fell out of the cloth, nearly amputating my left toe, and dented the champagne-puddled floor with its corner. It was the *exact* color of the strawberries.

I don't think it was until then that we heard them. My father and Fatima, I mean. I didn't know it was Fatima at the time. I only learned who it was later. At which point I was no longer in any position to care. But when the brick fell with a melodic thunk, I noticed their mingled cries coming from upstairs, voices pitched about the same, short and breathy. Digger clapped a hand over her mouth and ran onto the porch, and then ran back inside, looking ashamed. I'd almost finished unfolding the cloth the brick had been wrapped in, and I could see that there was writing on it. The cloth felt clean and light, the way new cotton does. You could catch that spacious smell of fresh cloth even at arm's length, and underlying it another smell, choking, somehow childish. Familiar, though. The bed screaked and the headboard flapped against the wall. I'm not trying to disgust you. But the sounds were an integral part of the whole thing, my father and Fatima fucking with a vigorous, mechanical regularity of rhythm. I'm just glad they were crying out in wordless pleasure and joy, though. And not talking to each other, I mean. That would have been unbearable. "Holy shit," Digger muttered. She sounded impressed. I have to admit I was, too.

They reached a raucous pitch now. Just going *at* it. I had opened the flag of cloth to its fullest, so I could see what message the brick thrower had printed on it. A cut bedsheet, still trailing threads from its edges. The handwriting was overperfect, as though the writer were illiterate and just copying lines and curves. My own scrawl is that of a retarded five-year-old. So clear, firm handwriting—and this was *musically* fluent—always impresses me. No matter what it says. "Dude, dude, dude," Digger kept chanting. She read the message before I could. It took me longer because I had to hold the cloth in an awkward position to decipher the words. Their message was terse and unmistakable:

SCARED NOW JEWBOY

ran across the top. No question mark, no comma. Across the bottom:

This lacked the exclamation point you'd expect. The source of the familiar childish smell was the black tempera paint the writer had used, which made each letter a knobbly landscape. The middle point of the upper W, in the first JEW, was closest to my face. I could see the hardened gobs and spatters in amazing relief.

And in between these two statements, one interrogative and one imperative, was a large, foursquare, steady-lined swastika. Which would have been as perfect as the handwriting, except that Lorriner had gotten the orientation reversed. So that it suggested the schematic sketch of a man running blind, pinwheeling his limbs. *Saint Vitus' Dance*—the phrase flickered through my mind. I could see the words, in violet on a night-dark background. Words appear to me that way sometimes. I'd started talking, to myself, to nobody.

"How does he like *know* we're Jewish?" I asked.

"Schacht *is* a Jewish last name," Digger murmured. And then: "He *did* have caller ID. Right? You said he did. He probably just looked your father's name up in the phone book. Your address." She stroked the banner between her thumb and index finger, as though to gauge the value of its material, and took a sharp breath in, through her nose, the sound a doe about to break cover makes. Upstairs, the steam-engine racket continued, and the mingled, exulting voices showed no sign of slackening.

IX.

PROBABLY FROM EVERYTHING I've written so far, ladies
and gentlemen, you've gotten the impression that my father is a
bad father. He's not. He raised me by himself. He came to parent-
teacher conferences. He arranged halfhearted birthday parties.
He cooked his repetitive meals for me when he got home early
enough and left me money for pizza when he didn't, until I was
fourteen. All the things parents do. But even to me it's obvious
that he's weak. Or that he chose to be weak. Maybe after my
mother died, maybe before—my knowledge of him, after all,
is restricted to the period of my own life.

His weakness is undeniable, though. Example: when I was
ten, I broke my wrist. I didn't do it in any extraordinary way; I just
tripped over my own feet and put out my arms to brace myself. In
front of our local library branch, where I once had a real craze to
go every weekend. My father was two yards ahead of me, sashay-
ing toward the car. I heard the bone crack as I fell, and he must
have heard it too, because he came rushing back, his face emptied
of blood, and he forklifted me up and put me in the passenger
seat. I was screaming my head off, I remember, in the embarrassing loose-mouthed way children have. Although the pain *was*
considerable. So we drove off to the emergency room as I wailed

and wailed, my gaze transfixed by the up-and-down of the telephone wires above the street. My arm went kind of numb after about three minutes, my howls abated to whimpers, the wires swooped and lifted and the sun shone. I was starting to feel better, like maybe I wouldn't have to spend the rest of my life in agonizing pain, which is what you think when you injure yourself as a child, that the hurt will be permanent.

And that's when I heard him, my father, I mean. He was weeping now, teary and windy, moaning, "Addison, Addison, oh, God, Addison, what are we going to do, what are we going to do." While he was driving! This, as you might imagine, scared the shit out of me. So I renewed my screams out of raw terror, which has that unique metal taste, and by the time we got to the hospital, my father and I were both completely hysterical. The doctors, of course, thought he had broken my wrist and was wild with remorse, so they took me aside into a room and asked me confusing questions. "Can you tell us how this happened, Addison?" "Are you sure, Addison?" "Addison, is this the *only* time you've had to go to the hospital?" I answered all these with my good hand clenching the guardrail of my rickety gurney. But—since I could no longer see my father weeping—I found myself getting calmer and calmer, to the point that it became difficult to keep my eyes open, and I drifted off into the sleep of shock. I must have passed their test, because they didn't arrest my father. We were released into the spring night, and drove home. I was ashamed. I couldn't say why at the time. My father would not look at me. So you understand what I mean by his weakness. Though I know it came out of love and concern.

Does the fact that my father is a *terrible* potter surprise you? It seems to me to go along with this weakness. I mean, there's no way of verifying this. But the available evidence suggests it is the case. He hasn't sold a pot in years; he just grinds along, and Viktor Something makes his occasional visits, and they commiserate. I'm willing to admit he's a failure, considered as a maker of pots. I have never seen the merits of the ones he throws. They remind me, as I said before, of him. Maybe that clouds the issue. But whatever his flaws as a potter, he is an unquestionably excellent maker of masks. We have a whole collection on our mantel, and dozens more in this pine crate he keeps in the basement closet where the water heater mumbles to itself. My father casts them with incredible speed and certainty. He doesn't agonize over them the way he does over his pots. He's also never sold a mask. He's refused to try. I think—and I'm speaking as a philistine here—I think they'd sell. Who doesn't want a mask?

Anyway, the collection on our mantel shelf has not changed in ten years. He's *made* other masks. These are the *icons* among them, or whatever. And he keeps them on permanent display. They dominate the room, as you'd expect an array of large-featured, final faces to do. From left to right, they are: a cartoony version of William F. Buckley, with a flaming hundred-dollar bill in place of a cigarette; a phallus-nosed mask for Carnivale, with almond-shaped eye slits; a bigmouthed Chinese demon; an old, wild-haired man, a deposed king, maybe; a gouty man-in-the-moon; the god Cernunnos, from whose forehead branch deer horns. He's on the right edge, and his right horn reaches up to the lip of the tall narrow window. And in the middle? In the middle there rests the oval face of a woman. The one female face. Unlike the other masks, this one is unpainted, and it has the blessing of eyelids, to relieve its empty, burning stare. My father made it of my mother when they were first married. And since she died, I always nod at it. For ten years, now. I nod at it when I go in or

come out of the house. Like I'm greeting or thanking her. Digger
is used to this movement of mine. She asked me who it was once.
I couldn't answer: my face burned with shame as I tried to speak.
I think she figured it out, and kept silent about it afterward. Even
that afternoon, when I lingered in front of it. The phone had just
started to ring. Ten, fifteen times. I didn't pick it up, just dropped
the banner and grabbed the brick (why?) and ran to the door.
Stopping to stare at the mask.

Digger gathered up Lorriner's banner and followed me out,
her quick steps filling in the gaps between my unsteady lopes. She
stuffed it—the banner, I mean—in her purse as we ran to my car.
I was glad she'd had the foresight to pick it up. I realized I didn't
want my father finding it or the brick. That would have been
awkward beyond imagining. A broken window—well, a person
can almost *ignore* that. If you see what I mean. I tossed the brick
onto the backseat and hurled myself into the driver's seat. Digger
didn't ask where we were going. I didn't know, either, until I
found myself turning Noel's corner. David Cash was outside when
we arrived, tipping the last of a forty down. He never wears a coat,
just a heavy workshirt and a canvas jacket over it. Not even in the
bitterest weather. He offered us a curt nod as we parked, and then
went inside to alert Noel. My car is recognizable: as I said, it's
orange, a car color that has suffered grave neglect for more than
two decades. Digger kept quiet the entire drive. Not the quiet of
fear, but the quiet of considering.

Noel, though he tried to hide it with a thick guffaw of welcome, was shocked to see us. He started talking to us, yelling,
when we were still ten yards away. I'd never brought anyone with
me to see him before. Can you be ashamed of someone you're not
related to? By blood or marriage, I mean. Ashamed of someone

you associate with by choice? He kept us on his stoop for a while. His eyes kept falling to Digger's tits. Against his will. It's *impossible* not to stare at them. She, I guess, is used to it. And so am I. To other guys checking her out, I mean. Even a twinge of jealousy would violate the agreement. So I don't feel any. Besides, how can you be jealous of Noel? When he greets you by saying, "Daaaaaamn, son! You all *shook!*"

Maybe I looked it. Maybe I was pale or something. No mirror was handy. Digger jerked back at the words, and I was afraid she would whip the banner out right then—you know, to make our point for us? The old black people who live in Noel's area tottered out onto their porches and stoops. Some junkie rocked himself on the curb, muttering and laughing. This is about par for the course where Noel lives. People call it, in the papers and things, a "transitional neighborhood." As we approached, I saw that the junkie was, to—please forgive me—my amusement, Stokey. Remember? "Don't Care?" He didn't recognize me. He didn't look to be in a recognizing mood. He was addressing himself as he swayed. I heard him mumble—I swear to fucking God—"It's eternity either way you look at it, my friends." He had on his blue corduroy vest. His open, working mouth still showed omelette-colored teeth. He moved his torso in countertime to his own speech. "Can we come in," Digger asked. Or rather instructed. And Noel, who despite his idiosyncracies is a polite guy, pressed himself against the wall and sucked in his gut, so that we could squeeze into his living room.

I expected more objections from Digger. Once we got inside and she saw the barrenness of Noel's house, I mean. There was an empty bottle of malt liquor on the floor in front of the couch, next to a pewter ashtray shaped like a smiling pig. Two metal folding chairs, chipped white enamel, that I had not seen before. Set out as if he'd been expecting us. Which was, of course, not possible. A bunch of two-by-fours in one corner. He was always planning some absurd home renovation project. I'd gotten used to this visual shittiness. But having Digger there made me *see* it, you know? The CHANDLER pennant still clung to its wall, immaculate red and white. David leaned against the grimy paint beneath it. Eyes 80 percent closed, lips immobile. Noel blobbed out on the leather sofa, fumbling with the empty ashtray. He had on this glare-blue shirt, which said SHABAZZ GEAR across the front, in an arc distorted by his bulges. No one had any idea how to begin.

"Yo, y'all wanna *smoke* or suh'in?" Noel asked without enthusiasm.

"He threw a brick through our window. I mean through *his* window. That guy you told Addison about." Digger was clenching the straps of her bag.

"The fuck?" Noel warbled.

"She means Short Mike," I explained. He heaved himself around a little.

"Naw, man, I ain't even say I *knew* that nigga." No one had accused him of knowing Lorriner. But Noel's scoffing, which he delivered with a little fartage of his bolsterlike lips, sounded irrefutable.

"No, man, I mean, it's fucked-up."

"And? Whutchoo want from me, nigga?" followed from those lips.

"Can you stop using that *word*, please?" This was Digger again. "You sound ridiculous." I swear to God that David chortled at this, although when I flicked my glance up to him he had recovered his shut-eyed, statue-proud poise. Noel tried to grin. It looked *sad*. I mean, it was a grin, in a *technical* sense. His cheeks had gotten this slight queasy shine, his eyes racketed back and forth. His breathing was loud, so loud you felt *bad* for him. He lives in combat with his own physical form, as all fat men do.

"Look, Noel, can you just like give us some *help* here. Seriously. Like *you* brought this guy *up*." He was already shaking his head, his lips were already in motion to refuse. So I kept talking.

"*Noel*. Don't be a *dick*. I'm not *asking* you for anything. To *do* anything. Just some information. Right? I'll fucking *pay* you. I have *money*. I'll pay you like a *thousand* bucks. I can go home and get it right now."

"Nigga, y'all think I need yo' damn money?"

"But it's like for *nothing*, man. You don't even have to like *sell* anything for it."

"I tole you I ain't even *know* the muhfuh, ain't I?" You had to admit, his lingo was holding up well. I'd upset him with my importuning. When you're that fat, all changes in your vital signs and emotions are apparent: sweating, breathing, they all get magnified by the effort of your suffocating heart. David was bouncing himself off the wall, using his back muscles, nothing else, making these deep slaps. Out of impatience or something.

"Ain't I *say* that," Noel almost pleaded, his voice going soft. "Ain't I say that." He looked frightened. I thought at the time it was of Short Mike. Later events convinced me that this could not be true. I think it must have been fear of *exposure*.

I'm getting ahead of myself. I had no time to worry about his motives, because Digger started talking. She was using her most reasonable voice. Which is always a sign of deep disturbance.

"You fat motherfucker," she began, "you're *going* to *help* us. We're going to *deal* with this. And if you don't, if you don't come up with some kind of contribution to this whole problem,

I mean, not the problem but whatever, you know what I mean, I swear to God I'll beat the shit out of you, right now. I can do it! I know I can! I will beat the *shit* out of you. I'll hit you with that fucking *plank*. And your fucking *boyfriend* in the *corner* over there won't do anything." David shouted with laughter at this, and jogged over to and up the stairs, as if in confirmation.

Digger yanked the crumpled banner out of her bag and hurled it into Noel's huge lap, as he was emitting the obligatory *I ain't no muhfuh faggot* stutters.

"Dude, I mean, I don't necessarily think that *violence* is indicated? But she's right in *principle*." I found myself addressing the white cloth, with Lorriner's message clearly visible in reverse. Noel had the banner up, screening his torso, two slices of which were visible on either side. Blue-white-blue, the arrangement of Israel's flag.

"Man, gimme like *two* gees and I like think about it, a'ight?" Noel mouthed this from behind the swastika, now reversed into its correct orientation. He let the banner fall and shroud his lap and asked us again if we wanted to smoke.

"Sure," I answered, an eye on Digger. I was worried. But she kept calm. She'd gotten it out of her system, I guess. Noel is a guy you can scare, yeah, and mercenary to boot, but you also have to play along with the whole notion that you're friends. So we'd smoke, and he'd tell us about Lorriner.

"Is David like *pissed* or something?" I asked while Noel was crumbling weed into a blunt wrapper he'd split with his horny thumbnail and reamed of its tobacco. He eyed Digger, and then the planks, before he answered. He believed her threat, ladies and gentlemen, and he was right to. Like I said, she's going to achieve greatness.

"Naw, son, he juss like *mad*. Nigga juss *get* like that." David was still stomping around upstairs. He was *rummaging*: you know, clanks and muffled self-questioning. The walls in Noel's house are sound-conducive, and the emptiness of the place doesn't help either, as far as acoustic amplification goes. Even your own speaking voice can blare into an aggrieved shout.

Blunt time! I told you Noel considers me a friend, and that's why he shares his made-up sex stories with me. He gets high with me as another unrefusable token/proof of this friendship. It's a little gross, the idea of a blunt, because it gets finished—the wrapper gets sealed up, I mean—with an intimate slurp: the whole thing goes into the roller's mouth and then is drawn out, moistened, and closed. *Kind* of horrifying, when it comes out of a cavernous, fat-guy mouth. But we were all polite. Digger's sole indication of hurry was her drumming heel, which made all the beads on her bag click. This solid-sounding *bony* click. She had a severe coughing episode after her initial puff. Blunts are harsh, the drags are copious, and the acrid cigar paper around the weed doesn't mollify the taste.

"My shit be *crucial*, though," cooed Noel. He was staring at Digger's tits again, brought to heaving prominence by her coughing fit. With the white cloth covering his legs, and his goggling eyes, he looked like some deviant, obese and prematurely aged, used to having his whims satisfied. Hermann Göring or something. I was also—I'll be honest—transfixed. By her tits, I mean. We were both lucky she was too busy coughing to notice our joint gawp.

And isn't this the *essence* of all social situations? A group in which lines of relationship exist as fragments failing to connect the whole? I mean, *I* was connected to Digger, and *I* was connected to

Noel. But they had nothing to do with *each other*. I had taken a long drag on the spit-wet, limpish blunt. Smoking weed always makes you think, even if it makes you think stupid things; it loosens you up, at first. I mean, we were sitting there with *nothing holding us together*. How did this serve my *higher purpose*? I wanted to stand up and shout. But it was too late. David quieted down upstairs. Digger got her coughing and her tits back under control. Noel had slapped on the fake-confident smile that means he's about to assent. All the stupid, senseless elements were in place. For your sake, I'm going to distill what Noel told us into somewhat *reasonable* English, condense it. It took him an über-long time to finish. He kept having to grab breaths, to squirm around in his seat. He speaks at a *canter* anyway, when he's stoned. Which just made everything take for-*fucking*-ever. So: Mike Lorriner, Noel said, was

like this nigga from like *Maryland* who like be friends with that shorty Kelly, you know that one with the mad thick ass? So like he like this real redneck nigga, nahmean, like real *racist* and shit, and he like came into D.C. like to handle his bidness and shit and like *party*. So like one weekend he had like been at the party like in fucking Chevy Chase, some shit like that, at some white nigga name D's house, nahmean, just like chillin'. And this nigga *Kevin* like was talking all this shit about how like *Maryland* was some like shit or whatever, so like *Mike* started talking shit back, and like *then* they was like pushin' each other and *screamin'* at each other and shit, and like Mike called him like a nigga, and then Kevin got like real *pissed* and shit and like took this cup of like *rum* or some shit and like dump that shit *right* in Mike's face. And *then* like Mike punched that other nigga, I mean that nigga Kevin, and like Kevin punched him back, and they was all like *hittin'* each other and like shoving each other and shit and everyone was like yellin', but like then these two *other* niggas like broke up the shit and like all the other niggas calmed down, and like Mike left but he was all like "I'm a fuck you up, son!" Then that nigga said like some crazy shit about graveyards, nahmean? At least, that's like what *Kelly* said, man, and she was like at this nigga's house, man, it like some fuckin' mansion she said. I think you prolly *know* that nigga whose house it is, man, anyway. Nigga like play *lacrosse* and shit. So like that's all I know about Mike, man, he just like a crazy white nigga, you know, like all racist and shit.

"Man, he like *you*, Addison," Noel finished, exhaling an impressive curlicue of smoke. "'Cept you ain't like *racist* and shit." He spoke as though *we* were being interrogated. Noel picked the banner up and began to fold it, hand over curdy white hand. Digger took another nostril breath. We would have had to go through another cycle of this, of her demands, his balks and feints, and my limp conciliation, if David had not, with his loud assured steps, come back downstairs, carrying something wrapped in a green-checked dish towel. No smile or frown. Just the same shut-eyed look—of disdain?—he'd been flashing us the whole time. There was a stitchwork dog on the cloth, and the excess gingham spilled over David's smooth left fist. Holy fuck! My balls retreated as soon as David *unwrapped* it, just the butt. You could see the gun's textured gray grip plate, which glinted in the subtle way concrete does.

"Shit, nigga, is you *crazy*?" Noel screeched, slamming his feet to the ground in an effort to lever himself off the couch. (Which failed.) David hushed him with a raised palm.

"It's *for* him. He should get something useful out of this, you fat motherfucker." This was the longest sentence I'd ever heard him speak. It gave voice to my own feelings on the matter, and to what I imagine were Digger's. But at the time all I could think, if you can even call it thinking, was, *Holy fuck, it's a fucking gun! For fucking shooting people!* Do you know what it means to have a gun? It's amazing! Not in some *my dick is bigger than yours* way. You have this *thing* that puts you in touch with the absolute. Everyone dies, no matter what. No matter what you do. *Everyone* dies. Including you, ladies and gentlemen, including all of *you*. David tucked the cloth back over the grip and handed the bundle to me.

"It's a Glock. You know how to use it?" I nodded: a complete lie. This moron's grin had smeared itself across my face. I could *feel* it. "Nigga all smilin' like it *Christmas*. Don't he have like a Christmas smile," Noel sandpapered out. It was heavy. It was *so* heavy.

"I gave you a clip, too. It's like folded up in there. I ain't load it, though," David told me. Though he might as well have said, *Four score and seven years ago our forefathers brought forth upon this continent,* etc., for all the attention I was paying. I was *floating.*

"Hey, Noel," I said. "Noel." I wanted to ask him about Huang and Baltimore, if he knew anything about them, too. But I realized this would require telling him I'd gone to the cops. Which looked to be perhaps the stupidest thing I'd ever done.

"Whutchoo want, nigga? You *scurred* or suh'in?" His whale's lips parted in derision. Just wanted to get back on the controlling side, I guess. But! My hands were moving now, unwrapping the rest of the weapon. Of their own volition. Amazing, right? I slipped the clip into my pocket and cradled the denuded gun. A Glock. Who even knew what that *meant*? Then, in the grip of a sure and perverse impulse, I aimed it at Noel's bobbing, pointed head and squeezed the trigger. "Addison, don't, come on, don't *do* that, Addison, please," he gasped, raising his arms in defense.

It took all my strength to pull, to make the gun give up its dry, thirsty, prefatory sound. Lick your lips and separate them. Like that. Much louder, more metallic. *Much* scarier. But identical in spirit. You know? Like it was preparing to *speak*. Like it had something complicated and awkward to say.

"Nigga, shit, naw, man, don't fuckin' *play* like that," Noel gargled. He'd recovered his lingo.

"Okay, man," I said. I mean, I was ready to rush home and bring him *all* my money, as long as it meant I got to keep the gun. To put a final shine on everything, I wrapped up the gun again, and offered to pack a bowl for everybody. Digger fished out her pipe, without objecting. She looked from Noel to David as though she were deciding between victims. She even took a hit after Noel, who lipped the pipe way too much. Even David partook, and he never smokes. He told me once it was bad for the heart. I tried to refute him—"It actually has many medical benefits," like what the legalization people say—but he just walked away from me without listening or saying anything further.

"So it's like a Glock?" I asked Noel.

"Yeah, nigga, just point and it's like bladow! Y'all can pay my ass lata, though." David was making the muscles on his neck fan out. He does this when he's bored, to kill time.

"And *how* much did you like want? Like two thousand?" I asked. Two thousand was less than 25 percent of my cash hoard. An über-reasonable fee for all this glory. David, emerging from glowering silence, cut this conversation off, shouting at Noel.

"FUCK you, nigga." This was the first time I had ever heard

him raise his voice. We all stopped moving in astonishment, including David, who was now wearing a surprised half smile. Digger released a squib of smoke. I swear to fucking God she gave a quiet accompanying laugh. Nobody *argued*. Nobody said anything *more* about money.

X.

THE REST OF OUR EXIT? Shrouded in a mental haze. Noel
had sulked his way downstairs to his monk's room. David watched
us leave. Stokey the junkie was still muttering to himself in the
dark. That much I remember. We drove not speaking, at least for
a while. We were both solemn and stoned. Then Digger said, "I've
never *seen* a gun before." No criticism. No *moral lecture*. Just the
same druglike, frightening delight coursing through me. Do you
even understand how rare coincidences of feeling like that are?
Another reason I value her company so much. It won't surprise
you to know that, despite the late hour—it was seven minutes
after eight o'clock at this point—we headed to the Dump. It's a
second home to us, sad though that may be, so confident are we
of our solitude there.

"Like what the fuck are we going to *do* with it," I breathed.
She didn't answer me. I was *speeding*, which I never do, for
professional reasons. The lights of the city rushed by in two
low glittering wings.

"I can't believe I've never even seen one, not a *real* one,"
Digger whispered, as my engine groaned and struggled.

We got there in twelve minutes, record time from Noel's
house. We parked in the jagged shadow of a trash hill, a tangled

heap of junked car chassis, and crouched in the brown dark. Digger unwrapped the gun with visible tenderness, lifted it, hefted it. We could hear each other's breathing.

"Do you have to oil it or anything?" she asked. I slotted the clip in. By some miracle of instinct.

"We didn't get the like *instructions*."

"What happens now?" Digger asked, fumbling with her lower lip as she spoke.

"What do you mean, *now*?"

"Aren't you going to *fire* it?"

"I like don't *know*. Should I?"

"How do we know it works? Right? I mean, consider the source. So I think you should at least *fire* it. It could be like a setup or something." A *setup*, ladies and gentlemen. How can you fail to admire someone so detail-oriented? We had a wealth of crap to use as targets, anyway, so we ambled around choosing. At random, with our appraisers' chin lifts, we chose a sturdy cardboard box and balanced it on a yolk-yellow chair. Then we placed a filthy bottle on top of the box and backed away comically far, as though the *chair* were armed. Digger quickstepped off to the side and palm-cupped her ears, crouching and ready. I lifted the gun—the weight strained my wrist—and pulled the trigger.

A huge percussive cough, from nowhere. A simultaneous kick from the gun itself. My nerves sang. And a reverberant gong-beat rose from the car heap and indistinct night birds took flight on both riverbanks. "Jesus *fuck*," Digger screamed, scuttling even farther away and shifting her hands: the right now tented over her heart, the left still over her ear. Posed like an old-timey phone operator. You know, a switchboard girl or whatever? Listening to some outrageous conversation. The swift, tremendous noise of the shot itself thrilled me. Just that simple: it *thrilled* me. I won't lie. Although the weird target we'd set up had survived my assault untouched. Digger walked back and slumped against me, shoulder-to-shoulder, in comradely praise. Her heart was vibrating, and I caught her scent as I massaged my tingling shooting arm. "Holy shit, man," she whispered. "Holy *shit*. Can I try?"

I handed the gun over, barrel first, and it slipped between our reaching hands and clunked into the floury junkyard dirt. We leaped back, screaming our heads off. It didn't fire. So Digger picked it up. "I feel like I don't know what I feel like," she said through clenched teeth, and turned her blue stare on the bottle. The river birds had calmed down. The yellow dump-light tinted everything. She dug her neat heels into the dirt, with two discrete squeaks. And pulled the trigger. Her entire small body was involved with the shot. The recoil shocked her; her shoulders heaved, like she'd let out one precise sob. There was the same from-everywhere percussion. The bottle shattered this time, and the pile of metal gave out a second lugubrious bong. Birds took panicked flight again. "Holy *shit*," she crowed. "Holy fucking *SHIT*." No humiliation! I'm not that kind of guy, I swear. I have a lot of *problems*—as you can no doubt tell—but it seemed *fair*, somehow, that Digger was a better shot. A natural.

I always keep a map in my car, a map of D.C., Virginia, and Maryland, which the map company considers part of the same unit, I guess. It's old and water-damaged, the pages scarred with creases, marked with the anonymous shit-colored stains that paper picks up when neglected. Or (in this case) crammed into the crumby, dank underseat on the passenger side of my car. I inherited this map from my father, as well as the paranoid tendency to keep it around. Digger, always, has change for pay phones. It's a neurotic habit of hers. Though we had given

Lorriner's banner to Noel, the brick it had clothed was sitting in my backseat. And now we had a gun. I know it may be hard for you to understand. But out of these simple and everyday components, we developed a plan. Or the plan came into spontaneous existence because these particular objects stood in close proximity for the first and last time in the history of the universe. That's how it goes. Think of those experiments with proteins and simulated lighting, in the sixties or whatever, that produced amino acids. You get the idea. We didn't even have to *discuss* it. We both knew what would happen: we would drive out to bumblefuck Maryland and return Lorriner's brick by throwing it through *his* window. The gun was just *insurance*. Which we didn't even need. We wouldn't write a message. We weren't a couple of racist hicks. Just a quick toss and "viola," as my father says. (He chuckles *every* time.)

Events conspired with us. We found a pay phone right after leaving the dump, columned in baleful and buzzing light, cradled against the wall of a urine-stinking gas station on New York Avenue. I can be sort of terrified by these places, because they're desert-empty, and because the name of one follows, eight times out of ten, the phrase, *She was last seen at*. Serial killers' natural terrain. But the 411 lady was just as helpful as she'd been the first time I'd inquired about Lorriner, and sounded just as delighted to help me. Although it was a different operator now. I remembered the bizarre name of Lorriner's street, even. I flatter myself that this impressed her. She gave me the exact address, which I'd forgotten. Then I was back in my retarded car, where Digger had lit a cigarette in mute joy, and we were off into the darkness.

All the kids in G&T hold it as an article of faith that Maryland contains the second-highest number of Ku Klux Klansmen in

America. There is some debate over whether Ohio or Indiana occupies the top slot. But Maryland, we *know*, comes in at number two. It's not impossible to believe this, in the long stretches of emptiness beyond the suburbs, which shade into genuine rural territory, with farmhouses and cows that look up with almost human stupidity as you drive past. In a winter dusk, you can pick out bare oak branches and black-looking ponds, and a sinister readiness breathes out of the whole landscape. I have no idea if these suspicions about Klan activity are true, or if they derive from the contempt for the white poor that educated members of the middle class in America are taught to feel and hide, from their earliest youth. Especially, I'd say, kids in the G&T Program at Kennedy, which is a *supercharger* for the development of bourgeois ideals. Good *and* bad. It's hypocritical to malign just your own class.

Digger and I held this belief too, of course. And to combat the stark sense of *expectation* it fostered, we screamed along with the radio, shoving our faces out the window. Stations deteriorate into static one after another out there, and soon you're left with anodyne and heart-twisting country music. We didn't know any of the words. But we managed. We had a lot of enthusiasm. We even got a few honks in approval. Including one from a huge truck, which we sped ahead of. The roadside arc lights got more and more infrequent, and their high whine sharper and sharper. We passed gas stations, with stolid-faced loafers our own age lined up under blaring fluorescents. The highway climbed; we were out in the empty fields, with green weather-pocked steel signage to guide us. We could not see much farther than the guardrail, which gave us a nasty, cloaking sense of the dark. Nauseating, somehow. No stars visible, and just the desert of the dead farmlands spreading everywhere. Monotony remains the most horrifying thing imaginable. It's why death is so horrifying, or a large part of why. Yeah, morbid, but what do you want from me?

Two hours we drove. Fuck! Even if you live in a small, pretentious city—like D.C.—the speed with which urban life fades astonishes. You can be out in the middle of real country, real agricultural shit, in ninety minutes, and then in the utter desolation of wild or fallow fields if you drive for another thirty. What's funny, though, here, is how *oppositional* everyone is on this issue. City people scorning country people, who in turn look with indignant suspicion on city dwellers. But they all share the same morality, right? Is the overt racism, for example, that you find among rednecks who say THE N WORD in casual conversation somehow *worse* than the covert racism of our teachers, who introduce us to a few nonwhites and then proceed to entomb us in our separate lives and consider their duty done? What about people for whom ethnic minorities serve an *instrumental* purpose? People who collect ethnic friends as ornaments, to show off to their other, white friends, and to prove to themselves their own tolerance and generosity of spirit? Can you say with any confidence that one of these is *worse*? I expounded these theories to Digger, who agreed and agreed, keeping her finger on the map. A pleasure über-masculine, to be pronouncing these judgments unopposed in a speeding car, and flinging glowing butt after butt out the window, where it would vanish in the slipstream. "It's like a *monument* to like all the *horror* of the twentieth century!" I remember screaming that. It made sense at the time, I promise.

The map became unnecessary, after a certain point: it all narrowed to one road, which wandered through clumps of houses, a few vague stores, back into open country, then more houses. This was Brander's Hollow, I guess. Lorriner's town. And then, out of nowhere, as Digger was mangling some more lyrics, something about a broken heart and wine, this *surge* overtook me. I felt like a *baby*. Adrift, alert, happy, secure. I don't know why. I don't know what caused it. Maybe the headlong murky nature of what we were doing. For some reason I wanted to *know everyone* in those decayed houses, know about their high school lives and friendships and misadventures. Do you ever experience that? When you stare out your window and into your city?

We'd been off the highway for a while, rumbling over a rutted surface road—withered clematis and creeper on the guardrails, that sort of nonsense—when Digger cried, "Hey, hey, stop. We're here." I parked; we climbed out to check the road sign. The yolky flames of our two raised lighters revealed the street name: FORK LUTE ROAD. The map had not lied. This always amazes me. It was now eleven minutes after ten. Digger chambered a shell and hid the gun, still gripped, in the pocket of her coat. I cradled Lorriner's rosy brick. "Okay, *you* like drive behind the bushes." I was whispering, pointing with the brick. There was a screening juniper hedge a little ways in from the road entrance. Digger reparked and caught up to me at the dark beginning of Fork Lute Road, and we shared a short silence. There were two houses we could see, one right off the main road, and another at the far end of the lane. The closer house's mailbox, subjected to my lighter's flame, was numbered 9778, in these saddening gold stick-on numbers, with some limp corners curled over. We got a muted chuckle out of those. And then we picked our way down the carious asphalt dividing us from the second house, through tea-stinking fallen leaves. "It must be this one." Digger sighed. There was another mailbox, and a small barn set right near the property edge. "It's gotta be, right?" Lighters out, mailbox examined: it was indeed 9780. Lorriner's address, according to the omniscient minds at the phone company. We had *arrived*.

The little barn proved to be a garage faked up to look like a barn. Red timbers, white crossbeams. These are popular out in the sticks. There *was* a fence, but it was just split-pine rail. Digger's breath was quickened by excitement and anger as we lugged ourselves over. I tossed the brick ahead of me, and Digger said, "Good arm." We both giggled and then shushed each other. I swear to fucking *God* we were acting like kindergartners. In the brownish half-light, we could see the blocky outline of a house.

"It's a rambler, ranch-style," Digger whispered, hoarse and tense. As though that made the problem of our brick hurling more difficult. "So let's like get closer and then like pick a window?" I had the brick clamped in my right armpit. It was starting to hurt. I loped ahead, but she hung back.

"Digger," I hissed. She took her time walking up.

"Are you sure this is a good idea?" she asked. And that did me in. Just destroyed me.

"Are you serious? Digger, you like brought the *gun*. Are you like out of *steam* after that? You brought the gun and now you're like Commander Moderate Violence of the Mounties or whatever?" I couldn't whisper-shout anymore, I was laughing so hard.

"The gun's for an *emergency*," she got out, but she was gasping with laughter too. We were more nervous than we'd estimated. We had been conducting this whispered conversation as we walked toward Lorriner's house, and we had reached the middle of a clump of pines, where we kneeled down in the fragrant needles. Digger had crammed a fistful of her jacket collar against her mouth, and I could see her ice-clear irises despite the lack of light. I put down the brick and she put down the gun, and she looked at me with this weird face, this open, appraising face; you couldn't miss it even in the dark.

"Hey, man," I started to babble, because this was moving into zones declared off-limits by our agreement.

I don't mean that we were about to have some stupid *makeout session*. But we just try to be adult about everything between us. Keep it free of entanglements. And certain moments imperil the agreement. But the whole built-up nonsense of the day, of everything associated with the whole enterprise, had come charging into the open, blatting and gibbering. I was *so* exhausted. She must have been too. So can you blame us? We'd driven out to this dark little *nowhere* with a map, a brick, and a gun—cavemen, or not cavemen, I guess, but total primitives. Can you blame us for almost violating the basic terms of our association? So I opened my mouth and said, "Hey, man," forcing a rich, witty tone into the words, to prepare her for I don't know what piece of offensive sarcasm. You know, to wreck the mood?

Digger beat me to it. She put her finger to her pursed lips. Lights were coming on in the house. Which was weird, because it was *night* and there hadn't been any lights on before. But hey, who knows what animates the minds of dumb hicks, right? Anyway, the lights were coming on, one at a time. The tenants were just waking up. Digger gestured with her head. She had picked up the gun, and she looked like a *squad* leader motioning me into combat or something. I hefted the brick and stalked out into the dim yard, trying to choose a window. I wasn't *afraid*. I was just calculating what would be the worst blow. I also kind of secretly hoped I'd hit Lorriner with the brick. All I could see, though, were unclear shadows moving around behind the curtains, which were blue and printed with green-headed ducks flying in endless fascist ranks. There were three windows within what I figured was throwing distance, so I set my legs and hurled. With two hands, a swaying, lolloping throw. The brick rotated stolidly as it flew toward the middle window. The one I'd aimed at. Happiness, ladies and gentlemen. Maybe the purest. The glass broke, with the universal confused chime breaking glass makes. The brick thumped into the house, pushing aside the curtain enough for me to catch a flicker of the room: a blue-glowing television, or maybe an aquarium? Whatever. I was already dashing back into the pine stand to wait and watch.

"I can't believe you *did* it, I can't believe you *did* it," Digger moaned in glee. At this precise instant, the security lights clipped to the rambler's eaves blared on. And we saw (*holy fuck!*) the front door flap open and disgorge the great Michael Lorriner himself.

He was indeed short, as his nickname would suggest—my height. Round and stodgy-looking. His face was as white as the missing moon, and disfigured with those thick-framed institutional glasses? The ones that give you the ape face of a complete retard? He was wearing a black Baltimore Orioles shirt, beaten-up jeans, and white clunky sneakers. Childish in general appearance. This was a disappointment. I mean, I had this whole *theory*. I wanted to be able to look him in the eyes. To *know*. To see that determination, that precision of intent. Whatever it was that had allowed him to march into Stubb's and execute three people. It *upset* me, the way he carried himself. A weakling, a nonentity. Then he started talking, and the tenor of the whole occasion changed.

"Someone out there? I hear yew, yew dirty fucker," he yelled. His voice, though loud, was shockingly even. Free of anger, you know? He might have been yelling for someone to pass the salt. It *was* the same voice from the phone call. That, at least, was satisfying. "That yew, Jewboy? Get off my property! I got my *rights*! I got my *rights*! Fuckin' *Jew*." And then he was off, stumping around the side of the house to check and see if the brick thrower might be hiding there. His walk was bowlegged and graceless. It reminded me of my own clumsiness. He was sort of *waddling*. Though he wasn't even all that fat, just chubby. And this was hilarious, I mean his *duckwalk*. I now had to clench my teeth to stop myself from laughing. Not even the fact that Lorriner had figured out it was me made a difference. It was *too* perfect, you know? Some guy in an Orioles shirt? What the fuck? The new laughs were making my diaphragm seize up. Digger pincered my hand, and I saw that she was fighting back laughter again, too, and we crouched there, linked in the semidark, watching Lorriner amble in fury around his flat-roofed house. A straw man wearing overalls slumped head-on-knees in a rocking chair next to the front door, and a plastic pink flamingo stood hammered into soil. You'd have been in a shit-fit of laughter, too, if you'd been there. "Come on, yew dirty fucker," Lorriner bellowed. "I know my *rights*. Yew fucking Jew!" The lights in the lone neighboring house, the one right at the turnoff, came on, and another male voice screamed, "Shut up! Wud you shut up!" "No, I GOT my rights," Lorriner yelled again.

So that was it! We'd thrown the brick; we'd seen the man himself. Done what we'd planned. Instead of righteous anger, there was this slack-muscled suppressed laughter. Digger and I decided to stay. Maybe it was the afterhaze of the comedy. Maybe it stemmed from the simple fact that human beings can be relied on to make as many retarded mistakes as possible. Maybe just because he looked so *harmless*. *This* was Kevin's murderer, this *ordinary* guy—we could beat him! I knew that. I remember *thinking* that. I didn't know what this victory would consist of, but

I knew we would win. In the end it doesn't matter *why*. We stayed, in the cold dirt, fallen needles rustling garrulously beneath us.

"I bet it's like *hard* for him now. I bet he's all terrified of getting caught. You know?" Digger muttered. It made sense. She has a real grip on the practical side of things. So we huddled there, freezing and expectant. Lorriner did not disappoint. With a final shout of "Jewboy!" he careened back into his house and out again right away, but better equipped. He'd put on a nylon jacket, bright teal, against the cold, which seemed much worse out here in farm country. The jacket made his moony face even moonier. In one hand he was holding a long black cop flashlight, the kind you read about in articles on police brutality. In the other, a racket of some kind. A tennis racket, but smaller. For badminton, I guess.

"Oh, come *on*." Digger snorted. "You still out there, Jewboy?" Lorriner advanced, shouting, to the edge of the light perimeter, and started hosing his flashlight beam in wild loops across his dark yard. It grazed Digger's face, the soft bulge of her cheek, and she slammed herself back against her tree, wrapping her torso in her own arms. "Yew dirty fucker! Come on out! Fuckin' Jewboy!" I won't lie: the slur got to me. I'm not stone-souled. And—in this blinding and glorious instant—I *knew* what I had to do. Doubt-free. I emitted a growl. Get it? Like a dog! And then some hoarse barks. Digger stopped embracing herself and joined in. Her dog voice was high and clear; mine was in the tenor range. Our imitations—which must have been terrible—set the neighbor off again, begging and begging everyone to shut up. To *please* shut up. "Wud you please, please just shut up!" "Get off my property," Lorriner answered, waving his flashlight and badminton racket in loose semaphore. For at least a minute or two, the misty beam careening all over the place, fence, straw man, treetops. Vanishing into the sky. Digger and I kept up our howls and yodels. They got painful. But I couldn't have stopped, some *joyous momentum* was driving me on; we barked and barked, high and low, till our voices went croaky and we had whipped ourselves back into a fit of comic hysteria. And, throwing down the racket but retaining the flashlight, Lorriner stomped around to the rear of his house again and vanished from our view. We'd *beaten* him! I'd known we would. Digger released my hand. We unbent our aching knees.

And a bass animal voice, a real voice this time, started belling and screaming. "Fuck," whispered Digger, as though in echo: she figured it out before me. I remained clueless until, announced by the light percussion of a screen door, Lorriner's dog came racing toward our clot of trees. Lorriner had released it in response to our barking. It looked as big as a steroidal horse, and its crimson pelt had this weaponlike gleam, and its ropy saliva trailed the brownish grass stubble it was loping across. Digger and I took off in a single motion, running blind into the cover of deeper trees farther back on the property. Lorriner started bellowing the word *Murphy*. The dog's name, I realized as we ran. "Murphy! Geddem! Murphy! Geddem! Fuckin' Jewboy! Geddem! Mur-feeeeeee!" he screamed, pumping his arms and bringing his white child's fists down to crush some invisible foe to dust. Digger and I stopped, panting, and pressed ourselves against a huge royal oak. I don't know why we thought this would help. The dog curved out from the glaring scrim of light and galloped straight at us, his shouts increasing in genuine rage. "Shut up, shut up, shut *up*," the neighbor at the road head chanted. Lorriner kept screaming, "Geddem." The world was whirling to an end. I was shit-scared. All the flatulent confidence Lorriner's physical appearance had inspired was gone. And there was this monstrous *dog* torpedoing at me.

Remember what I said about Digger being a natural? With the gun, I mean. Well, imagine what a natural would do in this situation. Being a natural at something, anyway, means that you *need* to do it. As opposed to *wanting* to do it. I'm not saying Digger was *eager* to use the gun. But she *did* bring it. She'd let David hand it over without comment, she'd fired it at the Dump and destroyed her target. All of those are signs of consent, right? Now, given that we were about to be mauled by this giant death-camp Labrador, she acted like a natural. No one can blame her. I don't. It's even *more* proof, I'd say, that she's marked out for an über-memorable life. So I stood there paralyzed, and Digger dropped into her shooter's crouch, forearms wavering, brows drawn.

Then the gun went off. Have you ever seen any living thing get shot? I doubt it. I hadn't, either, until just then. Nothing similar had ever come within the compass of my experience before. Absolutely nothing. I live in a crappy city. There's no need to worry about the violent death of animals in a city. And it *was* violent, in the worst sense of the word. Maybe the relative help-lessness of the animal made it more disgusting: it had no under-standing of its situation. Either before or after the shot—which converted it into something inanimate, except for a few final quivers of life. The dog jerked and fell, legs splayed, like it had run into some invisible obstruction. The howls of enraged pursuit stopped. It *sobbed*. You could hear a light glug of escaping fluid, a sucking whistle, undercutting its moans. Other dogs began bark-ing, in sympathy with their fallen comrade or whatever. All over the immediate vicinity.

. . .

Those empty-brained little sycophants! Where had they
come from? Where had they been when *we* were barking? There
weren't even any other houses! Lorriner rushed to the dying
animal and kneeled to shield it from further injury, with his
whole nylon-clad torso. Bending as though in reverence. Maybe
it was reverence. Who knows? He was speechless, at least. Silent
as concrete. Digger was already striding out from our thicket, out
into the glow of the security lights. *Covering* Lorriner with the
gun the whole time. So, even with all this confusion surrounding
me, what else could I do but follow? Murmuring, "Holy fuck,
holy fuck, holy fuck," as I ran.

XI.

THE NEXT TWO MINUTES I have no contiguous memory
of. Just chopped-up isolated moments in series. Life had been
replaced by still photos, or medieval tapestries or something. You
know? The ones where the perspective is all wrong, or it's not
adult perspective, and everything is the same size, and everyone
seems to be standing in the air, even if their feet are firmly planted
on that tan, ruined ground, and they all have those expressions of
empty piety on their faces. Never a smile, never a grimace. They're
content to live forever in their absurd poses. So: Image One:
darkness of the yard. Image Two: Lorriner standing there with
his dying dog lifted in both arms. Image Three: all of us in this
awkward circle, nobody saying anything. Image Four: a proces-
sion. Lorriner first. Digger is frozen at the sill of the door. She's
stumbled without making any noise, but Lorriner hasn't noticed.
Image Five: warm pear-colored light of the indoors. These *clean
cuts* with nothing connecting the images. Except their stark
contrast.

Time must have continued flowing by in its boring and
inexorable way, though. We *did* end up in Lorriner's house. And
the laws of logic or whatever still obtained. He *had* to let us in. We
were armed. I can't believe I just wrote that: *armed*. I blinked and

squinted to right my vision inside. Lorriner was carrying Murphy forklifted in two arms, as you would a dead child or a rolled heavy carpet, and there were broad swaths of blackish, viscous blood on the breast of his ugly jacket. Digger had recovered from her stumble, which I thought was awesome. I'd astonished myself by managing to not fuck any of this up, so far. We were *on the right track*, or whatever, to use one of Mr. Vanderleun's expressions. Despite the jerkiness of my mental record, everything was going according to plan.

The house we'd forced our way into was hilarious. I've already gone over the details of the outside part. Which might lead you to expect beer cans scattered everywhere inside, and carpets stinking of dog piss. Whatever rural squalor you want to imagine. But the place, first of all, was über-neat. Not a scrap of garbage, not a single disordered article. The living room was crammed with furniture, all carved stiffly from this heavy black wood. You know what I mean: knuckled spheres at all the joints, each piece weighing half a ton. Heavy crimson cushions. He must have bought it in a single go from some furniture barn. They have a lot, out in his area. No bookcase, no television, no rug, just a pseudo-royal two-ton sofa, two armchairs, and a coffee table. The blue light I'd seen outside came from an empty, totally clean aquarium. I remember one piece of decoration: a poster of a skier in mid-jump, launched by a ramp resembling a single sure ink stroke, vaulted high above the speckled crowd, arms rigid, legs rigid . . . There was a smell of chocolate. I swear to fucking God.

And Lorriner was pale, paler than before. I could watch him at leisure now, shaking with the effort of holding up the dog. His face had this doughy, unfinished look. Or not unfinished. *Unfinished* is an overused descriptor for faces, anyway. But too cautious, too constrained, the work of someone second-rate. A type of handiwork I am familiar with. A look of petty alarm smeared across it. What some rabbit-gazed embezzler would wear at his arrest. Murphy's sobs had quieted, and the start-stop gush of blood and fluid from the horse-size brisket (that's the chest part of a dog) had stopped. Even though I have no clinical training, I knew the dog was dead. Lorriner seemed to know it too, because he started snuffling. Just two or three times, and then he mastered it. With a brief reddening of his throat from the effort. I was beginning to have my doubts. But Digger's presence assuaged them. Or maybe it was just the gun. She was wagging it at him, now, telling him, "It's okay to put the dog down. It's okay. You can sit down now. We just want to ask you some questions." She spoke with a perfect and unhurried cadence.

"Her nayme's Murphy," Lorriner told us in his reedy, light-stepping voice. Knowing the dog's gender nauseated me.

"Yer that fuckin' Jewboy?" he asked me, still supporting the corpse of his Labrador. "Man, yew fuckin' *people*. Like what the *fuck*'s like the matter with yew fuckin' people."

"I mean, like it has nothing to do with *that*," I replied. What cutting intelligence! The bank-clerk's alarm had fled Lorriner's face. He was back on familiar ground or whatever. Jews are useful in that way. Providing a stable starting point for all *kinds* of rhetoric.

"Can I like sit down?"

"She like already *said* you could," I answered. He lowered himself, with labor, onto the throne-size sofa, and arranged Murphy's body on the coffee table. One of her legs was vibrating. To make up for my earlier failure, I added: "You fuckneck, I mean, you fucking redneck piece of *shit*." This sounded fake. This look of mortification pinched Lorriner's face. I expected him to get pissed. Kind of insulting that he did not, I guess. Some people just can't deliver insults with any authority. Even Digger, in my peripheral vision, was somehow expressing embarrassment and disapproval.

"Do yawl like want *munny*? Cuz I have munny." Lorriner smiled now. Which threw me. I mean, how does a guy with a gun pointed at his head smile? A guilty guy, no less. "I have like three-four thousand right here. In *cash*." He panted the last word. "I have like other stuff, too. Like good *shit*, mayn." I knew he meant drugs of some kind. Pot probably, also—given the rural location—meth, which is a going concern in Maryland. Another of the many reasons why it is the worst state. He directed all these offers to Digger. I wanted to tell him what a mistake this was. In case you haven't already figured this out, she's unbribable. I mean if the rest of her personality, flaws and all, is anything to go on. So she did not hesitate. Not even a fractional pause. The two of them hovered, eyeing each other. Lorriner, even seated, projected *injured dignity*. Fucking incomprehensible to me. Digger had this *clinical scrutiny* in her eyes. I might as well have been one of Lorriner's eighty-pound ottomans, gauged by my involvement in this situation.

"Why did you do it?" she asked.

"Mayn, I like *did* it because you fuckin' people thank you like own the *damn world*!" This was uttered with whistling smugness, a complacent body jerk, a tweak of his dull hair. You're thinking I was angry. Angry at Lorriner and angry at being ignored. I was not. I couldn't stop clenching and fluttering my hands, because they were itching for a weapon, not to use but to hold. I couldn't ask Digger for *hers*. She was sitting down, now, lowering her insubstantial ass (*white girl ass*, the argot goes) into Lorriner's heavy armchair. Her movement made me feel even more awkward. I would have launched into some diatribe. But Digger spoke again. She telepathically knew, apparently, that I was about to break into stupid speech.

"I don't mean throwing the brick through the window." She sounded calm and tired, nothing more. "I mean Kevin Broadus. Why did you kill him? Was it because he insulted you at that party? Because you like got in a fistfight? Is that really a good reason to kill somebody?"

"Mayn, I *don't*—" Lorriner began. Digger cut him off. Which she never does knowingly. She *always* waits for the other person to finish.

"If you lie I'll kill you. I'll shoot you. I don't care, Mike." Calling him by his first name—amazing, right?

"Yeah, she like *means* it, man," I informed him. I sat down now, too, with vicarious ease. Lorriner's round mouth hung open, his silent, stupid, ragged mouth. He tried a new tactic. You have to admire his adaptability.

"Look, mayn, do you all know how like *duuuumb* you all are being? They have like *rill* cops here, not like those duuuumb niggers you git down in the city." He had his old tone back: master of the domain. "I mean, like if they ketch yawl it's gawna be like rill bad. I mean like if you leave now, I won't call 'em, I swayer. They're not *like* those dumb niggers down in the city. You unnerstand?" Yes, he had that *tone*. But he was flutter-blinking now. Sweat emerged in pearls from the wide pores of his forehead.

"Don't use that word, please," Digger instructed him.

"No, look, mayn, like if yawl leave *now* I won't like *do* anything, awl right? Is that awl right?"

Digger sighed and steadied her grip.

"Please tell us why." She'd closed her eyes halfway to draw a better bead on his skull.

"Yeah, keep your like bullshit to yourself, man," I echoed.

"Addison," said Digger. Not without kindness. I shut up. Lorriner hawked back what must have been a *colossal* gob of mucus, to judge from the sound. Then there was this huge melodic clatter, and everyone screamed at one another in surprise.

Now, I know you've been waiting for our *massive fuckup* this whole time. Since the gun appeared. This isn't it, though it could have been. We were all über–freaked out by the sound, coming just when it did. Lorriner made a lunge, balked by the corpse-bearing coffee table, and I grabbed the iron-hard arms of my chair. It was the type of explosion that results in someone getting shot, in these situations. A flurry of chaotic motion, aggressive noise. But Digger did not fire. She's *that* cool-handed. The noise—it became apparent after our initial burst of terror—came from a dim corner, where a *cuckoo clock* was exploding into action, sending out a bluish knight through high wooden doors to chase a reddish dragon around a heavy, cheap-looking battlement. It played an infuriating song, and then chimed eleven times. Was it that late already? The burst of terror the noise inspired in me died out. Lorriner's breath came short and high and the pearled sweat on his face had spread to an even sheen. Digger kept the gun steady. Murphy's right rear leg kicked and kicked in the contractions of arriving rigor, scritching against the wood. We represented a whole microcosm of *vibrant activity*. I didn't blame Lorriner for taking so long to consider his answer. I mean, even murderers possess reason, right? Then the unique stench of human feces flowed up into our faces. I thought *I'd* shit myself, and shouted some inchoate noise of fear and regret.

. . .

I realized it was coming from Lorriner, who had also started weeping. He'd shit himself out of shock at the garish melody of the chimes. Writing it down, it sounds *sensible* and maybe even unavoidable. But still: he shit himself and started weeping. *Weeping*, ladies and gentlemen. A man voids his bowels and weeps. That's what all human purpose *comes* to. Fuck! You could still detect the under-aroma of chocolate that had greeted us, which made the whole situation *impossible*.

"Are you like a *clock* enthusiast?" I crowed in my utter perplexity.

"Addison," Digger repeated, in an exasperated tone.

"Look, like I ain't never, I mean, like it's just like I don't *know*, mayn, where yawl like *heard*—" Lorriner stopped for breath. "Just please don't, mayn, I like never even *knew* that boy." He was *hyperventilating*. "Did like Noel tell yawl that? Noel Bradley? Yawl like *work* for him?" I realized he was, at most, a year older than we were. How the fuck did he have this absurd house? And why? Where were his parents? "No, mayn, like no no no no no," Lorriner keened.

"Mike," Digger said, in that same sweet, low voice. "Shut up about Noel. Just don't lie, okay?"

"Why'd yawl like kill my dawg, mayn? How can I like believe what yawl like *say* now?" His hands were up, as though he could swat away the bullet when Digger decided to shoot. You think I was afraid, too. But I wasn't. Just *interested*. Fucked-up, right?

"No, man, no no like *please*, mayn, like *please*." Have you ever heard anyone begging for their life? It wasn't even clear to me that Lorriner was in real danger. The astonishment provoked by all of that night's anarchy kind of *dominated* every other emotion. We were holding someone at *gunpoint*. Have you ever tried *that*? It banishes other considerations. The idea of victory? Gone. Plans for vengeance? Double gone. I became a helpless retard, confronted with all this. "Like *please*, mayn," Lorriner was babbling, "I *swayer* I didn't. I *swayer* I didn't. Like *please*. Mayn, like do you work for Noel? Cuz I can pay you whatever he's paying you, I swear. I didn't *dew* it. I swayer. I didn't." He sounded . . . resigned. I guess this is how interrogations *work*. There's a point at which our fear of death vanishes, and beyond that point is the truth. Either that or permanent silence. Lorriner was not the silent type. "*Pleeeease*," he throbbed out. He steepled his hands. He was mouthing a prayer. Holy fuck.

"Mike, it's *okay*," Digger chanted in consolation, the gun steady. And—limber and warm with sudden rage—I started shouting at Lorriner. Just because he had the audacity to shit himself and cry, after dragging us all the way out here. He had no right! This white-trash asshole! That's how my inner monologue ran. I roared something unclear and rushed, with wild variations in pitch, about his being a racist and a murderer, about us *not letting his actions stand*, about justice. Justice! Oh, God, even as I was talking I knew he was innocent. No murderer *shits* himself. "And you think you can just do whatever you want, because you're fucking ignorant! You think you can just like go as you please and do like whatever!" I was shaking my index finger at Lorriner, who hadn't stopped weeping the whole time. If Digger were less moderate and sensible, she might have pointed the gun at me to shut me up, or maybe just coldcocked me with the butt. That would have done the job. But she continued to aim, enrobed in calm, and we all three sat there in the stink of shit, as Lorriner clucked and sobbed to himself. "Just don't like *fuck* with us anymore, okay?" I sputtered. As though this admonition were necessary. I said it because I had to go on, because momentum was pushing me on, I went on making the noises that the human animal makes, the noises of injured dignity and pious anger, the noises of falsehood.

Seriously, where the fuck do you go from here? Yes, Lorriner was innocent. But, I mean, in a technical sense, the evening counted as a success. Right? We may have had the wrong man. But our plan had gone off error-free. From conception to execution. A to B to C. Rushed and floaty as a dream. Shooting a dog doesn't count as a fuckup. I hate dogs. Digger does not like dogs. I'd say that anyone who does not hate them you should be suspicious of. (Do you know who has a picture of his dog Aurelius on his desk? Mr. Vanderleun!) Is killing a dog even murder? Who the fuck knows? Nothing *bad* had happened to us. And Lorriner *deserved* it. Right? Deserved fifteen minutes of abject terror and having his dog killed. Even though he wasn't guilty. Somehow, though, despite our success all our energy had vanished. Which is not supposed to happen. Success is supposed to lead you on to more success. Our whole society is constructed around this principle.

Lorriner was also robbed of whatever force had prompted his clumsy proud strut as he threatened us with flashlight and badminton racket. He looked even more childish than before. His whole slump had this weakness to it, this weird curvature. You know the way adversity affects little kids. It outrages their innate sense of fairness, it *hurts* them, even if it's nonphysical. It still *hurts* them. "Where are your like parents, man?" I found myself asking.

"Addison," Digger whooshed out. She sounded aghast.

"Whut," asked Lorriner, "whut the fuck is *rawng* with yew

people?" And you could hear the tears breaking in again. "My parents?" he blubbered. "My parents? Yew goddamn kike pieces of shit." His voice was in *tatters*. Digger flicked a glance of severe disappointment at me.

"I'm sorry about Murphy," she said. All that was missing was her offering Lorriner a handshake. Digger and I were both standing. It was time to leave. Lorriner hid his face.

"No, mayn, like it's like *fahn*," he said through his cradling hands. And from his tone it was unmistakable: he was *forgiving* us.

The night air smelled of cold. You know? That high, clean, bitter smell? Digger walked ahead of me, the gun dangling in her hand for a few paces, before she slid it back into her coat pocket. The clouds obscuring the moon had gone, and its dark light silvered everything as we kicked our way through the rattling leaves, back down to the turnoff. "Hey, man," I called to Digger. Who didn't answer. She just kept striding ahead through the leaves. The lights in the house by the road were still on, and she passed through them and into the further darkness, looking rigidly ahead. She didn't answer me, though I kept speaking. I thought she was furious. But she smiled—you could tell, even in the dark— when I got to my car, and gave a small sigh as we got under way and crooked a cigarette between her lips. She didn't even seem *perturbed* at all. We passed the truck that had honked at us before in appreciation of our singing, now stalled on the shoulder, its cabin lit and holding two leaden faces. I noticed the logo on its side for the first time, which made me slow a bit with surprise: our headlights revealed that it belonged to Rex Rentals. The maroon dog, the Rex emblem, stared out, mournful and docile, from its white panel into the third dimension. And then we were among the grass fields again, Maryland exhaling its dumb watchfulness.

. . .

If I were writing a novel, all this would precede a scene of obvious reconciliation. Quiet and subtle: *The road spread out ahead of them. Digger, without looking, let her hand brush Addison's knee.* Or with pyrotechnics, disgusting and overstated. Maybe we end up fucking in my frigid car, or in a shady roadside motel, or whatever. After all, we're just children, and that's how things work in books, right? Nothing *genuine* is ever at stake. And youth is resilient if nothing else. But what happened is this. We drove. Digger half slept. There was no need for navigation. There's one road, as I said, in places like that. It's a question of mere direction. Before two, we'd gotten back to Digger's house. I hadn't felt the cold of the night until then, as my blood crept back into my hands. We parked, and Digger clambered out of her doze. We'd been silent for the final hour of the drive. I found this long quiet provoking. So I started, as we sat in my car, *explaining* everything again. The whole stupid story. What you've been reading here, but the one-minute version. To myself as much as her. This time, without Short Mike. Inventing some other anonymous and powerful killer. (I almost preferred it that way.) She nodded in slow time when I finished, and bit her lower lip in concentration. I read this as a sign of encouragement. (Wrong!)

"Man," I went on, assuming a jocular air, "we just need to *find* the real guy and get him like *preemptively*." Digger did not respond. I was worried, now. Her silence suggested doubts. "Hey, Digger? Right? What should we do? Do you think." Still nothing. I rambled, trying to get her back in sympathy with the cause. I even brought up the racial angle again, which had worked before. She just asked me to be quiet. That didn't stop me. "Hey, look, man. We *both* thought this guy was the guy. We both did. Right? And now you can't just like *disavow* the whole idea? Right?" This prodded her into speech. Her voice, though modulated, got all thready—frayed, sort of.

"Don't use that word. *Disavow*. You go on and on about this guy and then we like go and kill his *dog*? Some poor fat guy. And it was *not* him, okay, Noel's a liar, and *you* are by extension, and it was all just some *atrocious* coincidence. Okay? Coincidence. Like everything else. It's all just appearances and coincidence. Maybe you're going through some weird *thing* about Kevin. And maybe I sort of like humored you. But it's like *bad* luck. Just bad luck. For everyone. I'm really tired, Addison. It's just like what you're always yammering about. From Latin. '*O Fortuna*' whatever. That stupid *song*. Like that." You could tell that she was, despite her controlled voice, angry. With me, with the *situation*. But there's no bigger reason than being wrong to turn on the old self-righteousness faucet, and I let out some gorilla breaths, nostrils flared, as I planned my response. I had a whole little speech ginned up.

She started talking before I could. About the last possible subject I expected her to bring up. Our agreement. I didn't realize it at first, because she failed to make herself clear. Or, I should say, I was too stupid to grasp what she meant by saying, "You're being really unfair to me. And you're pretending not to know it."

"Man, how am I being unfair? You're just like sitting there. I mean, yeah, we were wrong but you can't just sit there and not say anything."

"I don't mean that." She wouldn't look at me.

"So what then? What do you mean? Not telling me will not like resolve the issue."

"If you can't figure it out, why should I tell you? Don't talk to me like we're having some debate, okay? Just don't."

I took two minutes to respond, judging by the dash clock, pallid and blue. I had no idea what she was so pissed about, when I opened my mouth. So I decided to guess, like they tell you to do on standardized tests.

"Do you mean unfair about like the *sex*?" I mumbled.

"No. I don't know. No. But you're not some fucking person I don't know. So why are you talking to me like you are? Why do you say *disavow*? We're not on the debate team together. And yeah, okay, maybe the sex is part of it. Yeah, so we don't say that. But come on, man. Don't be fucking *obtuse*. So the sex is part of it. Okay? Okay? Is that what you wanted to hear, you fucking asshole?"

She still would not look at me.

"I thought you *wanted* that, man," I said. This turned out to be a terrible idea.

"So *you* didn't," she coughed back instantly, as though she had been waiting all night for me to say just that, and crammed a thumb into her mouth.

"No, Digger like you're my best *friend*, man," I mumbled, to my own mild horror. This is maybe the worst thing to say to anyone at *any* time. I waited, jaw clenched in self-protection, for her to scream at me, to make some wounding remark. That's what violations of our agreement deserve. What I'd said was, in addition to being intrinsically moronic, a *major* violation of the agreement. But she did neither of these things: no yelling, no sarcasm. She leaned over and *kissed* me, which she had never done before. I mean in public. I mean not while we weren't fucking. You know what I mean. We both failed at the kiss, too eager and inert. Also, considering that she had just called me a fucking asshole, I had not seen it coming. So maybe I am a fucking asshole.

"You're such a jackass, Addison," she said in an overprecise voice, after we'd detached. "And everyone else is such a fucking liar." She handed me back the gun. Grip-first. A professional. We gave each other a weaving, troubled mutual stare, an acknowledgment of serious intent. Or just the look brought-together strangers exchange after a bus accident or whatever. Then she got out of my car, went into her house, and her door shut behind her with a leaden clap, and I sat in my freezing seat, smoking cigarettes. I opened my glove box, to hide the gun, then changed my mind and flipped the safety and put it in my coat pocket. I figured I could hide it in my safe. I did see Kevin's file, sitting in the glove box: a bit grimy now. I wanted to pore over it for an hour. I didn't—not then—though the desire stayed with me as I drove home.

My father was out on the porch when I pulled up. He'd been waiting for me, but he said nothing. Just wanting the fact of his being awake to make me admit I'm indebted to him. Which I never do! He was wearing this beaten, creased look, his face drawn and furtive. *That* expression is how you know he's happy. The single sign. Can you believe I've forgotten to tell you his full name, this whole time? It's Theodore Franklin. He's named not after one but *two* grinning murdering Roosevelts. People call him Ted. "*Some*body broke the window, Addison," he told me. His constant and unconscious prayer to suffer some persecution had been granted, after unjust delay. I didn't answer. I was so *tired*. "It *happened* earlier this afternoon. Where have you *been* all day, Addison?" He never asks this. I can't even think of the last time he asked where I'd been. Or asked me any question about myself at all. Not that I resent him for it. I'm a private person.

Our living room lamps were all on. We have six, all antiques. Pewter bodies, multicolored glass shades—all the overornamentation my father loves. They give no real light, so you have to have all six lit to get even reasonable illumination in our living room. To my utter lack of surprise, Fatima was sprawled on the couch, smoking, dressed in a long blue man's oxford. The rolled-back cuffs displayed her furry forearms. I could have figured out it was her when I'd heard the sounds of their fucking, earlier. By a basic process of deduction or whatever. She pretended not to notice me. My father stood on the porch and gave the night air a coach's rundown of his afternoon and evening, as I walked away. His voice getting shallower with each step I took. "We cleaned up the *glass*, Addison," I heard my father yell. Still from the porch. Why was he not coming inside? Who *does* that? "The police came. They were very *respectful*. That tall one. You remember. Officer *Huang*." I was already scurrying down to my room, and I fell down the stairs when he shouted this. Just *lost* control of my limbs and slipped the rest of the way in a flailing tumble. The gun hurtled out of my pocket and skittered across our basement tiles, spinning. "They came and they were completely *respectful*, Addison. Where have you been? Are you going to sleep?" His words wafted down as the gun rotated and slowed, coming to rest with its small black gaping barrel aimed directly at me. I didn't even scream this time, just stood up and began to check myself for wounds. But you know what? *No injury*. Not a bruise, not a scratch. Just a mild haze of up-too-late nausea. And a dull ache I could not place.

XII.

NOW IS A GOOD POINT, I mean in the *narrative* or whatever, to answer a question I know must be on your minds. *Why, Addison, do you talk so much about the* Aeneid? Just to lead up to some big display wherein I compare myself to a noble mythological character, you're thinking. Maybe Aeneas himself! *He's* a totally sweet dude. Maybe Anchises, who got raped by a female deity. Maybe it should be Aeneas's son Ascanius, because he's innocent and good? Or better yet: one of the gods! That would be awesome, right? Let me disabuse you of that idea. I'm not much of an egotist, in any normal way, and the character in the *Aeneid* I most identify with is not morally splendid. He doesn't even come up to the level of Helenus or anything. He's not even a *Trojan*. He's this vicious kid named Neoptolemus. A minor character. A Greek. I doubt you remember him: the angry young man so crushed by the circumstances of his birth (he's Achilles' bastard son) that he murders Priam, the venerable, aged king of Troy. *Just some sociopath*, you're saying. His name means "New War," for God's sake!

There's more to him than that, though. Yeah, he's a brutal murderer, but he's kind of an interesting one: he's always doing something related to but hideously different from what he intends. Take the thing with Priam. What he *wanted* was for someone to tell him, *Your lineage is not shameful; you have nothing to be ashamed of.* Instead of finding such a person, he goes and puts on armor and then runs through flaming Troy and murders this helpless old man, as though there weren't dozens of other more *challenging* people to murder. He even kills Polites, one of Priam's sons, right in front of him, right in the royal apartments. And the whole time he's committing these stupid atrocities, he's showing how *unrepentant* he is, taunting Polites with his spear, ridiculing Priam before dragging him to the family altar and decapitating him. Which is all the proof you need of a confused conscience: grim, ceaseless, public insistence.

His story also demonstrates an obscure truth. Having a plan, any plan, means you know on some level you're going to fail, you're in the wrong. This contradicts everything I've been taught, all the larger principles of modern life, which are all *about* planning and calculation. But if you're going to succeed, how could you need to think it out beforehand? If you had the necessary confidence—in every case perfect, unbreakable confidence— the idea of a plan would make you *laugh*. Who even *has* that kind of confidence? Mr. Vanderleun says that no writing is worth doing unless you talk about it first. Talk it through, he advises. Every aspect, every thought. With a friend. With a committee of friends. He points to himself as an example of a "writer" shaped by this parliamentary process. Total horseshit! How would *he* know anything about actual writing? He's living with one eye on some invisible audience. He can only think of how his *gestures* look. So he imagines that *other* people are consumed and ruined by always looking over their shoulders, out into the darkness of the theater, the unresponsive darkness. Virgil didn't suffer from that species of vanity. How could he have survived for two thousand years if he had? It's a *convention* now for artists to be looking over their shoulders for approval, to make these *demonstrations* of their commitment.

I can't claim to be innocent of this. Not as an artist. I'm no artist. I mean as a human being. On the first of October, as I was leaving my house, an unsupervised boy rammed my shin with his blood-colored tricycle. The stony, constipated frown on his face as he rocketed away, hunched and huffing, would have done credit to a victorious dictator. "You. Are. *Defeated!*" screamed the tricyclist. I watched him careen around the corner. My backpack was weighed down with all my money. Literally all of it. In two plastic grocery bags. This was one of those lead-colored indeterminate days prefiguring winter, which in D.C. is late to arrive. Our citizens grow hysterical at the first bad weather. You can go to any grocery store and find the bottled-water supply cleaned out. Car accidents abound, after which the drivers gather in lugubrious duos or trios accepting fate, their scarves leaping and fluttering with release from all that leaden expectation. And the snow, when it comes, which is not until late December or January—the snow itself is always minor, a grayish dusting. Fragile. It never achieves that *white darkness* quality. The thwarted desire for which, I think, makes children so high-strung here in the winter months.

Picking this up again was hard, I won't lie. You see that I've had to ease my reentry into the world of writing with speculative material. What happened that night at Lorriner's house turned out to be a watershed moment in my *social career*. And not the harbinger of some tremendous positive change. Writing about it exhausted me and I had to rest before I started writing again. I don't want to sound dramatic or mysterious. All this *is* going somewhere. Even Mr. Vanderleun would approve. He's very big on *resolution.* He cleaves the air with his finger-missing hand when he talks about it, as though he had some deep and personal stake in the successful conclusion of stories. Trust me, though. I *do* have a massive closing circus-type event coming. I just need to put in some explanatory stuff beforehand. I mean, I *could* just lay it out all at once, but then even *I* wouldn't be able to make sense of it. And it *happened* to me. I hope you can excuse me for making such an abrupt new beginning. I'll try to summarize, below, so you're not lost.

#1. Digger and I killed Murphy on September 12. For the rest of the month, my energy levels plummeted. In school, I mean. Though my teachers considered this an improvement. Mr. Vanderleun took me aside after class to tell me how much my attitude had improved. "I'm really surprised at you, Mr. Schacht. It begs the question where *this* Addison was hiding before." His stump waggled in appreciation. And he still did not fucking know what *begs the question* means. He was referring, I guess, to the fact that I did the work I was assigned, all that sort of thing, as though doing my teachers and the school a *favor*. (Which I believed I was.) But I started letting all *kinds* of things pass that I wouldn't have before, I mean not without deliberately offending the speaker. Alex Faustner spent an entire English class mispronouncing the word *foliage* as *foilage*. I said nothing. I stopped shouting out the correct translations when my classmates fumbled in Latin, an activity that Ms. Erlacher could never punish because *technically* it proved that I was both involved and apt, though you could tell from her white-lipped smile that she couldn't stand it. I did it to humiliate people. Though it wasn't humiliating for anyone, because they themselves didn't care; they were *relieved* to let me take over in midsentence their blabbery wet-mouthed translations. They shouldn't have *been* there in the first place. Stopping was easy. What do I care if some random guy fails to learn Latin? *Better* that he doesn't. Knowledge should not be shared out among the giftless and clumsy. Nothing is worse than presumption.

#2. My father—and this, really, I don't even have adequate language to describe—bought a Sherlock Holmes costume for the Cochrane Institute's October Gala. You'd expect this gala to be on Halloween, right? Wrong! Those pretentious fuckers can't even observe the old pagan holidays with the rest of us. It's always on the second Friday in October, usually about two weeks before everyone else is celebrating, it's always a costume party, and my father has gone every year since his initial employment. He starts talking about it in late September. He brought the costume (and Fatima) home the day he purchased it. He made her dress up in drag as Dr. Watson. To try it out. And the party wasn't even for more than a week. This was the *dry run*. I was present when this travesty occurred. My father was so *committed* to it. He was running around, looking for his pipe, his deer-stalker, the magnifying glass, all of these trappings that he had paid some exorbitant price for at a costume shop, like it would somehow absolve his dull ways, his grinding habits. Fatima was sitting smoking on the low red sofa in our living room, staring. The look of contempt on her face was all the more corrosive for lacking a visible object. She was half dressed as Watson, wearing this houndstooth pants-and-vest combo, fingering the sideburns and mustache my father had wheedled her into applying with some high-grade adhesive, smoking and smoking. "Are you ready yet, *esteemed* Doctor?" My father yelled this again and again—what a great joke!—from his bedroom upstairs. It took them a while to get back into civilian clothes and leave: they dragged back and forth, and my father's rare laugh, which is almost always fake though it is rare, rang out again and again, like a dropped piece of pewter.

#3. I felt *no* further fear of Mike Lorriner. Anyone who shits his pants in front of you and a gun-waving girl isn't going to call the cops. That would just *confirm* his own humiliation. He'd bury his dog and shut up about it. Tell people she got run over. I mean, what could he say, anyway: *I threw a brick with a Nazi banner through this guy's window and his girlfriend killed my Labrador?*

#4. Digger and I had not spoken since the morning after we killed Murphy. I mean, *technically* I had spoken to her. That Monday I'd approached her in homeroom, ready to make some quip about the weekend. Sunday passed for me in this slack-muscled mist, a golden mist of languor. I couldn't understand it. I had no idea what to expect. Not that we would abandon our agreement. Never that. I stumbled into school, mouth tacky with anticipation. The noise of my contemporaries swelled in the hall. I crossed the steel threshold. I saw the cropped back of Digger's head, midturn.

But now she had this *look*. I'd never seen it before. A look of *woundedness*. Like I'd shot her, instead of her shooting Murphy. Lips flat. Eyes gleaming. She said nothing, literally nothing, when I said hello. It winded me, sort of, but then there was just this airy unconcern. Which lasted till the end of the school day. Then it turned into panic. I spent the afternoon calling her house and hanging up before the other line rang. When I did wait for an answer, I got the machine. I left three messages, each less comprehensible than the last. On my fourth attempt her mother picked up, made a predatory squawking sound, and said—with the suppressed glee doctors harbor in their voices for announcing deaths to family members—"Please stop calling, Addison. Phoebe doesn't want to *talk* to you." Then a breathy sigh. Then: "And do you know what? I'd like to take this particular moment in time to tell you that I've *always* thought you were a creep. A little alcoholic creep. You *and* all your alcoholic friends."

"Her name's not *Phoebe*, you cunt," I muttered, and hung up, the huge obscenity making me sweat with brief pride. I'm still proud of saying it, showing zero hesitation. Why Dr. Zeleny called me an alcoholic, or assumed I had friends—this I cannot explain.

There were other attempts, in the initial days of this exile. Or whatever it was. This *internal exile*. At lunch, I tried to bum a cigarette from her. She just sat there, taking precise bites out of her sandwich. She said, again, absolutely nothing. After school that day I chased her down, ran her to ground on the sward of rusty grass between Kennedy and where the houses of the neighborhood begin. I grabbed her sleeve. She whipped around to face me. I was expecting anger, disgust, revulsion . . . I was *hoping* for any of those. Anything would have been better than that look, that mute, even look of certitude and pain. I let go of her coat, its rough-woven wool scraped my fingertips a bit, and then she walked off and got into her car, which backfired twice. I watched until she drove away, my knees getting weaker and weaker with despair.

I know this sounds sort of overdone. You have to believe me: I had no idea it would affect me this way. So it had become sort of obvious to me that she felt . . . betrayed, maybe, by the way I'd acted in Maryland. That was the only way I could interpret her remark about being on the debating team. But fuck! If her feelings had changed, she would have said something, right? If she wanted out of the agreement, she could have just said that. I have no experience with women, other than her. And the one time I'd ever come close to behaving inappropriately with her, she'd just gotten sort of pissed. Right after we met, I asked her out. We hadn't yet had sex. I was operating according to the protocols I observed my peers using to prosecute their social lives. She just laughed, not unkindly, but still right in my face. Weirdly, I didn't feel any hurt or humiliation, just like I'd misunderstood a math problem or something, and then everything was fine. Our agreement kind of developed out of that event: we still ended up sleeping together three or four times a week. There was no one, literally, I could ask for advice. And having no idea of her reasons made the exile worse.

Digger and I still had to *see* each other. In school, I mean. In the halls. We had homeroom together. The kids in G&T are divided into two blocks, and they observe complementary class schedules—while I take English, Digger has World History, *etc.* So there was that fifteen-minute chunk of homeroom to be gotten through every morning, and then the eye avoidance between classes. Twenty-eight, twenty-nine minutes, total, per day. Excruciatingly, spine-slumpingly painful for me. Which I had not been expecting. And this, in turn, was a new humiliation—to feel pain when you have no idea if the other person feels the same pain. That would be the ultimate expression of slavishness and dicklessness. I mean, what's the point of having an *agreement* with someone at all if not to prevent emotional nonsense from happening? Why had we *observed* all those rigid protocols? So Digger and I shuffled past each other in the halls. No more cock-stiffening knee-to-knee contact. No more fucking. It killed me. I didn't understand why, was part of it. The pain was an affront to my honor! If you see what I mean. And to hers. It was this *testimony* about the shameful and emotional side of our relations, which we tried to ignore so that we could focus on more important things.

She *was* being consistent. Without sentiment, without remorse. She was following the terms. Not even the extraordinary, not even the inexplicable, could justify departures from them. I said she's destined for greatness. I meant it. That unswerving will is the *qualifying* mark of greatness-to-be. I had to admire it. But fuck her! Fuck her anyway. I didn't need her, and fuck her for thinking that I did. So what if it made me miserable every time I saw her stonily walking away from me in the hall. It wasn't about *her*! There was more at stake here. I'm putting this down so you don't think it was all about Digger, just so you don't think I'm this weak love-addled moron. The fact that I could imagine everything being different was what made the pain murderous. What if we hadn't driven out to Maryland? What if I never made that stupid call to Lorriner? That's the real *fuck you*! That your mind offers all these *alternatives* to your current situation. Mine was not one of despair. Or sadness, even, sadness does not properly describe it. It was the pain of *nothing*. What if I'd just kept my intrusive Jew nose out of the whole affair to begin with? Wouldn't that have made moral sense, anyway? *Oh, some random innocent kid gets shot? Here comes that crazy kike Addison Schacht with his puffed-up sense of obligation to remind you of it! Look at him! He's rubbing his hands like some spiritual usurer! And what's more, he's discovering will and intention where they can't be found! What moral genius!* This kind of thinking, I mean when you attribute mind in cases where it does not exist, is called the Pathetic Fallacy.

#5. I had three weeks. Three weeks of this shit! I got things done, though. Not seeing Digger freed up *huge* swatches of my time. I had no one else to talk to, remember? Do you know how much money you can earn in three weeks, with no one to talk to? I made three thousand dollars. I didn't spend a dime of it. My industry impressed Noel. I'd never had to re-up three times in a month before. Dealing with *him* was easy. He didn't know about the whole catastrophe with Lorriner. He never asked. I never told him. He would have thought killing Murphy was funny, though. I can just see it. He would have said, "Daaaaaamn, son! You shot the mufhuh's dog? White people be crazy!" Maybe that's why I never told him, because I didn't know if I could stand hearing that.

Noel was now a bigger part of my life, anyway, so it made sense to hold some stuff back. He and David and I shared a number of nights in Noel's freezing house, Noel jabbering away while David downed forty after forty. He could drink ten or eleven of them. He's a fucking *building*. They never had any effect that I could see. His voice didn't slur. If his eyelids slipped down, it was from pride. Noel, as he got higher and drunker, would become incoherent. The stories of his conquests entered the realm of obvious fantasy: hackneyed "Letters to *Penthouse*" tales, Jacuzzis and lesbians and oiled limbs, filtered through Noel's self-limited vocabulary. Punctuated by an occasional incredulous whinny from David. I just nodded and agreed. Noel took no notice of either stream of commentary. Fun times! Three guys in a brick-cold, unfurnished house. You understand why I never brought up the thing with Lorriner. What would have been the point? It might have gotten me a beating from David. Noel's not a psychopath, but he has his interests to maintain. And so what if Lorriner had known who Noel was? So what if maybe he was also one of Noel's retail distributors, which more and more his words that night led me to think? It meant nothing and it proved nothing. Nothing at all.

. . .

Apart from these jolly interludes, I spent hours, every evening, serving my customers. Not well. I raised my prices. I stopped extending credit. And you know what? Instead of alienating them, instead of driving them away, it made them more serious and loyal. More respectful of me, even. The worse I treated them the more they wanted me around. There's some lesson to be derived from that, I suspect. Even if you don't make it an iron rule of your conduct, you can learn something from it. I ferried around enough weed to ensure jail time if I were ever caught or searched. But, as I said, you're invisible to cops in D.C. if you're white. You have to do something amazing to get their attention.

Names, you say? I'm *happy* to give them. The customer is always wrong, remember? Jason Rosset; Tim Carcanet; Hannah Loughlin; Mason Chatto; Blake Bonder, who despite the Harvard-beats-Yale name is a girl with a widemouthed melodic laugh; Evan Osterreich and Katie Bayern, the other gold medalists on the National Latin Exam in my class; Hamilton Bray, whose father is ninety-two years old; the Eichman twins; Andrew Bammler, a gaping and universally despised asshole ("Fuck, man, Andy *Bammler*'s here!") and ex-Chandler classmate of Noel's; Magdalena Beinmark, Digger's next-door neighbor—I won't lie, I spent the whole trip to Magdalena's house fantasizing about running into Digger and flaunting my über-casualness; the supercilious, unspeaking Amanda and Pyotr Metzger, twins and bandmates in the Bringdowns; Octavio Machado, shaver of notches into his eyebrows; Tehran Wall, five-foot-nothing, our champ debater, and, after Kevin's death, 20 percent of the black population of my G&T class; Victoria Blanning; Alex Hamden-Court; Ashton Denvir; Drea Skalnick. At least six people named Jonathan.

. . .

My *tribe*. And, as I remarked before, I know as little about them as you do. Beyond these incidentals. Warm and identical houses: check. Square-built, money-sturdy furniture: check. Sound-eating inch-piled rugs: check. Parents pretending to be oblivious: check. Warm and insincere greetings: check. A dust-filmed piano, a cloudlike Samoyed, an inquisitive younger sibling, a disintegrating party, a wretched solitude, a fistfight, a theatrical tongue-thick kiss, a recent-dyke mother, a mirror edged in knurled bronze, a fake Ming vase with a trembling sheaf of catkins, check, check, fucking check! The solitary trip back to my house, occupied by my father, my father and Fatima, or by nobody at all. Check. Leaden, vacant sleep. Check. Morning. Check. Et cetera. It's all *scenery*. The underlying quality, somnolent ease, never dissipates, and there isn't even any intruding authority to give your activities the spice of crime. Everything is permitted. When everything is permitted, mediocrity is the rule. Nude trees arcaded every curb, their nets of branches like diagrammed lungs, and baleful street lamps hovered above. It's all so calm, it's dizzying.

Some people probably can draw *inspiration* from this, from a great regret, from nothingness. I'm too much of a philistine to do that. *Philistine* is one of my father's favorite words. Though he's never directed it against me, I know that I exhibit a lot of philistine tendencies. It means being cut off from higher things, which I certainly am, and it means not having explosive emotional reactions to things, which I certainly don't, only glacial responses, numbness or fear or on the positive side awe and gratitude. And sometimes these rainstorm bursts of happiness, but even those are sort of calm, not at all fit for discussion, the way my father is always talking about his most private inner activity. The stuff about wanting to throw himself under a bus, I mean.

. . .

I think you'll agree that the other activity consuming my time during these weeks belonged to the kingdom of philistine behavior. I was über-dedicated to it. During the minutes spent stuck in traffic. During my now-solitary lunch periods. Waiting for customers to meet me. In the twilight before sleep, when it replaced my obsessive rereading of the *Aeneid*. I'm talking about Kevin's file. Even more worn than it had been when I'd stolen it. I knew it, at this point, backward and forward. Not that it was hard to memorize. It was just a two-page list of classes and grades, with a note at the bottom, in blocky printer script: NO LONGER A STUDENT; a friable newspaper article; and a crease-seamed photo. Scraps. But there *was* nothing else. And every spare moment I had, though, every moment not given to selling weed, eating, sleeping, or school, I gave to the study of this file. As though it would yield up some answer about Kevin's murder. I can *still* recite large chunks. Fuck, I can probably draw Kevin's face blindfolded, gripping the pencil with my teeth. Though I haven't tried this. You'll have to trust me.

That's all there is of you, in the end. These meager public traces. Nothing beyond that. And if these public facts remain striking or original, you get called a genius, and if they involve the deaths of millions, you become a hero or a tyrant. And either way cities and governments erect monuments to you. Which no one ever notices, unless they're on a tour or doing some kind of historical research. Monuments are just weighty guarantees of your consignment to oblivion. So it doesn't matter if you leave behind you a war, a cathedral, or just a thin pile of paper. You're fucked, eternally. Which is, I assume, why you have asked for so much documentation, and why you want me to put my answers to your questions down on paper. Because you know that what we call *inner* life has no external meaning.

· · ·

Example: about a year ago, on an airless subway in winter, I saw a guy get on, not too old, not too young anymore. He had short auburn hair, big glasses, skinny wrists, a premature paunch, that sort of thing. Two bags, a man-purse and a canvas tote, which I thought was strange, one of those small inexplicabilities. And what was he doing? Picking through the man-purse, as soon as he sat down. I was leaning against the doors, and he sat on the same side as me, facing away. So I could look down into his lap and see him yanking open and closed every compartment. I had no idea what he was looking for. He sighed, an angry androgynous sigh, as he came up with a *fucking crayon*—in mauve, no less. The kind of color eternally unpopular with children. Then—and this impressed me—he reached with grave dignity into his *other* bag, the tote, and pulled out a dog-eared sheaf of pages, the corners foxed. The whole thing grimed. He had been searching for a pencil to correct his pages, I saw now; he was frantic to correct them. A point in his favor. But he was doing this in public, which meant either that he was a horrible cretin or that he was so gifted his talent made him indifferent.

Needless to say, it was the former. And what he was doing was amazing! He would change a word, the word *dirty* to the word *filthy*, for example, and then slash out the change. He changed semicolons to periods/initial capitals and vice versa. He crossed out the word *asphyxiation* and replaced it with *suffocation*, he misused the word *inveigh* . . . And so on and so forth, his white, clean hand darting around on the beaten-looking pages, making these minor corrections. I started to feel sick. Whenever I see people taking out private matters, like manuscripts, in public, it sickens me, but I can't look away from the horrible humiliation of staring into someone else's mediocrity, which illuminates your *own* choking mediocrity. He was so *defeated*, this man in his late thirties, about twenty years older than me, with a manuscript that looked to be years and years old, maybe started when I was a child, a book he had great hopes for, still, even now, despite the manifest evidence of his failure, his hand darting with precision and care, correcting and changing things that would make no difference. And the crayon! A loose strut, an atmospheric gauge of some kind, something no longer human, something degenerated. He caught me staring, of course, and looked up. I whipped my face away. The insectile rasp of the crayon never ceased. He got out at the next stop. I was leaning against the doors, like I said, so he had to pass me, which I was dreading. He only smiled, though, untroubled, blind-looking. We *all* sit in public correcting our insufficient manuscripts, hoping that God is watching, whom we all believe in as some kind of *spectator*; we believe that our useless devotion *proves* something, that it *demonstrates something about us*, that we're *all* artists. His smile of angelic completion revealed this to me as five or six other passengers, total strangers, looked into my face with burning and indifferent kindness.

XIII.

WAIT, THOUGH. I have to do some more *backgrounding* here. I've gotten you up to speed on the first five major aspects of my life in the weeks after Digger shot Murphy. I left out the sixth component. Six is what's known as a perfect number: it's the sum of its positive divisors excluding itself ($1 + 2 + 3 = 6$). Why that makes it perfect, I don't know. But a lot of mystical carrying-on about the number six has derived from this fact. So maybe it's *auspicious* that I'm getting into this now. I had been, alongside all the other nonsense and running around, engaged in *another* Kevin-related activity. A last-ditch effort. It had borne no fruit so far.

On the first of October, an unsupervised boy rammed my shin with his blood-colored tricycle. I had my backpack with me, nothing in it except for a bit more than twelve thousand dollars. And, which I did not mention before, a thick sheaf of posters. I was on my third. Sheaf of posters, I mean. IF YOU HAVE ANY INFORMATION ABOUT KEVIN BROADUS, PLEASE PAGE, and then my number. Remember? I'd already gone through two stacks. Much faster than I'd expected. I also had a staple gun and a roll of invisible tape. These were the posters I made the morning I stole Kevin's file. *Ille dies primus leti*, to quote Virgil. It means (in very rough modern English) "That's when everything started to go wrong." I won't waste your time with a literal translation. He was talking about the first time Aeneas and Dido—the insane queen of Carthage, remember?—have sex. In a woodland cave, during a thunderstorm. When he leaves to continue his quest, she burns herself to death on a pyre composed of all his ambassadorial/courtly gifts to her. I think I mentioned her insanity before.

Anyway: *Postering*. (#6) Like Kevin was a lost cat. Putting them up anywhere and everywhere I could. I found the sheaf of old posters on top of a bookshelf, where I'd stowed them to avoid thinking about them. I mean the first-generation ones. I found them the afternoon Digger's mother called me an alcoholic creep, actually. A small sail-shaped polygon of white, the corner of the poster pile, obtruded itself into my complacent solitude after I'd hung up. I took them down and knocked off the blue house dust. It took no time to find the tape and the staple gun. My father keeps it loaded. As part of his artistic mission, in case he wakes up one day as a painter who needs to frame canvases, or maybe as some staple-loving conceptual artist. Then I was bolting out of my house, in a frenzy, affixing flyers to every friendly surface I saw. I got through the whole stack in two hours. I even had to tear the last-affixed one down. Otherwise I wouldn't have had a template to use, moving forward. The naked trees lining my block all had their quivering squares of white. I was out of breath. I'd been jogging. No coat, no hat. The cold of the falling evening burned my lungs. Et cetera.

That's how I went through my first sheaf. I blamed its eventual failure on the small distribution area and the posters' lo-fi overall appearance. It looked like some overly focused crazy person had assaulted this one chunk of D.C. and left it at that. A sad old man, or a pervert, or a bearded schizoid type. You know: a haunter of public libraries. Wool hat in all seasons. Binder of manuscripts shouting with ALL CAPS. The kind of person who leaves cheap flowers at a public memorial for the dead. I improved, on the second go-round. I spaced them out, made the civilians think I was taking my ease. Which was a misrepresentation. You can't let anyone know what you're going through, though, or you'll just get corrosive ridicule heaped on you. My second sheaf, in bright colors and with Kevin's obstinate photo Xeroxed in, lasted longer. I was more judicious. I spread them out. Crossing and recrossing the city. Enduring the uneasy looks of schoolchildren, shelf-assed cashiers, bus conductors, guys hanging out on corners, staunch lawn defenders. The entire *typology* of life here, which is a good general simulation of life in second-rate cities everywhere.

Postering, after all, is one of those skills that you learn only if you're involved in some stupid group activity. Putting on a play. Or advertising some political protest or whatever. A lot of the kids in G&T do this, put up political flyers that they get secondhand from older siblings. Or in some cases from Mr. Vanderleun, who believes himself to be a real *inspirer* of youth, and wants to bring our social consciences to new and passionate life. The art of postering was alien to me, because I'd never participated in anything, play or protest. And if Mr. Vanderleun ever gave me flyers to hand out, I would have dumped them in the trash. Not that he trusted me. He gave them to his in-class henchpeople, foremost among them Alex Faustner. As a result, I was über-terrible at it, when I started. I see that now. I did not understand what I was doing. When you poster, you're asking the Great Anonymous for help. The fervency has to be like sublimated. Not that it's *praying*. Not that I pray.

. . .

I've *thought* about it. Praying, I mean. But what's the point? What you want to happen never happens anyway, by definition. And the one thing I'd ever wanted badly enough to pray for—that my mother not be dead, I mean—well, according to my cursory readings on the subject, you're not even supposed to ask for that. For the past to be different. Some Catholic theologians even say that God Himself cannot change the past. Which is one of the paradoxes inherent in the idea of omnipotence, I guess. Or just part of the natural comedy of our higher aspirations. Mr. Dwight, my religion teacher, is the one who told me about that theory of omnipotence. He's actually been everything from a Buddhist to a Trappist monk. So I have a weird respect for his opinion. Although I think that if the God of the Jews wanted to change the past, he could. For all the ambivalence about him in the Bible and stuff, you kind of have to believe in his limitless power. Which is maybe why the Jews get shit on by history so much. In compensation.

You're getting off topic again, Addison! That's no way to behave! Sorry. Once I *cooled down*, once I lost the postering habits of a fervent Stalinist, I started using our city's public transportation systems. Which in D.C. comprise buses and subways. You can get anywhere by subway or bus. You just have to use the two in conjunction with each other, because the subway is built on the same plan as the streets: axial lines crossing uneven concentric rings. So you miss a lot of fertile ground if you stick to the subways. But if you use the buses, you can get by. I bought student monthly passes, these demure pink cards. They give you the same color if you're a senior citizen, I think. The subways in D.C. are constructed, city lore claims, to withstand nuclear attacks. I doubt this is true. You can trace the blackened rust-bloomed courses of leaks from the street, rain runoff. Sometimes, in the grates over the railside fluorescents, moss and tendriled plants even sprout from fallen seeds, watered from above and lit from below. The stations themselves have high, soaring ceilings paneled in pressed concrete, the damp odor of which permeates the still air. Sub-aqueous whitish light makes everyone look lost and unhappy there, and weak. The trains stink of tatty fabric and usually of urine or dog. You have to feed your ticket into a thick-lipped reader twice: there's no standard fare; it's calculated by distance. The employees hide in dark aquaria, irregular polygons of glass, and if you go up to ask them anything you can see the blind glow of the security monitors, and sometimes even a walleyed version of yourself bent to the metal mouthpiece in supplication. Ochre hexagonal tiles. Ochre bulwarks. Long waits. Officious and ineffectual cops: wavers-back from the platform edge and bike ticketers. Misery. And indifferent, bureaucratic malice.

Our buses are fine, though. Blue and white, tinted with the free-floating gray filth of cities, yes, but still blue and white. Kind of *noble* colors. Hard to say why. A lot of graffiti scratched into the Plexiglas windows. Kids use chunks of concrete or razor blades to do this. Not so many obscenities. Just the announcement of names, an understandable desire. Some of the buses are old, dating back to when you could smoke on public transport. Before black people were allowed to sit at the front. Some of them are newer, but they're still uncomfortable and ridiculous-looking. Always late, too, and the drivers are surly exiles from the human race. I started developing eye-meeting relationships with some of them, despite this. I never learned their names, so I made up designations: Doctor Shortcakes, Fat-ass McGee, Madame Sassy, the King of Comedy. The King of Comedy was this crumple-faced old man with a shrub of white hair, who mumbled incomprehensible jokes and monologues into his mike the whole ride. There *and* back. He drove the M2 on weekday afternoons and evenings.

"Mama lama hama namahamanownow wamalamanow." Then the digital voice system, sexless and happy to assist, would announce the stop, and the King would go back to orating. "Nah *teya* damalamanamanow!" I think he was close to retirement.

Despite the problematic means, you can get anywhere. And I did. I just went blindly, getting off after a random number of stops and, with supreme coolness, postering a neighborhood. I got some looks, I'll admit. But being young deflected most of those. Nobody really cares, if you look like you're under eighteen, which I definitely do. Even in a for-shit pseudocity you can find facelessness. I did this before and after school, and on the weekends, so I saw neighborhoods at their most vulnerable, full of sleepy, irritable people or relaxed and happy ones. Once, at the edge of a crowded shopping plaza, I even saw David Cash, and we locked eyes. But he turned away with a visible smirk of disgust. Didn't even faze me. The weight in my backpack of the posters still to hang comforted me. I put up my quota—getting one on a barbershop window, which I asked the barber guy if it was okay, something I'd ordinarily feel too awkward to do. I was proud of that one. It was goldenrod, and it stood out like a petal in the midst of all the city colors, brick and asphalt. Like it was *natural.*

Every day I did this. I should have said that before, but I thought it deserved its own space. Because it was such an undertaking. And it had zero returns. I did not get a single page about it. Maybe people thought it was suspicious because I'd put a pager number, which has certain *connotations.* Every time I saw an unfamiliar number march across the dented strip of my grayish screen, I got this queasy heartsickness. But they only ever wanted to arrange a time to buy weed. I consented, lips cold with disappointment. The thing about selling more drugs is that word tends to get around that you have more, and it can actually increase the demand. There's some stupid economics term for this, I have no doubt. But economics is an elective at Kennedy, and I opted to take religion. Our economics teacher, Ms. Mehta, is as wide as she is tall. Which maybe is why I didn't take economics. Nonetheless: that's the choice. So I have no idea what the correct term is. I only have my practical firsthand knowledge, which, if you lack proper credentials, is worthless. Otherwise I'd be able to write a book. About stupidity. About how to get no results.

This failed to change my ambitions. I just kept on with the procedure: make copies, hang them up, wait. Isn't that someone's definition of insanity? To do the same thing over and over while expecting different results? You kind of get a picture of a guy in a straitjacket bashing his forehead into a white-padded wall, or someone picking up every scrap of tinfoil they see outside, or someone counting out loud, all the time, and waiting for the moment of their redemption. What I was doing bears a family resemblance to those activities. I can admit that now. I remember the day my second clutch of posters ran out, because the bus I was on broke down, not far from my neighborhood. I'd made five hundred copies, in vivid colors—violet, sky, and grass—and included Kevin's picture. The one from the yearbook, the one Digger had given me, that showed Kevin poised with his enormous saxophone. It came out fuzzed and somehow *more* tragic-looking. But it added a heretofore missing *human* element to the posters. Which would make responses more likely, I figured. It was evening, green and purple. It gets that way here in the late fall, the light, I mean, these lurid colors. I'd done a good afternoon's work. My legs burned. And then the bus, with a flatulent, mephitic, mechanical grunt, jarred itself to a halt and we all jerked forward in our seats, releasing a unitary cry of consternation. We were on Connecticut Avenue, near the Maryland border. Pretty close to the Camelot, actually. The King of Comedy was driving. He sounded delighted to explain our trouble: "Hamanowlamanownowmamanow!"

After this rhythmic and vowel-heavy announcement, I stood and walked to the front, where he cranked the door lever with a decisive and memorable motion of his forearm, and I trotted off of Connecticut, onto one of the residential streets, tree-lined and hard to tell from my own, though the houses were bigger and in better shape. Some of them had those fake gas lamps out by the curb, extending metal arms from which hung the numbers of the address. Each number on its own armorial plate. Some had beards of ivy hiding their cross-timbers. It was that universal hour of warm interior light among the bourgeoisie. You could see families at dinner, or on separate floors. I heard a kid practicing drums with incompetent vigor. And I kept on walking into the dusk. I'd recognized the street: McKinley, named after the first president to use the telephone for campaigning and the sole one to be assassinated by an anarchist. My bag was light. Kevin's file, a pack of smokes, and nothing else. A sudden, stupid happiness settled on me. McKinley Street was familiar to me, though I had not set foot on this block of it before. Why the familiarity, you ask? Because of a certain house on this street: 3549. I was just leaving the 3400 block now, the street signs informed me, and my throat was thick with giddy joy. It was an omen. Proof that I was doing the right thing. That all my (so far) fruitless drag-assing through the streets of my shithole of a hometown had meaning and purpose. Do you know who once lived at 3549 McKinley? Do I even *need* to tell you?

His parents, I now assumed, panting like a hound, were still there. So let me introduce them a bit. Because you're only going to get a fleeting glimpse of them in what follows. Stanford Broadus, Kevin's father, was born in Grimshawes, North Carolina, in 1948. He studied at the Franklin Institute, *an historically African American college*—how pretentious is that *an*! Thanks, Archer B. Sexton, you goddamn motherfucker!—*graduating with a master's in public administration*. His mother, Ellen Maskelyne, graduated from Antioch College in 1964, and then from Columbia Law School in 1967, after which she was employed by Godwin Howe— *an historically African American firm*. Who was copyediting you, Archer B. Sexton, you cocksucker! *The Broaduses have been D.C. residents since 1970.* Kevin, their only child, was born in the spring of 1981. (*March 19*, according to the article.) *Kevin's legacy as a student at John F. Kennedy Senior High School is perhaps best expressed in the words of Conrad Vanderleun, an English teacher in the Gifted and Talented Program there: "Kevin was a strong and quiet presence, though blessed with a genuine musicality, a strong rhythm. He'll be remembered and missed."* Can you *believe* a human being would write that way? Our species is a disgusting one. Though you've determined that already from observing me.

Five minutes' walk and I was there. Not a kid in the street. My cigarette tasted sweeter than normal. Or more complicated. It hurt my lungs more than usual too, which I welcomed. The wind, just barely, worked over the stripped branches. Ten or so yards away from the house, I stopped walking. I could see even from a distance 3549 was largish, with those unbearable, sad green shutters, like leaves of a useless plant, and a trained yew hedge around the front, flashing its poisonous flame-orange berries. A brick walk, of which each brick looked dusted. But all these undeniable facts interested me much less than the tall, paunched figure I watched emerge from the front door and climb into a dark blue sedan, whose engine sputtered to life. Kevin's father, going about some trivial evening task. I almost puked from happiness. The car passed my way, and I caught one frame of Mr. Broadus in the driver's seat. His face was calm, empty. Faint music, a piano, wafted out of his car, despite the closed windows. The car made the corner and chuffed away, taking the undertone of music with it. I ground out my smoke and kept trotting and panting, my feet lighter than ever. I was about to lose contact with the pavement. Just a few more paces, and I arrived at the first lip of the brick walk. Couldn't go forward, at least not for a long minute. I watched a light traveling in the house from window to window, a dutiful servant. The blue aura of television wavered in an upper bedroom. My breath tasted of smoke and leaves, of some burning. Sweat rilled down my rib cage, tickling me. I swear to fucking God I could feel every hair on my scalp and forearms.

The brick walk gleamed in the streetlight. I didn't know how long it would be before Mr. Broadus returned. But I had to act. I had no plan, just this ungovernable tide of impulse. And before I could stop myself I'd dashed to the front door and thumbed the brass handle. The door was unlocked. I guess I'd been subconsciously counting on this. In Kevin's neighborhood many don't lock their doors. A fact Noel pointed out to me once. I hadn't even thought of entering the house, at first. I hadn't even wanted to. Now I was fumbling with the door, conspicuous as a government. A stripped finger of elm branch kept scraping the roof slate. It was the last thing I heard before I crossed the threshold. The house, inside . . . holy fuck! The air warm and heavy. The intoxicating scent of floor polish, and some common but unidentified spice. Doilies, looking leprous as always. And glass-fronted cabinets. One of which contained thirty-one (yes, I counted; what else did I have to do?) porcelain parrots of varied color and size. All that was missing was a table of votive candles, to add the waxy scent of holiness. I wandered on tiptoe around the living room, fingering the openwork lace of the doilies, pressing my palms against the parrot cabinet. There was a grandfather clock as tall as I am next to the kitchen entrance, at the rear of the room. It needed winding. Seemed to have been in disrepair long enough for its counterweights to be cowled with grime, which I fingered off in streaks. Nose-breathing the whole time. Sounding like some obscene phone caller, I have no doubt.

I didn't notice the whistling, for at least the initial moments of my trespassing. Mrs. Broadus was whistling to herself upstairs. She was good at it. A full tone, a steady breath. I picked out the melody with not too much effort. The opening aria, the theme, of the Goldberg Variations. Don't think I'm some kind of *classical music expert*, just because I cite the Goldberg Variations so casually. I'm not. I don't know *anything* about music, as I've said. It's just that my father puts his record of the piece on our stereo a lot. And you have to admit it's fairly goddamn memorable: a geometrical ascent of some mountain into the purest, liveliest solitude, some meadow where all human imperfection is gone. I love it. I hate it. It makes me clench my fists and jaw and curl my toes with tension.

It was calling me upstairs. I decided that it was a sign, beckoning me upstairs. Moving was tricky. Staircases are loud, in movies and other situations where someone is trying to sneak around. In real life, too. I risked it, though. I couldn't stop myself. As I climbed, taking these arched, agonized, careful steps, Kevin's face at every age stared out of the pictures on the wall, ascending with me. All set in uniform black frames. He'd been even plumper as a child, with that fat-kid shine of jollity and fear in his eyes. Then he started resembling anyone (and everyone) else going through adolescence. He had the same chubby solid build his whole life. He looked capable of enduring anything. He got his glasses young. At eight or nine, these huge ones that made his round face even younger. He had a grin in that photo, with a missing tooth, a grin betraying no awareness of anything. And despite his submersion in the generality of adolescence, he had not lost this original childish smile as he aged. That's rare. I can't smile the way I did as a child. Being able to demonstrates some tremendous inner reserve.

The pictures stopped when Kevin was seventeen. At the top of the stairs. Where I paused as well. No idea of where to go next. Luckily it was decided for me. A floorboard whined beneath my sole. The decorous whistle stopped and Mrs. Broadus called out, "Hello? Hello?" I held my breath and crouched. And a second later the whistling started again, taking up at the precise place she had stopped the recitation, and I tiptoed back downstairs. I couldn't go forward. I just couldn't bear it. I sneaked back down into the Broadus's orderly, crammed living room, and then into their kitchen.

What I saw then made my stomach lurch. Not that what I saw was fucked-up. Just sort of nerdy in the way that parents overly concerned with decorating schemes are. It made me sick, though, because it was so domestic and well-executed. A sign of the life I was invading, I guess. It would have been totally impossible in my own house. They had decorated the whole room, with what looked like tremendous and painstaking effort, using fruit-themed objects. A clock in the shape of an orange, with a slice cut out from it between eleven and midnight. Alternating columns of pineapples and bunches of grapes stenciled on the walls. Pot holders the color of black cherries. Napkins emblazoned with nippled peaches piled up in the glass-fronted cabinets, next to dishes painted with images of papayas. Salt and pepper shakers shaped like red and green apples. Curtains printed with waterfalls of chemically yellow lemons. Every goddamn thing. And then I noticed—I swear this is true—a figurine about nine inches high, one of those hideous racist caricatures of black people, in a jockey outfit, embracing with both arms a huge, wet-looking watermelon standing on its end next to the spice rack. I fingered the manikin's lumpy skull and stroked the melon in unbelief: ceramic, with a small dimpled handle on the upper end. A cookie jar, filled almost to the brim with gingersnaps. In retrospect, it kind of makes sense. I mean, like Digger and her nickname. A way of offering a preemptive *fuck you* to anyone with bad intentions. At the time, though, I was stunned. And amused, in a horrified way. *Why would they have this?* I thought, and smothered a laugh. Then I whispered, "I'm sorry, I'm sorry." Out loud. To the dead, spiced air. My paltry voice disgusted me.

How long did I stand in their garish kitchen like some hesitant rapist? No idea. The orange clock's hair-thin second hand jerked itself into each upcoming empty moment. Then my trance dissolved: the harmonious, skillful whistling was getting louder, accompanied by footfalls, and the front door slammed. I hadn't heard the car return, and now everything was happening at once: Mr. and Mrs. Broadus were greeting each other in the front hall, they murmured warmly to each other, and I couldn't understand, he was *so* much taller than his wife and she had a blue towel wrapped around her hair. I stood in utter stillness, having shoved myself against the fridge (for camouflage). They held each other for five, ten seconds, her voice muffled by his sweater, his by her hair towel. Talking the whole time, in friendly undertones. She was the one who broke the embrace to lead him upstairs by the hand. Their treads matched, receding. An upstairs door closed, with grave delicacy. And then, hoping they would not hear, I crept out of the kitchen and slid through the front door, opened just enough to let me pass. I was *freezing* now. Slicked in sweat. But despite my all-body shivers I followed McKinley Street up the slight hill into the dark. Toward home. Maintaining the walk of innocence, my retarded bantam strut. September 27, 1999, 7:48 p.m.

XIV.

FOR THE *THIRD* FUCKING TIME, ladies and gentlemen! On the first of October, as I was leaving my house, an unsupervised boy rammed my shin with his blood-colored tricycle. I was all primed to go distribute my sheaf of flyers. I had resigned myself to a life of despair, without Digger, I mean. It's quite a voluptuous feeling. I had my backpack with me, with the dumb-ass posters and my rubber-banded, sorted bundles of money. As the pain of the tricycle blow receded, and the afterecho of the boy's shout thinned, my pager went off. This was at nine o'clock in the morning. It was the earliest daylight page I had ever received. The number was unfamiliar. A D.C. number, an exchange (that's the first three digits after the area code) I knew: 202-364-1889. But at nine o'clock on a Saturday morning? The thought of someone needing weed first fucking thing in the morning kind of wowed me. I mean, it's not heroin. It's just pot. How strong can your craving for it be? There's no physical dependency. Yeah, some kids pretend that they're *total addicts*, but that's just the exuberance of being young, rearing its clumsy, horned head. So I decided to ignore it.

Four days since my intrusion into the Broaduses' house. I lost track of things in the interval. I can't remember anything *specific* happening. I mean, when you're in *free fall* from some bizarre event, as I was for those days and the preceding weeks, some catastrophe, time takes on this amazing *uniformity*. One day becomes indistinguishable from any other day, simply because the dominant fact illuminating them all doesn't change, I mean the constantly present fact of your loss or your crime or your remorse or whatever. Probability dictates that, in the ensuing ninety-six hours, I showered, took a shit, ate, slept, went to school, sold drugs, jerked off seven or eight times, pretended not to think about Digger. The chill I'd felt the night of my trespassing had stayed with me, as an irritating tautness at the back of my throat, a sandy pain behind my eyes. The one thing I remember from this period is my growing determination to get rid of my money. I mean the weed money. All of it. I wanted to burn it, originally. But that would be too conspicuous. I thought of my father's kiln. This was ruled out by the possibility of his discovering the cash, even a burned fragment of it. I had fantasies of giving it to some bum or something, though I realized this would create more problems than it solved, if anyone found out about it. So I started thinking about throwing it in the Potomac, and as soon as I pictured it I knew it was right.

Twelve thousand dollars. In an absolute sense it's not that much. But it was more than I'd ever had before. Three thousand of it came from the relentless sales push I'd made in the past month and a half. I hadn't even counted it. I'm estimating here. I wanted to throw it in the river. The Potomac, which varies in autumn color between black and gun blue. With webs of gray foam veining the surface. And even some gulls, even this late in the year, pell-melling back and forth looking for scraps. The river's the one thing in D.C. that has no opinion or ideas on any subject. Making it the ideal candidate for propitiatory offerings. Who or what would I even be appeasing? The Great Anonymous, the mute steely river?

I didn't know. I'm not some believer in the wet-locked, classical water deities, despite my involvement with the dead culture that venerated them. Whatever. I was a wreck that morning.

So I ignored the page and drove off, down Wisconsin Avenue. Most of the main traffic arteries in D.C. are named after states. As a gesture of Federalist unity or something. I was going to just drive straight down it, south-southeast. It kinks a bit east and west out of true, past Kennedy, past the Cochrane, all the way down to M Street. Where the land humps down to the water, under a thunderous overpass buttressed with steel fins. These are the exact dirty-cotton color of old ice, but all year. Remainders of some frozen sea or something. Once there, I'd heave the money in. The bundles would spread out, a flotilla drifting toward the Chesapeake Bay. With luck none of the insane autumn anglers (yes, they exist, and even in the summer the river's not alive, really, at least where it passes through the city) that line the thin promenade north of the Roosevelt Bridge would snag any. There would be no questions. That kind of human-interest bullshit always makes the papers here, because nothing else happens. And I believed with all fervor that if I did this and then put up my whole sheaf of posters before sunset, then whatever god watches over rivers would grant my petition. And I'd find someone with the information necessary to lead me to the man I'd imagined, the man with the hideous purpose lighting his eyes. Not Lorriner, who violated all my aesthetic ideas of what a murderer should be. But a calm-handed and indifferent killer. Never subject to any emotional upheavals. A free man. In some sense an enviable man. If it's permissible to speak that way.

Wisconsin and M. Remember? That's where the Stubb's is. Where Kevin got killed. I'd chosen my route *symbolically*. I have a tremendous sense for that. Empty gestures. As you've seen. Everything looked normal, at first. I'd beaten the Saturday crush of late-morning traffic, and that weird preactivity staginess had settled on the streets. All that remained of Kevin's hideous memorial was a long bow of weather-lightened purple ribbon kicking in the river breeze. And then I got this weird dislocation, a recall failure. A construction crew, four fat guys in orange vests over their sweatshirts and trucker jackets, was moving with infinite slowness and carelessness. There was an empty storefront. Roughly where they were digging up the street. It was, I realized as my sense of having *lost* something broke, where the Stubb's used to be. "Fuck!" I screamed and punched my horn, and the construction guys whipped their heads toward me in outrage. One of them offered a middle finger! A classic gesture. So classic I failed to realize he meant it for me. Following its line of motion, looking for the man who deserved this gesture, I craned my neck like a trapped animal and holy fuck! They (they? what?) had opened another Stubb's ON THE OPPOSITE SIDE OF THE STREET.

This shouldn't have hit me the way it did. I mean, that's the company's *business plan*. You can find a Stubb's at each five-block interval in any neighborhood. In any city. In the world. Their stupid green logo, with this piratey-looking guy on it in that fake-woodcut style, you know? Pipe in his mouth, brandishing a cutlass at the sky? Everywhere you go. They don't even have *commercials*. They have achieved ubiquity. So why not! Why not across the street? Acceptable and even praiseworthy, according to the natural order of things. Yet I stared and stared. The crew member holding the STOP sign flipped it to GO, red to green. And I started to make the turn down the short hill to the water, when I saw that they had blocked off that chunk of Wisconsin, and that I'd have to keep going.

. . .

The stop-sign guy had started doing this deeply satirical dance before I got my shit together enough to drive on. He and his coworkers waved their arms at one another, to communicate my failure, and I drove east on M and took the dogleg onto Pennsylvania, and then turned down this dinky little exit until I hit Rock Creek Parkway, now heading northwest. I could have stayed on M and made a turn down to the water later. I mean, the whole of downtown abuts on the Potomac or the Anacostia. They flow into each other and vanish on the long meander to the bay. But this *certainty* overcame me: the offering would be refused. The downside of large empty gestures! When they fail, you can't do the logical thing and accomplish your goal some other way. You have to do the *symbolically coherent* thing. Which is, nine times out of ten, nothing at all.

During the course of my drive, the unknown number paged me and paged me. Three more times. It was starting to worry me. I mean, what the fuck could anyone want from me that they wouldn't wait for? I ran through everyone I suspected it might be, as I drove, muttering to myself and looking around for tails. *The cops.* No, that didn't make any sense. Why would they page me? *Digger.* As much as I wanted it to be true, this didn't make any sense either. I knew her number. Unless her mother had gotten her a cell phone. *My father, calling from the Cochrane.* That would just be crazy. I was sure he didn't even know I *had* a pager. And he's way too languorous to page someone four times in a row. *Alex Faustner.* Just to fuck with me, you know? Or maybe lure me into some clever trap. And so on and so forth, calculating all the stupid probabilities. I followed the parkway. I knew it would turn into one of the roads that wind through the northern mass of the park, and end up among a mansion-filled glade of hills and declivities. But I wanted to go through the silent woods, at this point, to rush through them. As though I could get away from the money that way. From the unknown number. I knew if I just gave myself enough time, the leaden feeling would leave, I'd be able to make a real decision, to develop some stratagem for making my offering, or abandon the whole enterprise entirely. I was stuck in this *twilight* for now, yes. But it would go. I just needed patience. My pager was buzzing again. I didn't even bother to check to see who it was. *Just have patience, you stupid asshole*, I kept telling myself.

Which is, as you've guessed, the one thing I lack. During normal times, when it's not required. And when I most need it. I didn't drive until my mental twilight dissipated. I didn't pull over and breathe deeply, or meditate, or any of that shit. I only made it to a bit north of the zoo before I lost control of myself and turned back out of the leafless twilight. I screeched into the first free parking place I saw, just bucking back and forth with these shrieks of the rubber, and rammed a quarter and a dime into the pay phone on the corner. I was *calling* the unknown number. The worst thing to do. Answering the provocations of mystery, I mean. As this whole endeavor should demonstrate. It had gained me nothing but confusion so far. And I wanted more. The line rang three times before someone picked up.

"Yes, hello? Hello?" I yelled, loudly enough to make an old lady passing on the street stop and look. She was pushing a grocery cart, one of those oblong personal carts, not a store cart, from which two stalks of celery dangled like broken arms. There was only light breathing on the line. "If this is you, Lorriner, like *fuck* you," I screamed. The old lady pushed off again. Whoever it was hung up. I stomped back to my car. And noticed, for the first time that morning, where I was. About a ten-minute drive from Noel's house. *Not by chance*, I promised myself. *Not by chance.* I was, at this point, absolutely sure that it was Lorriner, calling from a shadowy associate's house in D.C., trying to fuck up my life in some unspecified way. Maybe he was in secret league with Huang and Baltimore. Maybe he had found an armed and willing friend. It didn't matter. *Noel would straighten everything out.* My neck started to throb, right when I thought this. The ache served as further proof of my correctness. As did my chills and grinding jaw.

No one answered the door at Noel's. The street was empty, but I still felt watched. I kept pounding, though. My pager was going off again, which increased my determination. After (I counted) seventeen thumps on the door, three locks, two tenor toned and one bass, tumbled open. The door opened inward, drawing the security chain tight. Just enough for me to see David.

"Addison, we *busy*, man," he said.

"No, I need to see Noel."

"Yo, man, like come back in like a hour. He busy." This low-frequency *hum* was drifting out of Noel's house, along with David's voice. "You a'ight?" he asked. "You look sick, man."

"I just like need to see *Noel* like now. It's like über-urgent. David. Like just let me in. I'm not going *away.*" David clicked his tongue and shut the door. He clicked a couple more times. A calculating noise, abacus beads or whatever. Then I heard him sigh, and the security chain clattered and he opened up again, and I was inside. The thrumming was louder. "Dude, what's going on down there?" I asked before I could stop myself.

"Shut *up* a second, man," David said. "Just wait." I listened to the noise: it was unmistakably the murmur of a crowd of people. Coming from nowhere. I wondered, with no fear or even concern, really, if I had gone crazy.

"Do you like hear that? All those people?" David gave me an empty look and opened the basement door. The noise swelled and resolved enough for me to make out single voices. Somehow, despite the fog in my head, a suspicion began to announce itself to me.

"Just wait here. Just wait." Then he was gone, and the noise dimmed back to a dull thrum. I occupied myself eye-tracing the crimson lines on Noel's Chandler pennant. About all I was good for, at this point. Nothing else to look at, anyway. My pager went off again, and I yelled to no one, "Do you like have a phone in here," before some still-operating sense of abashedness shut me up.

Then David reappeared. "Look, man. This sound weird, but I need your coat and bag. Pager, too. I need you to hand them to me. And then I need to frisk you." I shouldered off my bag and the coat, which David set down with real care. He then frisked me. First time it had ever happened. Not even the cops had frisked me. I slumped there as he patted my back and chest. His behavior confirmed my guess about what was happening in Noel's base-ment. You'd expect him to be cursory. Some skinny-ass mother-fucker like me presents no threat, right? But David takes his work seriously, and he did a thorough, efficient job. He pocketed my pager. Turned it off, to my relief: I'd missed a few more, just standing there. I never even felt awkward when his hand approached my scrotum! A sign of skill. "A'ight, shit, man. I guess you good." He hefted my coat and bag in one hand and beckoned me downstairs. The passage, narrow and alley-dark as ever, was made worse by the increasing noise.

He left me at the bottom, telling me once more to wait, and opened the door leading into Noel's room. I saw a slice of dead-white fluorescent glare and one rumpled edge of a crowd. And

I knew I'd been right. It was a fucking dogfight. The door was opened fully, and Noel was trotting across the room to shake my hand. "What up, my niggaaaaa," he cawed, and we leaned into our usual handshake. He reeked of sweat. A happy sweat. The room was hot as fuck, anyway. There were about twenty guys there, ranging in age from mine to my father's. All dressed the same, though the older guys were wearing more muted colors. Jeans, too-large T-shirts, ornately knitted sweaters. Enormous shoes. It's weird to see a forty-five-year-old man in huge spaceman shoes. I didn't stare too much. Or I tried not to. Other than Noel, who was doing his host act, and David, who looked worried and embarrassed on my behalf, no one was paying the slightest attention to me.

A long trestle table had been set up along one wall, on which lay a pile of coats, a heap of pagers and cell phones, and several handguns. At the end opposite from these piles, the battered old money counter. You know: it's this thing that looks kind of like a scale, and you drop stacks of cash into it and it whickers through them and gives you a digital readout of the amount. Above it, at shoulder height, the small blackboard was covered—the first time I'd ever seen it used—in small, clipped, legible handwriting. Which I knew without having to ask belonged to David. Who was now placing my hole-elbowed gray coat with the others, adding my pager to the heap. David dangled my bag from his hand and stared at it, and then kicked it beneath the table.

I read the blackboard: just a bunch of initials and numbers, divided into two columns, one headed by the word *Shazam* and one headed by the word *Trojan*. "So what you want, nigga?" Noel asked. Through the human voices bouncing between the concrete floor and the baffling on the walls, I heard different, animal sounds, a growl and a whine.

"Man, am I like interrupting a bout, or something?" I asked. I was sure, now, that I was. I noticed the pen, made of scuff-clouded black plastic and hinged with oxidized metal, that had been set up in the room's center. This was what everyone was crowding around. It rose to hip height. Noel's bed was gone to make room for it, a fact I accepted with feverish equanimity.

"Shit, nigga," Noel breathed out. "You too funny, man. You wanna like bet or suh'in?"

Noel would straighten everything out. Not wholly wrong. I remembered my purpose in coming here. For literally two seconds. And then, louder than I'd meant, I yelped, "I have like twelve thousand dollars in my backpack." This caused the other spectators gathered to pay attention. "Shit, Richie Rich!" one of the older guys said, in this gravelly voice. The guys standing with him cracked up and they all went back to ignoring me. Noel was restraining laughter, too. David still had that tight-lipped look of professional concern stretching his face. "I'd like *like* to bet man. I'd love to," I gushed. David crossed back to us to interfere, but Noel was already asking me who I wanted to bet on. It took less than a second for me to reply, "Trojan." Symbolic coherence, ladies and gentlemen! I was sure he would lose. Based on the name. That's what Trojans do. They lose. Greeks win, Trojans lose. Kind of the story of everything, right?

David rifled the money from my bag, at a two-finger gesture from Noel. "You all *organized* and shit, Addison," David gritted out, when he noticed my über-anal bundling system. Pissed, yes. His voice well under control, despite that. As always. He fed the bundles through the money counter. The whiffing of the machine, which took its time eating through all the bills, made everyone go sort of quiet. The group gave me another stare, and the older guy piped up again: "He really *be* Richie Rich." He got just as big a laugh as before. Why mess with success?

"It's like twelve," David called to Noel, as the machine finished up. "Like twelve four." He was crouching under the table, twirling the dial of Noel's fire safe, which had been dragged from beneath his mattress for the occasion and sat beneath the table in stolid shadow. I heard the door chunk open and closed, a heavy chord.

"Man, he a'ight," Noel said, as David noted me on the board with the rest of the players, in the TROJAN column: A.S., 12,447. "You bettin against the favorite, though." Noel chuckled. This reassured me that everything was going to be fine. "Like three-to-two, son," he continued.

After some more communal mumblings, things quieted down. Noel had gone back among his crowd of bettors. And two guys came out of the subrooms at the back, each with his dog on a leash. The dogs were a lot calmer than I expected. They didn't go for each other at all. They didn't strain at their leashes. One was cotton colored, and one was brick red. They both had this squat, foursquare build. Pit bulls or half-breed mastiffs or something. The owners approached the pen. I can't tell you what the owner of the white dog wore. But the red dog's owner had on this mango-colored tracksuit, with a blue racing stripe from heel to shoulder. "Which one is Trojan?" I whispered to David. He pointed at the red dog, and then walked over to stand guard by the entrance, resolutely not looking at me. The owners both lifted up their dogs, with visible tenderness. Noel raised his open palms. The crowd took a breath. You know how crowds, even small ones, can sync up at moments of tension.

What happened next I did not participate in. I didn't even *watch*, really. I stood in the corner of Noel's basement, flexing and unflexing my fingers in my pocket and quivering like a fool with my chills. The crowd had heated the air. There were enough people gathered to generate heat, a low earthbound heat, even at the ragged edge of the crowd. I'm not the kind of person who hates crowds. You feel more solitary in a crowd than anywhere else, because it deemphasizes the physical side of your solitude. You know? Leaves you with the intangible and more important side of it. And there was this air of businessmen's camaraderie emanating from the group, though there were clearly two opposing sides. As Noel lowered his hands, the owners placed their dogs in the pen and clicked off their leashes. *That* I saw.

Then the crowd obscured the action. Everyone was yelling, pumping their fists. David grew more and more still. Noel's face glowed with social happiness. I kept having to shut my eyes and swallow, from the dizziness and growing dryness in my throat. A window in the crowd opened for a moment. I saw that the dogs did not seem to be fighting so much as struggling. The crowd wove together again, and I contented myself just listening to the sounds of the fight, grunts and outright barks. The animals were speaking to each other. You could pick up the rhythm underneath the hum of human voices, which had blurred into static-like noise.

"Dogfighting," Noel told me when I'd asked him what the soundproofing in his room was for. I laughed. Big fucking joke, right? But it makes sense if you think about it. Another of his *gestures*. Constructive of the illusion that he's friends with his business peers. I had no idea who these guys were, but in my memory their clothes were clean, expensive-looking. Their faces well fed. They looked prosperous, if not 100 percent legitimate. The crowd was leaning left and right, arms around one another, faces hectic with hope or worry. I counted up the numbers on the blackboard, or tried to. They didn't make any sense. I got different totals each time. One of the dogs howled. The white one, Shazam, I was sure. A howl of victory. I expected everything to stop. Probably I *wanted* it to stop, the crowd buzz and the smoky, used-feeling air, rich with human exhalation. The fight continued, though. The howl wound down, and the back-and-forth of brief cries rose again. One of the crowd members leaped, off the balls of his feet, and muffed his landing so that he fell on his ass. His gap let me see the action again. My lips were numb.

The dogs were just going *at* it. The white one scrabbled its forelegs up on the red one's shoulders and gnawed at the back of his neck. But the red one bucked him off and lunged, opening a gash in the white dog's flank. They circled and snapped, without getting real purchase, as the fallen guy moaned and everyone ignored him. The reddish one, broader built, lower to the earth, dove at and gripped the white one's throat and drove his enemy with a writhing twist to the floor of the pen, jerking his head and grunting through the mouthful of flesh. The white dog waved its legs, a recognizable gesture of dismissal. This was greeted with a huge unitary roar, cheers of approval by some and cries of defeat from others. We'd entered the final stage. Everyone was delighted or devastated. As the red dog crushed his opponent's throat, the shouts and catcalls dwindled into an abashed, almost awed quiet. Then the fallen man was back on his feet, obstructing my view of the slow death. It distressed me, though. Not out of empathy. I hate dogs. It was *not* out of empathy.

"Shit," someone said during the hush, his voice hollow. Then everyone backed away from the pen. Not a crowd anymore, just a bunch of guys. That likable cohesion gone. The losing owner, the forgettably dressed one, scooped up the white dog in two arms, staring down into his burden. A forking blaze of red and pink at the throat. Eyes rolled back. My stomach heaved. *Not* out of empathy, again. The winning owner, the man in the mango tracksuit, was surrounded by the people he had made money for. Patting his back and congratulating him. He'd released the red dog. Trojan. The white one was called Shazam. Trojan, who was still alive. Which meant that I had just won . . . I couldn't do the math then. I was too out of my head. Noel was slapping me on my back, asking me jovially if I wanted to bankrupt him. ("Or suh'in," he appended.) To show me, I guess, that he could handle basically any action. He does usually have a huge amount of cash on hand. I mean, was he going to put his profits in the bank? Buy fucking bonds, or whatever? A short line had formed by David. He'd opened the safe and was counting out money for the winners. After he paid them, they'd get their coat and pager or phone back. The guns stayed on the table. There were only three.

When David had stowed my money, the last of whatever weight was connecting me to real existence vanished. This *certitude* overcame me, about Kevin, about the killer . . . every-thing. All I had to do was *to not do anything*, to cede the control I'd been trying to exert, and I'd be set free. Have you ever joyrid-den? Just cruised down a steep hill, letting gravity and the other natural forces do their work? A sense of soaring liberation. Lasting less than five minutes, it must have been. Holy fuck! All that money, which I'd been sure was gone, had now come back and *fructified*. What the fuck was I going to do with *more* money? This is why I waited until everyone had gone before I approached David. I didn't even go to him. He called me over, with soft contempt in his voice. Noel had followed his guests upstairs. "Look, man," I said. But he held out my original stacks of cash, bound again in their ratty rubber bands stained with my father's sketching ink. And six more. One was a centimeter thicker than the others. I figured it held the odd bills. "Look, man," I repeated. "I want to like *donate* it. Like donate it to you and Noel. For like your home improvements. Is that okay?" I was cradling my money, half shoving it at him. The soundproofing had killed my voice, damming it within the confines of my skull. "Like, David, *please*. Please, man."

He didn't hit me. He didn't have to, though his jaw was set like he might. He just *looked* at me. His eyes half-lidded. That hard-to-decipher expression, or lack of expression, calming his features. Then he gave me my bag and coat, my pager, and thumped up the staircase. The throb of gathered voices leaked into the basement. I was alone. So I put the money back in my bag, shouldered on my coat, and activated my pager: I'd missed five pages since David had shut it off. No one looked at me as I stumbled into Noel's living room. No one looked at me as I flat-footed it back onto the street. The forgettably dressed man was just closing the rear doors of a white van parked in front of Noel's house. He sat on the bumper, which made the van bob tinily, and massaged his chin and cheeks, staring at the concrete. This is the point in the story where, if I were a professional writer, I'd insert a meaningful, beautiful scene. A disgusting showpiece of talent. I'm *supposed* to be trying to impress you. Pulling out the old *look at how gifted yet modest I am* routine might help my cause. But I don't have anything like that to offer you, only a fragment of ordinary memory. The loser bobbing on his chrome bumper, his breath streaming up in a vanishing ribbon. My stupid car, the same orange as the inflamed autumn sun. And, stretching in all four directions, the trackless kingdom of nothing at all.

XV.

I MIGHT NEVER HAVE FOUND OUT who was paging me all that day if I had not, as soon as I'd gotten back into my car, vomited all over my lap. Yellowish bile. It burned, coming up. I'd eaten nothing, which made it worse. I gacked and harrumphed, and pounded the horn, and started—though I knew I didn't have any—to rifle my glove box for napkins. Which is how I found out. I mean because Kevin's folder was what I dug up. I took the contents out, the sheaf of documents, and tore a corner from the etiolated cardboard of the front flap, and scraped the strings of stomach acid and mucus from my lips and chin, and tried to get some of the shit off my thighs. Having done this, I lit a cigarette. Having done *this*, I'd exhausted my options of in-car behavior. So I sat there, sucking down the smoke, which hurt my astringed throat. I picked up the pages. Not against my will, but without will. Some dinosaur-brain tic, moving my twentieth-century hands and arms. Almost the twenty-first. Can you believe that? In like less than three months we'll see if all the prophets had it right, if they outguessed us, or if our long-lasting whatever-it-is will last a bit longer. I, for one, am excited. Either way.

Another gout of bile surged in my throat. I gripped the wheel. Even when you don't puke, the odor of it still permeates your pharynx. Hydrochloric acid, with large quantities of potassium chloride and sodium chloride. What metallic-sounding shit! Numerous secretions get human-specific names—adrenaline, dopamine. *This* was just raw chemicals, salts, and acid. I defeated it, though. When it had stopped fountaining up to my uvula, I picked up the pages from Kevin's now-ripped file. Nothing else to do, other than sit in the private stench of my vomit. The top half of the sheaf dimpled and percussed as I locked my thumbs. KEVIN BROADUS. 3549 MCKINLEY STREET NW 20015. 202-364-1889. I read the top line five or six times. KEVIN BROADUS took on a random look, like the street signs you see in dreams. My pager went off and I slid it from my pocket. Another spurt of bile tickled the inner cavities of my nose. And there on the display was the number listed for Kevin in his school records: 202-364-1889. I dropped pages and pager and shouted in fear. Struggling to get away from them, belted in though I was. My cigarette tumbled into my lap and I punched myself in the nuts trying to swat it out. Chills were rocking me now, much worse than before, and I had to sleeve the sweat from my wet neck. I checked the numbers again. They matched. And I knew where I had to go, no matter who or what was paging me. I had the address, after all. I'd *been* there before. I'd even seen the porcelain parrots. The losing owner had not moved from his bumper when I drove off. He was talking to someone now, on a cell phone. Or listening.

Busy! That's what the drive over was. No other word for it. I had a long and energetic talk with myself. About ghosts! I'd come to that. I'm not saying I was *absolutely* positive that Kevin's ghost was somehow paging me. I did think about it, though, every time a red light came up, as I wiped the sheets of sweat from my face and neck, and hunched closer to the steering wheel for imaginary warmth. Noel's house is due southeast of McKinley

Street, and it's basically a straight shot once you get past the old soldiers' home. I'd missed the first gout of morning traffic during the dogfight. So it didn't take long to arrive. I covered a lot of paranormal ground, all the same. I *may* even have wagged a finger at myself in reproof, between dabs at my perspiration and muscle clenching to suppress my shivers.

It didn't take long to arrive. There was even a parking space, right across from the Broadus house. It took me *forever* to actually go and ring the doorbell, though. The morning light was gray, literally gray. It made everything look carved and weighty, the kicking branches, the bricks of the walk, the helpless screwed-back shutters. All of it. I knew that if I got out the cold would assault me again. I wanted to go to sleep. I wanted to smoke cigarettes. I wanted to smoke weed. I wanted to do anything other than what circumstances required of me. So I hunched there and hunched there, until I looked up and saw, through the open green curtain of a first-floor window, Mr. Broadus shuffling back and forth, and before I could stop myself I charged up the walk to the door, jabbing my thumb into the fingernail-colored doorbell. It released a silvery chime. I heard some more shuffling. The instant stretched and stretched. I remembered I'd forgotten to lock my car, and muttered, "This is the second doorbell I've rung just *today*," as I patted my cheeks with my sleeve.

The door creaked. And he was there. Just as tall as I'd remembered him being on TV, his stoop just as slight. In a knit Christmas sweater—gray, showing three rearing maroon reindeers with white tufts for eyes.

"If you're selling firewood, I already informed your friend: no good." He ticked his glasses back up onto his nose, and a fragment of torn dry leaf snecked into his line-free forehead.

"No, I'm like not here for firewood." Eloquent, no? He wasn't convinced.

"So what *are* you selling?"

"Am I *selling*," I echoed.

"Are you all right?" he asked me.

"No, man, it's like, I mean sir, I just wanted to *see* you about something." He held up a *wait* finger, and leaned back into his house from the threshold. Returning with a piece of cornflower blue folded paper. Which he unfolded. "Is this you? Have you been putting these up?" he asked. Kevin's Xerox-fuzzed face stared into the world of objects, looking somewhere over my left shoulder. "Sir, it's like you paged me all this morning."

"And you couldn't *call* back? Why did you *come*? Why are you here *physically*? That's *one* thing I don't understand."

"I was a friend," I told him. This time, it did not leave my mouth with the smooth hurry of a lie. Mr. Broadus wet his lips.

"He did not have a lot of friends. Who are you?" I said nothing. Standing with my arms tight-crossed against the cold. How did he not feel it? He paused there straight and still, in his sacklike sweater. "My wife's out. I wanted to talk to you before she got back. I guess now I'm getting what I want." He moved aside in the doorway, with an exaggerated sweep of his arm. And displayed a stiff, stiff grin that should have warned me away. A car alarm began shrieking just as I crossed his sill.

This physical sense of *tactical superiority* poured into me at the sight of the living room. Through the growing incoherence of my bodily sensations. Nothing had changed since my visit; all the doilies and porcelain parrots had kept their sad order. And this made me feel like an equal to Mr. Broadus. You know? My violation of his home entitled me to equal rights within that home. Or superior rights, even. That's how the human mind works, I think. Virtue is its own punishment, if you see what I mean. He was a large man, slack-gutted, yes, but large-built. Competent-looking. The shapeless and juvenile sweater could not conceal this. He did not resemble his son, whose face had still carried indecisive fat. Mr. Broadus was staring at me as we stood near his threshold, a trickle of cold air singing in under the door. He was barefoot. That much I remember. Going around barefoot in front of strangers takes a lot of spine, in my opinion. I can't do it.

"Sit down, please." He pointed at a rocking chair. "And your name would be . . . ?" I made for the couch, assuming his point was a general gesture. It was not. "No, there," he instructed, giving the chair a shake by its shoulder, as though he were trying to rouse it from the trustful slumber of objects. "And what's your name? You're slow with questions, huh? Is that vomit? Did you vomit on yourself? Have you been drinking?"

Do you know how humiliating it is to be interrogated while sitting in a rocking chair? It's worse when you're embracing yourself to fight chills.

"It's like Addison, man. I mean sir. I mean my name. It's Addison Schacht."

"Addison Schacht." You probably assume he said it "venomously" or something. Like how novelists write: *He looked at me as though I were an insect. He said my name as though it were the name of a disease.* Nobody does that, you know. Such ideas of human nature come from TV, where people *do* use that hilarious sneering emphasis. But Mr. Broadus was just trying to get it clear. Or maybe he thought he remembered it.

"You have an unusual name, Addison. I like names like yours. Always have, although I could not tell you why. It may be due to my own name, for which I was mocked a lot as a child. On the other hand, it's easy to look at other people's affairs through the lens of your own. It's dangerous to do that. I apologize for rambling. Though I was complaining before, I'm *grateful* that you decided to come by, Addison. For a number of reasons." Here he lowered himself onto the brown couch across the room, without averting his sharpened gaze. "I think it's important that you have your say," Mr. Broadus continued, "because all angles must be considered, correct? In any important issue, all angles must be considered." The chalk-stiff smile stretched his face. Before I could speak he held up a massive hand—bigger than my father's, and free of the pointless art-caused scars and discolorations that mar his. A prick of fear, here. But he went on. "Wait, wait, wait, wait, wait. I've been *rude* to you, Addison. I was just about to go make some tea. Would you like some tea? Young people like yourself often don't enjoy it. But I find it relaxing. Will you have some? I insist that you do." And he got up, still speaking, and wandered off to the fruit-walled kitchen. *He has no idea that I know how his kitchen looks!* Again, that pompous little thrill of superiority.

"Yes, it's quite relaxing," he yelled, over the sound of the water and the minor clanks, "and being relaxed, you'll find, is usually the most necessary thing in any situation. Don't you agree?" He'd returned, by this last question. "Don't you agree, Addison, that being relaxed is the *important* thing?"

"Sir, like I just wanted to talk about Kevin. I see you found the posters. I think the posters are like a good thing. I've like been doing them like after and before school. I think they can help bring out uninvestigated aspects of the case." I was panting by the time I finished. I knew it sounded mechanical. I couldn't think of anything else, between the cold, which had somehow gotten indoors, my worry about ghosts, and that tickle of superiority. He didn't answer. Instead, he asked me, low and calm, "Well, do you or don't you, Addison?" I noticed that he had a pen clipped to the neck of his sweater, which went with the meticulous gait of his speech.

"No, I'm *very* relaxed, thank you."
He unclipped his pen and sighted me down it.
"No. No, Addison, that is *not* what I asked. I asked a general question of principle. Not specifically related to you." His grin only got stiffer and wider.
"I agree," I said, with high and vacuous sympathy.
"You agree what?"
Another tide of sweat burst out of my pores. "I agree that like what you said about relaxation? Is important?" This elicited a nod.
"Well, I suppose I have to accept that, Addison. Although you might be just telling me what you think I want to hear. You have to admit, there's a good chance that you're telling me what I want to hear." As I listened to the easy, full drone of his voice, this weird *seizure* of sleepiness gripped me. Fucked-up, right? "Addison? Hello? Hello in there?" He was snapping his fingers. "Your attention wandered, Addison. That's sort of rude, wouldn't you say?" Before I could agree, the kettle gave a high harmonic moan. "*There* goes the water," Mr. Broadus chimed. "Please keep talking." And so I did. After agreeing—"Yes, I would say it *is* like sort of rude, Mr. Broadus"—I explained everything. Explained it to that chocolate-colored couch. Above it hung a lithograph, an old map of the city, still a whole rhombus then, before the government had given the ragged quarter west of the Potomac back to Virginia.

I offered all the pathetic fragments I had. The assembly. My idiot teachers. Mr. Vanderleun. My theft of the file. Noel's statement about Short Mike. The lax behavior of the police. Lorriner's assault on my house. My trip to Brander's Hollow. Murphy, Murphy, Murphy. The postering. The dogfight. My money. And this newest moment. Oh, ladies and gentlemen, *you* know how empty and sad it sounded. You've heard it already. The way you lie to your teachers. Or the way you lie to whichever parent you love and trust more. I didn't care. I thought I sounded *amazing*. The rocking chair plunged back and forth beneath me. I did not mention weed. I did not mention the *Aeneid*. I did not mention Digger. I did not mention Holocaust jokes. So Mr. Broadus—or rather the air where he had been sitting—got the whole story. Minus the useless personal information. My voice had come apart. Luminous haze had started seeping from every object I could see, through the fishbowling of my vision, through the bone-cold of the outdoors that had gotten into his house.

"Is your like heat working?" I shouted at the end of my précis.

"Our heat works fine, Addison," he called from the kitchen. "It's a new renovation. I can send firewood sellers away because of it." I shivered. In agreement, I guess. The trails of glowing vapor followed my glance, whenever I moved my eyes. And I just forged ahead.

"And I've like lost a loved one *too*, Mr. Broadus," I gasped. A loved one! The big finish! Kevin's father was still clattering away with the teacups and kettle. He wasn't much longer about it, though. "Sorry about the delay," he sang through his rigor-mortis smile as he sailed in. He'd brought only one cup of tea. I didn't object.

Water chunked through the second-floor pipes. Mr. Broadus blew on the limpid surface of his tea.

"Now, Addison, you were telling me before that you had some evidence? About Kevin, I mean. And that you were his friend. Although, as I said, he did not have many friends. His schoolwork was very important to him. I believe in attending to your studies. It's how I became successful. And I think I would remember you. Wouldn't you say so?" I tried to slow the squeaks of the chair.

"Well, Mr. Broadus, I wouldn't say we were exactly *best* friends or anything like that, and I *certainly* didn't *mean* to give you the *impression* that we were best *friends* or anything like that." I was starting to sound like a querulous spinster, and Mr. Broadus only widened his grin.

"I didn't *ask* you if you were best friends with my son, Addison. His best friend is named Tarasac Choulamontry. He's Laotian. I asked if it wouldn't be likely, given that you say you were friends with Kevin, that I'd remember you?"

This high *buzzing* distracted me, right as he said that. More of a ringing, or the onset of deafness. I almost asked him, *Do you hear that?* But I restricted myself to a direct answer.

"Yes, I think you would remember me, Mr. Broadus. And I think like there's been some like miscommunication here?"

"You mean that you told me you were his friend and you were not his friend?"

"No, I didn't mean . . . I only meant that we were like *acquaintances* more than friends, if you see what I mean, and that really I never met you before the whole thing, so that's why you don't remember me." The spinsterish whine had crept back into my voice, so I shut up. Mr. Broadus seemed to accept this, although his smile did not vanish, as I'd hoped it would. He only shielded his neck with two hands as his glasses blanked into discs of light.

"No, but, Mr. Broadus, really I think I can help. I'm sorry but I know I can help. The posters can help." Mr. Broadus ran a gray tongue over his large lips.

. . .

"I talk to myself, Addison, sometimes when I'm alone. Do you ever do that? It's a bad habit. But we all have those." He blew on his tea some more.

"No, I *respect* everything that you've gone through." I told him this without managing to meet his eyes. "I respect *everything* you've gone through and I really *feel* I have something valuable to communicate here." (What?)

"Yes, I *know* you do, Addison," cooed Mr. Broadus, in his clipped and equable voice, and apologized for not bringing me a cup of tea. Then we said nothing more to each other, for a long moment: Mr. Broadus staring at me over the rim of his cup, me in my frantic stillness, trying to prevent the chair from rocking.

"I just think if you'll let me move ahead with my *investigations*," I stuttered. Mr. Broadus slurped down the rest of the tea.

"Why are you here? Really?" His voice contained no recognizable emotion. Only interest. "Do you know what you're *actually* doing? Do you *know*?"

"I can sympathize with everything you've like *gone through*," I repeated, because there was no other coherent reply I could make. I'm sure you all can agree: I am a stupid and useless motherfucker. Because of that little tickle, that little hint of *saintliness* I was groping after with him, that glint. So instead of answering his question, which would have required me to reveal myself as a full-bore fraud, I blurted out, "Can I leave my pager number with you?"

He waved the blue poster at me. A shade I'd chosen with special pride.

"Addison. Addison, Addison. You forget that I have it right here. You even mentioned in this flyer that it *was* a pager number. And you were saying something before about killing some dog? About money? While I was out of the room. As I said, I also talk to myself when I'm alone, so I understand. You were talking to yourself. All your theories. I heard all of it. But it was just something you imagined, Addison. Wasn't it? That you were discussing with yourself. I can understand that. How could it be real? Nobody decent would behave in such a way. Nobody would do something like this"—and here he waved my poster again—"for reasons that thin. Nobody decent. Do you understand what I'm saying? You look confused." He'd crossed the room and was kneeling to look into my face, hands on his ponderous knees. The bulge of his gut filled out his sweater, elongating the reindeer legs. I managed to meet his eyes. A glaring and icy green, behind the large glasses, under the gray bush of his eyebrows.

"Don't you have a better reason, Addison?" The chair groaned beneath me. I groaned with it. The ache in my neck had reached a grinding and miserable pitch. I groaned and covered my face. I could form no words. "Come with me," Mr. Broadus was saying. "Come with me. Come upstairs."

"I haven't *been* upstairs before," I blurted out as I struggled to my feet. Mr. Broadus turned his green gaze on me again, squinting at my non sequitur or maybe my drunk's wobble.

"That's neither here nor there," he clacked out. And in my single lucid moment so far that day, I came up with a great retort: *You sound white! I have a white friend who sounds black! Isn't that funny!* He was already halfway up the short staircase, where I had been perched less than a week ago listening to his wife whistle. So I never said it.

The pictures of Kevin had been taken down. That shocked me. The pictures had been taken down and my pompous inner voice decried their absence. As though that were my right. The pictures were gone, leaving lighter patches on the white walls of the stairway, and little holes, which looked like dead gnats. The floorboard sang beneath his feet and then mine, and we were upstairs. The layout was simple, a big entrance area with a schoolroom piano, which I had not seen from my previous vantage points. And next to the piano a saxophone on its stand, smaller than Kevin's. An alto. Kevin played the baritone. There were pictures of the Broaduses as a family on the walls, of Mrs. Broadus and Mr. Broadus when they were younger, one picture where she was wearing a bridal gown and he was wearing a dark, wide-lapeled suit and a dove gray vest and a top hat. He was motioning me on.

"You went to school with him?" he asked. "You had that same teacher? Mr. Vanderleun, yes? You're also gifted and talented?"

"All of those things are true," I mumbled. We had stopped before a door to which was affixed one of those joke road signs, in crimson and white: KEEP OUT.

"He liked his privacy," Mr. Broadus said. "I feel no compunction in telling you that." Then he opened the door, without saying anything else, and we stood on the threshold and stared.

Ghosts? Let me tell you what I saw: nothing. The walls had been stripped bare. Paler squares from posters, awards, whatever, all the furniture, bed, dresser, etc., all gone, no blinds on the windows, no dust on the floor, in the gaping closet only quadrangles of shadow, not even bereft hangers. Nothing but pale winter sun and the heavy air of the house. My breath speeded up, and two tearlike drops of sweat plashed down from my eyebrows. He was *there*. The emptiness itself proved it. I withstood the view. Gnawing my lower lip. Then I turned my face to Mr. Broadus, and I saw that he had clenched his jaw. I was close to tears—not from exhaustion, or guilt and shame, but tears of an emotion beyond those, which lacks a definition and does not need one. Greeks always win. Trojans always lose. Virgil had to weave a large and specious story to redeem their sad fates. The gate of ivory. Mr. Broadus spoke into the desert of his son's room.

"You didn't know him. You were not his friend, and you did not even know him. He had a pager. I don't know where he got it. He had it for about a year. He had a pager, and he liked his privacy, and spent a lot of time out at night. I never asked him about it. I always believed he should be independent. I taught him that. I trusted him. I found certain *indications* in his room. After. The police did not find them. He hid them too well. It was like him to do that. To be methodical. I taught him to be methodical. I could show them to you. I can't show them to you. I destroyed them. This is the first thing I wanted to tell you. Do you understand? Are you sick? You seem confused." His voice never wavered or lost its metronomic pace. "Do you understand? Are you sick?" He looked at me. I nodded. My one honest answer to him. "They took his *watch*," he said. His jaw now shut. "The murderers took his watch. Only the police know that. That was the *one fact* they kept back. Out of everything. All of it. They planned on verifying the killer. Or weeding out the false callers." He made a noise, a long, windy huff, high-pitched. "The second thing is that I wanted to see you. To see your face. I thought you'd be older. I don't know why. We always imagine these things differently." He moaned again and spoke no further.

I could have left then. Only the staircase separated me from the street. I could have left and gone back to my false life, and come up with some piece of explanation for why even Kevin's own father was not on my side. Normally I would have started doing this while I was still standing in the man's house. But my creative powers had left me, for the moment. There was only

Kevin's empty room. That was the only fact. The ringing in my ears had ascended to this impossible vacuous whir, the noise of rapid wingbeats or an engine. My jagged fast pulse fluttered above my larynx. I had no response. I had to respond. You see that, right? I had come to this point, and action was demanded.

"I think I can help find out who killed your son." My teeth knocked against one another as I spoke: *I think I c-c-c-an.* I was gripping my upper arms in the bitter cold, embracing myself. Mr. Broadus did not seem to have heard me. "I can help," I clicked out.

"Addison, are you aware of the fact that right here in Washington, D.C., more than thirty percent of murders go unsolved? That's what the *police* told me. Do you really think it even matters, now? Why are you here? What are you doing?" He was still looking into his son's empty room. "They took his watch. It was some psychopath. Nothing else was stolen. No money. No wallets. Don't you think, Addison, that this indicates some irrationality on the part of the killers? Couldn't you have just called me and asked? Before you did all this?" He brandished the blue poster. No words exist for the undersounds he made as he spoke. So I took off my backpack. I offered it to Mr. Broadus. "There's the money," I murmured.

For the first time he raised his voice. "You don't understand this! Don't *think* you do. You never *could*. You don't understand the *situation*." His voice came from everywhere. I swear to fucking God. He was shoving me, not shoving me, he was jabbing his enormous first and second fingers into my chest, and I was backing up and backing up. He took the bag from me, jerked it away, and lifted it over his head with his left hand and he stabbed at my solar plexus with his right. He did not lumber. He moved with smoothness. And, so to speak, with justice. That I recognized.

I knew he was going to hit me with my bag. I wanted to raise my hands in defense. They would not rise. "You cannot *understand* this, Addison," he was chanting, blinking hard behind his glasses, "you cannot *understand* this." He backed me into the corner with the piano and the saxophone. We had no more space. Nowhere to move. I bowed my head and waited for the blow.

The lock of the front door clicked open. I recognized its sound. My eyes still shut, I heard a woman call out, "Stan? Who's that? Stan? What's wrong?" She had a beautiful voice. As good as her whistle. The bag did not strike me. I opened my eyes. Mrs. Broadus was climbing the stairs. Wearing a reindeer sweater identical to her husband's, except that the colors had been inverted: it was maroon with gray deer. "There's the *money*," I repeated, "all my money."

"Who *are* you," asked Mrs. Broadus, no more music in her voice. I started to speak. My legs quaked out from under me. And just before I was gone, just before I slipped into that waiting and echoing dark, the back of my head hit the keyboard of their piano. I can hear the broken chord it made to this day.

XVI.

THIS ISN'T ONE OF THOSE ABSURD pieces of writing where it turns out that the narrator *has been dead the whoooooole tiiiiiiime!* I would never abuse your trust and impose on your goodwill in that way, ladies and gentlemen. My father brought me such a book while I was convalescing. He'd picked it up from the best-seller racks, where he buys all his books. It was called *Rage*, by Nathan Levitan. The narrator (it turns out) is this already-dead college student who got killed in the Vietnam War. Telling the convoluted story of his own death. He gets into a good college, and he gets showily disgusted by the innocent vulgarities of his classmates, and then he starts to "rebel," gets expelled, loses his academic deferment, ends up in the war, and thus gets shot. I don't want to sound harsh. I mean, this guy is a published writer and everything. But what the fuck? Do you need much help in guessing what my opinion of *that* concept is?

Rage had on the back flap this photo of him, of Levitan, I mean. He looked like a successful insurance salesman, divorced maybe. Really unhappy. Something in the set of his mouth. After I got out of the hospital, I read up on this guy. A, he's seventy years old. B, in all of his photos he has that same weird, unhappy look, although he is—as far as I can determine—a famous and successful writer. So why does he look so miserable all the time? He writes kind of like he's miserable, too. You know what I mean? So grim! Why? Why this grimace in his author photos, a look of chagrined concentration, like he's trying to take a highly spiritual shit? What more does he want out of life? I can't figure it out. My father brought me this book instead of my Loeb edition of the *Aeneid*, which I asked him for when he first came to visit me in the hospital. He forgot the *Aeneid*, as I half expected him to, and he covered his mistake by bringing *Rage* instead. "It was a *staff* pick, Addison." He grinned as he handed it over, and I faked a really good smile right back at him. "They all seem intelligent there. *Very* upper-percentile." He's the one person I know who uses that phrase. It makes me nauseated, sort of. He must have stopped in a rush at a bookstore on the way to Sidney Memorial when he realized he'd forgotten. More than a few bookstores exist on the route from our house. D.C., like most fundamentally barbarous cities, contains a large number of bookstores. As a kind of camouflage to deceive unwary visitors.

I wasn't in Philip Sidney Memorial Hospital for long. Four nights, three days. Hospital life is boring and difficult. They had me on an IV, and I had to take it with me everywhere. To the bathroom or to go get examined or whatever. It goes alongside you on this tall, ill-balanced metal tower with squeaky wheels. You move like a weak old man. You have to wear those ass-baring sterile gowns. I slept a lot. I was tired. I felt like I'd become over-sensitive to gravity, or something. Every movement cost two or three times as much effort as usual. You ever get that feeling? It's frustrating, even sort of terrifying. But it helps you sleep. I have trouble sleeping. Everyone who knows me knows I have trouble sleeping. My sleeps in Sidney Memorial Hospital remain the most accomplished of my life. I slept and ate the putrid hospital food, all of which tasted sweet, eggs, sausage, whatever it was. It all had a horrible sweetness. The food nurses or whatever arranged it on trays, put all this aesthetic effort into it.

I had a nice little room, or what I call a room to save time. It was a curtained-off alcove. It did have a window. You could see a vista of bare trees and sky. Sometimes a cloud. I was in a bad state when I first got there. Mr. Broadus took me after I collapsed in his house. I cut the back of my head on his piano keys. There must have been a lot of blood. He put a wadded-up hand towel to the wound, and somehow managed to get my father's name from me, and then called him. I don't know how he accomplished this. I was delirious. But the doctors told me that Mr. Broadus sat with me till my father arrived, holding the fruit-printed dish towel against my wound. I found it, after I'd been admitted, and hid it at the bottom of the garbage pail in my room, while my father was out taking a leak.

My main doctor, Dr. Paull, told me later I'd been running a fever of close to 105, the temperature at which your brain denatures or something. He suspected it was viral, just a virus that had gone untreated. Gotten out of control due to *poor health maintenance*. Nothing remarkable at all. Which insulted me. Who wants to hear that his disease is nothing special? He asked me if I'd been under a lot of stress lately, or gone through any traumatic events. I told him no. He said he understood. He said he had a daughter my age, and he understood that young people think they're invincible. "But you only get one body," he admonished. "I had to stitch up the back of your head. You fell on a piano, you say? First time I've ever heard that!" He tugged at the golden flukes of his mustache. Then he said, "I guess you'll *see sharp* from now on!" and permitted himself a full-throated chuckle. His mustache I can only describe by saying that if a six-month-old baby could grow a full and luxuriant mustache, it would be that corn-silken color and texture. His skin was baby pink with the flush of permanent health.

All this biography comes *after* I resurfaced. I spent my first day *under*, with this viral issue Dr. Paull told me about. I told you about the echoing darkness. That sort of continued for a while, and then I slipped in and out of consciousness. I felt too hot, I felt too cold, sweat glued my flimsy robe to my shoulders, my joints throbbed. I kept thinking that there was a weird skylight directly over my head, one looking out onto a glaring white sky. This turned out to be an über-normal fluorescent panel light. I figured *that* out the day before my father brought *Rage* for me to read. That's when my fever broke and my perceptions returned to normal. He was sitting in the low wooden chair across the room from my bed. That's when I asked him for my Loeb. He nodded glumly, and said he would bring it tomorrow. He sat in that chair for at least an hour every day, till the end of my short stay. He didn't ask me anything, at first, about what had happened. Just fingered the tip of his ponytail. But midway through his second visit, some minutes after he'd finished enthusing about *Rage*, he directed his glance to the floor and asked me a question.

"Addison, we need to talk. Something has been *going on* these past few weeks. I know it. Call it intuition. You know how intuitive I am. I want you to tell me. I won't be angry. But I want you to tell me. I mean how you ended up in here." Right out of a parenting textbook, ladies and gentlemen. I blew air through my nostrils.

"It's nothing, Dad. I just made a mistake. I had like a viral thing, and I got all confused. Okay? You don't need to worry. Okay?"

I expected him to give up, then, as he normally does. This is about as far as his questioning goes. But he kept his eyes on the linoleum, and kept talking.

"Addison, Mr. Broadus told me that you've been putting up flyers about that classmate of yours? His son? And that you came to his house? He told me he thought you were on drugs. He said you fell and hit your head. Are you on drugs?"

How is it that an adult, like my father, who has *obviously* at least smoked weed in his life, and maybe even dropped acid, can use the word *drugs* like that? It's like saying, "Did you eat food? Did you drink liquid?" If you're "on" something, it's drugs. So why not specify? I gave him the obligatory answer: "No, I'm not on drugs." He still did not lift his eyes.

"You can, you know, *tell* me stuff, Addison. I'll understand. We *all* make mistakes. Was it part of that project you mentioned? I mean, I can understand *that*. If it was for school."

This made me even more tired.

"Yes, Dad. It was for school. It was part of the project. Okay? Is that okay?" I heaved the lie out, not caring that it sounded false. He went quiet. My blood beat at my temples. In the hall, a gurney wheel squeaked and a wave of cross talk followed. Then my father spoke again.

"Addison, is Phoebe pregnant?"

I couldn't restrain my laughter. I just couldn't. It bubbled out of me; exhausted as I was, I heaved up and down in my bed with it, chanting, "Yes, Dad, she's pregnant. Okay? She's totally pregnant. And we're totally getting married and having the baby. Okay? Okay?" By the time I'd finished, he had lifted his eyes from the floor, and the hurt in them was visible enough to shut me up. We didn't speak too much, after that.

. . .

I had two other visitors. I was more popular in the hospital than I am outside of it. The first person to come and talk to me other than my father was Archer B. Sexton. Remember him? The man with the interchangeable name? The man who wrote the disgusting article about Kevin? *An historically black institution*, etc.? That guy. I'd never met him before. Despite the considerable part he played in the events of my senior fall. He'd heard about the posters. He wanted to ask me about them. For an article, he said. I'd never considered that they would catch the attention of the media. Otherwise I would not have put them up. He was out of breath when he arrived. He came when my father had gone out to get a soda. Sexton still had his weird pomegranate facial coloration, and his voice was still extra gay.

My interview with Interchangeable Archer didn't last long. He introduced himself—"Hi, Addison. I'm Arch Sexton. From the *Post*"? With a pause, maybe in case I said, "Oh God, not *the* Arch Sexton!" and started hyperventilating. I just stared. Bugging out my eyes on purpose. To freak him out, you know? Then he started talking about the flyers, how he thought it was noble, he was interested in how I'd come to do it, whether I'd accomplished anything. Et cetera. He talked and talked. I cut him off by saying, "Kevin was a strong and quiet presence, though blessed with a genuine musicality, a strong rhythm. He'll be remembered and missed." Sexton scribbled this down in his little notebook and looked to me for more copy. Eyes round and ready. Avid, even. So I pulled my blankets up over my head and ignored him till he went away. It took almost twenty minutes. Stupidity can be a form of strong character. "Why are you *lying* like that, Addison?" my father asked when he got back. I peeped out. He had a sweating maroon can of Shasta Cola (a product I have only ever seen available in the vending machines of Philip Sidney Memorial Hospital) and took a long slurp when I failed to answer.

So that was a big letdown for Sexton, I'm sure. If I ever get to a point in life where I can fire him, or maybe run him over with a car and make it look like an accident, I will. That twenty minutes made hospital life even worse. All I had to read was *Rage*. Only my father to talk to. And then Sexton. I mean, what the fuck? I guess when things start sucking, they just get worse, and if they're going well, they just get better. Or I *would* guess that. But on the third morning, when I had just opened my eyes from a real champion sleep, I saw Digger poised in the dropsical-cushioned muddy mauve visitor's chair, where my father normally would be.

"Hey, man," I croaked. She was clenching her turquoise-beaded bag. Lips parted for speech. She'd put a crimson streak in her hair, above her brow. She had on her necklace from Chile and a black T-shirt with a picture of this musician she admires, Lou Reed. And she was wearing makeup, which she never does. I know I told you she's not hot. But I swear to fucking God: at that moment some beauty was in her or shone through her, a beauty that demands respect and even fear, but *good* fear. I had never seen anyone or anything so infused with such impersonal beauty. Even in the dead light of my room you could see it.

"Did you call my mother the C-word?" she asked me, as her bouncing heel made the beads on her bag clack.

"No, I don't *know* your mother," I said. It took me a while to wake up during the days of my short convalescence. I think they were medicating me or something.

"Addison. Addison. Earth to Addison." Snapping her fingers.

"Oh, wait. Yes. Yes, I *technically* did," I answered. I knew what she was referring to now. The phone call. That put me back on *terra cognita*.

"Yeah. She said you did. A couple weeks ago. On the phone. I was just checking."

"Digger, man," I stammered.

"Addison," she interjected, then pitched a sigh, clapped her hands once. "You're not *dying*? Your father seems incredibly worried. I spoke to him. He's outside. He's looks mopey, sort of." Big surprise there.

"No, it was just like a virus. And I got stitches in the back of my head. I think I'm *basically* okay."

"Seriously, though. Why did you *call* her that?" She was not accusing me of anything. Maybe she just wanted a valid reason why. Maybe she kind of *admitted* the possibility that her mother might be a cunt. Digger's honest about people. She was spreading her hands now.

"I don't know, man. Because I was pissed off at you. I mean at her, at her. I mean at her. Just about everything. About. Well, you know." The beads rattled, but she stayed calm.

"Don't call her that. I don't even call her that. Maybe you can call her a bitch. But not the C-word. All right? Is that going to be a *problem* for you? How did you cut your head?" I fingered the sticky, tight, wiry comb of sutures, and the thrillingly bald region around them. I hadn't *seen* the wound. You need two mirrors to see the back of your head. I didn't even have one.

"From a piano. I cut it on a piano," I continued.

"What do you mean?" She shifted her eyebrows into the double uptick of incredulity.

"From the keyboard?" I said, suddenly interrogative. She has that effect on me.

"Okeydokey. From a *piano*. Pianos are like *known* for their deadliness. Are you coming back to school soon?"

I nodded and she sighed again. "Okay. Okay. You're probably all doped up. I have to go. And I can't believe you called my mother the C-word. It's totally unconscionable to do that. I have a French test."

"Okay, man," I mumbled. I'd been so shocked by her appearance that I had no time to feel happiness, and now that she was leaving I was too shocked to feel unhappiness. So I tipped her a salute, two fingers, über-professional. She gave me one of her looks. Like she was a grizzled old gunnery sergeant, and I was a green recruit. Exasperated and amused. Then she returned my salute.

"Digger," I muttered.

"What? What do you want?" She was poised in the doorway, ready to go to war.

"They're showing that movie. Like part two? At the Camelot? *The Sorrow and the Pity.* Do you wanna go?"

"Are you asking me out?" This is her standard response. Whenever I suggest we do anything. And my standard response is, "Only in your wet ones."

This time, I did not say that, but rather: "Yeah. It's in November, according to the calendar. Near the end of November. We already missed a showing." She started gnawing on her thumb knuckle. I looked her in the face. I didn't feel ashamed, although according to our agreement, I should have. But fuck the agreement. I was in the hospital. And if Digger could bend her principles enough to break her vow of silence, I could say, *Yeah.* She gave me a nod, almost imperceptible, frightened, except she's never frightened. And strode out, back to Kennedy and her French exam. She maintains a ninety-nine average in all classes. I was confident she was going to ace it. *Andromaque, je pense à vous!* That's from some poem she had to read in French. (You are a classy motherfucker, Addison Schacht!) Except Digger's fifty times better than Andromache. Who was, after all, a consummate Trojan.

"I'm still not talking to you, by the way," Digger shouted from the hall. Other than that, I don't have much to say about hospitals.

XVII.

THEY DISCHARGED ME the fourth evening, Wednesday evening. Took me out to my father's car in a wheelchair, which humiliated me. Then we went home. My room seemed strange. I slept, though, which as I said is rare for me. I slept well that night, and the next night, and the next, and the next. Nothing had changed! All the dumb artsy objects still cluttered our house. I don't know what I was expecting. Some visitation. Who the fuck knows? My father said I didn't have to go back to school until I felt "up to it," as he put it. He told me he would write me a note. I ended up missing the rest of that week and all of the next. I didn't do much on my unforeseen vacation, though. I didn't sell weed. My pager's memory was maxed out, so that every new page coming erased the previously oldest one. Some ancient cultures used to think that's how birth and death work. Over the centuries, that idea was refined into what we call the transmigration of souls. I lay around like a sack of shit. I reread book six of the *Aeneid*. (Holy fuck!) My father kept coming down to check on me. He also asked me if I had enjoyed *Rage*, which I told him I did. He had gotten über into it. I looked through college mail, which had started arriving last year and had continued. Those sumptuous brochures.

• • •

My father cooked for me, the same meal every night. Bitter salad and scrambled eggs. Impressive, for a man who never eats. My father is not the best dinner companion. He's silent and he chews with his mouth open. Two traits you'd think would not occur in the same character. He *did* refrain from giving his suicide-by-bus speech. Mark that in the positive column. And he did not try to get all buddy-buddy with me, to work up some fake friendship between us, to compensate for his usual neglect. You have no idea how grateful I was for that. I mean, it would have just been *impossible*. If you see what I mean.

I still had some business matters to deal with, after my discharge. The disappearance of my money had made these considerably easier. I figured Mr. Broadus had kept it. Otherwise I would have heard something about it from my father. That, ladies and gentlemen, would have been a real fucking disaster. My pager, my safe, even the huge amount of Biggie bags and the scale I could explain away, as long as they were not discovered all at the same time. But eighteen grand? That's a major piece of evidence. I spent a bad couple of days biting my nails over it. What could I do, though? It was completely out of my hands. It's not like my father would turn me in to the cops. He might take away my car. But, like I said, I'm not a huge fan of driving. So I stopped worrying. Maybe Mr. Broadus would keep it, as compensation for my idiocy. I had invaded his life. Or launched a lateral assault on it, for the worst reasons. Maybe he thought I owed him. I did. Maybe he'd buy a new car, something other than that age-dulled blue sedan. He never showed up to accuse me, and my father never found out about it.

The first of the remaining to-dos was getting rid of my industrial-size supply of Biggie-brand bags. This was harder than you might think. I had a case of them that I bought at a bulk store with Digger. We'd gone as a joke. I saw this palletload of Biggies, and it was a hundred bucks or something. I'd been using it for two years and had made this tiny dent. The columned boxes, blue and green, overladen with praiseful copy, line the whole left side of my business closet. So I had to sneak them out in leaf bags. In six loads. I did this in the middle of my first night back, rushing back and forth across our backyard to the spot on the alley side of our fence where trash is left for pickup. I was barefoot in the cold. You get, if you're a D.C. resident, a huge green container for regular garbage and a smaller blue one for recycling. Our green bin was already full. So I just left the bags in kind of a mound at its base, hoping for the best. The chill stung the shaved spot on my scalp, and made the healing lips of the wound pucker. My scale I left that same night on the curb in front of some random house a few blocks away with a note: *Perfectly good scale.* I put on my shoes and coat to make that trip. It had been taken when I looked the next day. I just chucked my plastic tub of orange peel scraps. That was easy. This left only my pager, my weed, and my gun.

My pager. My line of communication. It had sat at my hip for most of my adolescence, at this point. You could say it was the most human thing about me. Through it and through it alone I had traffic with my species. Lacking the pager, my existence looked doubtful. Which may be another reason I'm going on at such length. Getting rid of it was the easiest thing I'd ever done, though I waited, I admit, until the Sunday after my discharge to do it. I wrapped it in an old sock and put it in the garbage. Then I took it out of the garbage and dropped it into the drain of our sink. I checked to see if my father was nearby. He has a real neurosis about the garbage disposal. He's always fishing things out of it, like eggshells, which he claims are "bad for the machinery." But he was not nearby. I had no idea where he was. So I shoved the pager down into the drain, down to where I could feel the block-blunt, slimy blades against the back of my hand, and then I pulled my forearm out and with a grope flipped the under-sink switch, letting water flow into the drain from the faucet. That's another thing my father claims you have to do, to lubricate the crushing process or whatever. Some beetle-crunching sounds came out, under the circular groan of the blades, as the disposal ate my pager. "Is there a *spoon* caught?" my father shouted from his bedroom when he heard the noise. He has good ears.

And you know who was paging me, right when this happened? For the first time in a few days? You guessed it. Noel Eleuthere Bradley. The page arrived just as I shoved it down. Symbolic coherence, right? Oh, I hesitated. Not from uncertainty. To enjoy it more. Noel I'll never be able to feed into a wood chipper, the way he deserves. Too big! Too corpulent! Even filleting him into small enough steaks to get into a chopping or grinding machine would cost too much effort. So it's into the garbage disposal with *you*, you fat, grinning, lying shithead!

I have no idea how much experience with drugs you have, ladies and gentlemen. There is a hierarchy of retention. Losing coke or heroin is a tragedy. Losing acid or mushrooms or ecstasy is a major party foul, a depressing albeit bearable event. Losing weed does not rank. Except, of course, for the man who sells it. Who knows it, sells it, who wants to protect it, to see it blossom into pleasure and vapidity. I love my weed. Even though I knew this tag end of the package would be the last, I still cared about its fate. If I'd had enough friends to throw a party, I would have had a last smoke with them. If Digger and I had been on easier terms at the moment, we could have gotten *destroyed*. I theorized about smoking it myself. Just over periods of time. It would last, I extrapolated, until the middle of November. I couldn't actually, though. I didn't want to, and when I tried to force myself I just chuckled. I couldn't throw it away, though. It's the same with food. You don't want to throw it away. You want to see it used. I tabled the issue until Friday, nine full days of laziness after I'd been let out, when I woke from a real marathon nap ablaze with what I thought was an über-genius idea. You find that alarming? I don't know what to say. You'll just have to trust me. I marched upstairs, up to the second floor, and opened my father's door.

He was standing there dressed in his Sherlock Holmes costume. I was stunned; I thought he was mocking me, until I remembered that I'd forgotten that this was the night of the October Gala at the Cochrane. The second Friday in October, remember? Because they're too cool to have it on real Halloween? Which meant that Dr. Watson was either already in our house or soon to be. I wanted to get this exchange out of the way before she arrived.

"Ah, Addison Schacht, I presuuuuuume!" my father declaimed with a weird plummy quasi-English accent, and stared at me through his magnifying glass. I don't remember Sherlock Holmes ever saying that. I think it was the Stanley and Livingston guy who said it, though I can never remember which is which. I whipped out the bag of weed I planned to offer him. *That* was my brilliant idea.

It came to me in a dream-free sleep. So it had to be sort of valuable, right? I mean, because it wasn't born out of any romantic self-torture. I just thought of it and did it. No discussion, no plan. "Like maybe you and Fatima would *want* some," I explained, waving the bag. "For the party. Like after the party. You're *going* to the party, right?" I'd put fresh orange peels in with the weed. It was a fragment under two ounces, first-rate stuff. Red-haired, dense, tender buds. Good weed is nice-looking. Comforting-looking. Six feet of air between us. His left eye warped by the lens. Beneath his nails, at his cuticles, glittering clay. Ineradicable deposits. My fake smile hurt my maxillary muscles.

"Addison. Where did you *get* that?" He'd lowered the lens from his face, and his shoulders sank in despair. He was looking at the floor, just like he'd done when he questioned me in the hospital.

"I got it from a friend. I was like holding it for a friend. It's okay, though. You can have it. I thought you might want some. It's okay, Dad, really."

He tapped the magnifying glass against his lowered chin. The high collar of the costume shirt pushed its hard wings into his flesh, wrinkling his slight wattle. "Addison, while I have smoked dope in the past—"

I cut him off. "No, really, Dad. It's like not a problem. Okay?"

My cheeks had heated up and my sinuses began to burn. A sudden fear that I was going to weep made me grind my teeth.

"Can't you just *tell* me what's going on?" he asked. "Can't you tell me? Is this related to the conversation we had at the hospital? I feel as though it is. I feel as though it is and you're not *telling* me." His voice was tight, higher than normal. "Where did you get the *drugs*?" That word again. And I had just shown him it was weed, and he had recognized it as weed.

"There's nothing going on, okay? I promise. I don't even know what you *mean*. It's just weed. Okay? It's not even anything *bad*. Everyone smokes it. It doesn't even do any *harm*."

"Addison," he groaned, and hid his eyes with his free hand. He kept them covered for what felt like a full minute. His lips whitened and reddened as he pressed his mouth into a kinked prim demi-smirk. I'd never seen a similar expression appear on his face. I thought he might actually scream at me, might call me out for being a secretive little shit. This thought lifted my spirits. I don't know why.

But all he said, after unshading his eyes, was: "Can you at least tell me why you threw out all those plastic bags? There were six garbage bags full of perfectly good plastic bags. I found them where you left them with the trash. Were you just not going to *tell* me? We could have *used* them. Some of them." He spoke as though in visceral pain. I *wanted* to tell him, for a second. To tell him everything. What would have been the point, though? My face was even hotter. My eyelids trembled, the muscles at the top of my cheeks quivered, and horror at the tears I knew were coming constricted my throat.

And then I was saying, "It's like *all right*, Dad, like it's all right. I just like don't think it would be a very good *idea* to tell you." With a spurt of shame I started weeping, loud and windy sobs. Standing leaning at the threshold of my parents' bedroom and crying, palming my face. My father wearing his costume, the deerstalker slipping back from the crown of his head. God, it was painful. The crying itself, I mean. Humiliating. Crying at my age is the ultimate symptom of dicklessness. And why is *crying* painful? What sense does *that* make? Though it does lighten your burden, I guess. The pain didn't subside. He put his arms around me, which is something I can't even remember the last time he did, and I stood there shuddering and choking back my cries. Of what? I have no idea. I waited until I was calmer to break away, we exchanged a timid nod, and then I ran downstairs and lay in my cold bed until I heard Fatima arrive. They made less noise than usual, getting ready to go. My father was not cracking his desperate jokes. While they were at the party, I slipped the gun out of my now-empty safe and into his kiln. He had it going then, most of the time, attempting I think to re-create his Greek urn, the one that had exploded in the first days of the fall. A real spasm of productivity. And when I went to retrieve it the next morning, as he and Fatima were sleeping off the champagne and my weed, I saw it had been melted and warped into a thumby fist of metal. No longer recognizable as the work of human hands.

That night I could not sleep. Spare me your theories about my wanting to open a new chapter in relations with my father. Wanting things to be different. People are what they are, and wishing them to change is foolish. And insulting. I was not even thinking about *him*, anyway. I was thinking about something Mr. Broadus had said to me. About Kevin's having a pager. About there being certain "indications" that he had destroyed, before the police could search Kevin's room. You have to understand that what I'm about to say I mean as a strange compliment to Kevin. *He was a drug dealer.* A fellow of the craft. Maybe he was less of an asshole than I am. I don't know. I didn't know him. I do know, however, what all the evidence suggests. So I felt even worse. His death was my fault, somehow, right? Because we both sold weed? I know it's confusing. Narcissistic, even. But I wouldn't let go of it. That whole long night. Lying in my bed, hands folded on my chest, forcing myself into guilt. Maybe getting rid of all my business equipment had freed up my mind to focus on stupid shit. I even got a little proud of my guilt. I was a sinner, and therefore all the sin of the world touched on me. I didn't think of it in those terms. I just kept forcing myself to think of Kevin's face and then forcing myself to feel awful. You can do that, you know, with enough practice. And then the awfulness wouldn't come on command, and that's when it got so ridiculous that I jumped out of bed and smashed my knee into my night table, which knocked over my lamp. The bulb flashed blue as it died.

Kevin's death was *not* my fault. Many, many other things were, but not that. I'd never even felt guilty for it. I had just tried to make myself feel guilty for it. And how fucked-up is that? To seek the pleasure of guilt, the pleasure of self-abasement. And I knew, in that moment I knew: now or ever, there would be no answer. I was certain of that. The thing Mr. Broadus said about the watch made me certain of it. There was no plan behind the death. There was no cause. Some trophy-collecting motherfucker had taken Kevin's life. Someone with a windowless white van. No *business killer* would do that. I mean, David Cash wouldn't. Not that he's a killer. But he's a better businessman than Noel, and will someday eclipse him. He's another natural. Just with a different upbringing. No, Kevin's death occurred at random, along with the deaths of Turquoise Tull and Brandon Gambuto.

Remember them? They died too, except my stupid obsessional personality erased them. So what if Kevin took the most bullets! Maybe the guy who shot him hated his invulnerable smile. The blank-faced man. You might as well just call him Mr. Circumstance, because that's what he is, was, and will be. Yes, the police failed. Yes, I failed. We all failed. Remember what I said before about how you can't manage tragedy? You can't. You can't stop Mr. Circumstance. He waits everywhere, with infinite patience and zero mercy. You can't avoid or efface the bleak sight of the wrecks and ruins he leaves among us. Kevin. Stokey the bum. Noel Bradley. My father. Mr. Vanderleun. Mr. Broadus. All damaged, all injured and stunted, because they were guilty or because they were innocent. You're laughing by now at all this *grimness*. But I was there. I saw it firsthand. I'm not lying. Don't think I'm lying because I'm young. You think I'm lying, I'll introduce you to six million dead Jews, including a million children, and the tens of millions of others who died in our wonderful century, crushed, mangled, raped, tortured, frozen, mutilated, buried alive, burned, gassed, garroted, starved, drowned, impaled, fed to their bunkmates, injected with phenol, flung into the ripped-open hillsides and left for the frost to cover, eyes and mouths agape. So fuck you. Fuck you! That's your answer. Unless some miracle occurs, you have to accept it. *I* had to accept it. You've seen what I had to *go* through in order to accept it. Now *you* accept it. You motherfuckers.

XVIII.

LADIES AND GENTLEMEN, you've asked me to explain what my best and worst qualities are. As a prerequisite for admission to your university. This essay was choice number two, of six options. The other topics, frankly, I found insipid. *Explain what your name means to you, and why. You're having a conversation with Plato: what is the first question you ask him? Write about one of your friends—who's at least fifty years older than you.* I mean, come the fuck on! *What is your best quality? What is your worst quality?*, on the other hand, is intriguing. I've provided all the necessary transcripts and whatnot, and you'll have all of it by your admission deadline. So everything's clear. And we're finally there. At the answer, I mean. If you've read this far, just have a scintilla more of patience.

Do you know what November Criminals are? It's kind of a magical-sounding term, right? People who steal winter, some fairy-tale bullshit like that? Or a band name, some über-pretentious band name, and the band is nothing but a drum machine and a French guy playing the electric cello. But, happily, November Criminals were real. At least conceptually. The term was developed in Germany in the interwar years. It came out of the fears and hatreds of a whole constellation of political interests.

High-ranking government officials. Demobbed soldiers, many of whom were injured and prevented from earning a living. Impoverished working-class people whose lives had been wrecked by the economic catastrophes after the end of the First World War. German patriots, both of the real and rabble-rousing kind, lowborn and highborn, philosophers and political criminals. Protofascists. And, of course, Germany's most enduring political group, anti-Semites.

November Criminal was originally a slur aimed at the German politicians who signed the Treaty of Versailles, whom the above groups considered to be traitors to the causes of Germany in the war: glory, military science and potency, and the right for their nation to retain its eccentric and undemocratic political arrangements. Although these arrangements were not *illiberal.* At least when held up in comparison to the political lives of the nations making war on Germany. Especially the United States under Wilson, a president who resegregated the federal government, launched campaigns of terror against perceived internal political threats, and involved American military might in a European conflict, at a huge cost, for no reason other than to gratify his bloodthirsty belief in historical progress. Let's give it up for Woodrow Wilson! Racist and authoritarian. And proud of both! Now there's like some institute named after him at Princeton University. I learned this from the brochure they sent me. My textbook skips all of this stuff. About how bad Wilson and FDR were, I mean. Dr. Karlstadt, who describes Wilson, FDR, and Kennedy as the holy trinity of American presidents (that's *verbatim*; she actually said *holy trinity*), doesn't want to discuss these issues. So I had to read up on them in a book I dug out of my parents' bookcases. Which is to say my mother's bookcases. My father's not much of a reader. Best sellers, but the kind pretentious critics back. My mother, though, had wide-ranging tastes. Including a lot of European history. She had this one book from the 1970s called *Before Us Darkness*, about Germany in the interwar period. Written by this guy Jürgen Bitzius.

An awesome book. Calm and somber. In its pages I found out all that stuff about Wilson, and also about the November Criminals. A term that, as things worsened in Germany, became more popular, expanding to include supporters of the Weimar Republic. It took on a metaphysical aspect: someone who, through weakness and disingenuousness, betrayed his country. Not by spying or profiteering, but by morally undermining the war effort. Yes, the concept *November Criminal* is a spacious one. And it enjoyed—I'm sure you're shocked to hear this—considerable overlap with Germany's traditional object of blame, the Jews. Who had been assigned the broadest responsibility for all inequality and hardship in German society. As had been done for centuries, and as the German spirit would continue to do for two and half decades longer. Germany only stopped *then* because the government had killed 89 or 90 percent of the Jews remaining there after hostilities had opened, so *blaming* stopped making a great deal of sense. I mean, not that it ever made sense, but you can't whip people up into a frenzy against some group if the group has already been *eradicated*. You can't destroy what no longer exists.

Now, just as a side note, I should point out that Germany's Jews were *extremely* patriotic. They were not November Criminals. Tens of thousands died in the First World War. They were not patriots out of fear, either, but because they *wanted* to be Germans. Blaming them for the fall of Germany, when it was a simple case of inferior numbers, bad luck, and inept leadership, as is the case with every defeated nation, was just absurd. That didn't stop anyone, though. And everybody knows what the eventual consequences of that hatred were. That *insistence* that Jews creep around corroding everything. That we're treasonous by some ontological quality. We don't have to *do* anything to commit treason. Other than exist.

So what the fuck does this have to do with the essay question you set me? I believe with all firmness that I am a November Criminal, a betrayer by nature. Someone guilty at the feet of everyone else for his petty, sordid life and his petty, sordid crimes. An ontological failure. If you see what I mean. There you go! An answer to the second half of your essay question. As for the first, I'd argue: a November Criminal *by definition* does not have *any* good qualities. So there it is. All of it. All the emptiness and moral vacuity you could want. The killer: gone. The implements of my quest: gone. Kevin, my secret brother in the craft: gone. The whole result of my investigations amounted to a single dead dog and a four-inch gash on the back of my scalp. Nothing is ever explicable in full. Only human character reveals anything worthwhile. I am a November Criminal. That is my worst quality. Every man has to be a literary critic at some point in his life, drawing retarded comparisons and making psychological deductions. Most of these are wrong. I am right. I am guilty. I fucking know it.

And as a November Criminal, I can say that, while November Criminality may not have been prevalent in 1920s Germany, it sure as shit exists in contemporary America, where it thrives in the most educated stratum of society. I know you don't believe me. I know you don't believe thousands of reasonable, bourgeois people violate and corrode *through their mere existence* the principles of equality, of exceptionless equality, of impossible equality, that the founders of our country articulated and betrayed. No one would disagree that a guy who owned slaves, in the context of the ideal America, is a November Criminal. A traitor. Not in a legal sense. But that's the *point* of November Criminals. Their treason isn't *legal*. It's spiritual. Which leaves room for all sorts of less obvious, *sublimated* forms of treachery. You can decide for yourself, though: I'm going to tell you now what happened to my money. The eighteen grand I won at the dogfight, I mean, won with the savings I had tried to sacrifice to the Potomac. The money that got left behind at the Broadus home during my collapse, and gave me some worried hours during my convalescence. Ladies and gentlemen of the admissions board of the University of Chicago—if that is in fact the appropriate manner of addressing you; if you do in fact constitute a board—I *promised* you a circus-like closing event. And I'm going to deliver. I just have to explain the setup a little more, so you can appreciate the real piquancy of the whole thing.

I got back to school on Monday, October 16. My absence had not caused any real commotion. No one asked me why I had stopped answering my pager. There are, after all, plenty of other retail vendors in my particular market. Though the hair had grown back in over the scar a bit, Mr. Vanderleun was obsequious about my wound. I guess he thought I'd received it in a just cause or something. As he'd gotten his. Classwork and homework stopped enraging me. The impulse to shout down everyone in the world seemed to have vanished from my character. Even Alex I could stand. I no longer had to stop myself from correcting her. And there was one really, really awesome thing about going back. I discovered that Digger would sit with me, even if she didn't talk. And I was okay with that. Talking is overrated. We sat saying nothing, eating our sandwiches and pears; we walked side by side saying nothing in the halls. Silence from her is better than conversation from anyone. Even the decisive way she swings her arms is better than other people talking. And I appreciated her generosity. No one wants to be around people who have involved them in failures. Especially if you have as fundamentally *noble* a character as Digger does. It made homeroom bearable and lunch downright idyllic. And we walked to and from class together, fellow cadets. We always parted ways when school ended. I didn't try any more stunts. No grabbing her coat. We shook hands, and that was it. That was how it had to be.

So we pressed on, for a week, for ten days. Ms. Erlacher, perhaps assuming that my having been out of class for so long had blunted my skills, picked me to do a sight translation of a text no one in class had seen before. This was her way of pop-quizzing us on grammar and syntax. There'd be a block of Latin on the blackboard when we walked into the classroom, and all the idiots would groan about it. We had to translate it, or as much as we could, in the first five minutes of class. And then she would choose one person to read his translation, as a way of keeping all her students subdued with fear, I guess. This time we were being grilled on the ablative absolute, which is this really economical way Latin has of explaining the specific secondary events and conditions under which another, primary event occurred. Like, for example, *Urbe capta Aeneas fugit*. Which means literally "With the city captured, Aeneas fled," or "The city having been captured, Aeneas fled," and in smoother English "After the city was captured, Aeneas fled." *Urbe capta* is the ablative absolute, in this example: a noun (*urbs*, *urbis*, feminine, city) in the ablative case coupled with a modifying participle (*capta*, the ablative feminine singular past participle of *capio*, *capere*, "to take, seize, or capture"). Get it? There are four basic flavors of ablative absolute: one each using the past and present participles, one where one noun modifies the other, and one where an adjective modifies a noun, although a lot of the time that adjective is itself derived from a past participle, so it's debatable whether that's its own thing or not. Whatever. Not that hard, really.

The chosen passage did not ascend the heights of difficulty Ms. Erlacher thought it did. It was long, yes, and syntactically involved, but once you figured out that it was just an extended series of ablative absolutes explaining the various things that had happened before Caesar sat down to dine in his tent—some tribes were subdued, some soldiers got paid, that sort of thing—piece of fucking cake, right? She never told us the sources of these quotes; she wanted us going at them blind. And that morning she picked me to share my work, her eyes dimming with rage because I finished writing after about a minute. "Mr. Schacht! You seem to have hurried through. As usual. Would you care to share?" I got a hundred. As usual. This happened two Fridays after my return. I really wanted to tell Digger, but I refrained. I managed not to call her that weekend, although the urge had gotten stronger than ever. Instead, I started looking through the college brochures. I found that I could not take my eyes off the totally ordinary people photographed for them, in libraries or on greenswards. And I found myself thinking a lot about my high school's motto.

Yes, we have a motto. Yes, it's in Latin. *Haec olim meminisse iuvabit.* "Someday it will make us happy to remember these things." It's from the *Aeneid*, actually. Although, with typical dishonesty, my school has shortened it and considerably altered the meaning in doing so. Big A says it during a pep talk to his crewmen. The "things" he's talking about are the loss of thirteen of his army's ships, the wreck of Troy, and other catastrophes. And what he actually says is, *Forsan et haec olim meminisse iuvabit*, which means "Someday, perhaps, it will make us happy to remember even these things." You see the difference? Kind of a hilarious source for a high school motto, right? I cannot figure out what the fuck our founders were thinking, in both choosing it and then editing it.

It was with this dubious precept in mind that I walked into homeroom the following Monday, the penultimate day of October. The usual halfhearted Halloween decorations, the orange and black streamers and crepe that were used interchangeably now and during Thanksgiving, defaced our hallways. Once everyone had quieted down, Mr. Vanderleun informed us that he had a "very special" announcement. After some stump wiggling, he revealed that I had, in fact, missed out on something important in the life of John F. Kennedy students. At the beginning of the month an anonymous donor had given the school a "very gener-ous" sum to set up a yearly writing award. It was going to be called the Kevin Broadus Memorial Prize. We all remembered Kevin, didn't we? (I was tempted to say, *Yes, and he'll be missed. He had a genuine musicality.*) He outlined the requirements of the prize: a two-thousand-word essay on a socially or politically "relevant" topic (that's the word he used, *relevant*), to be judged by him, Dr. Karlstadt, and Ms. Arango. "We had a real flood of applicants," he huffed, "just an *avalanche.*" His tone made me suspect there had been almost none. You know? Over-insistent. Then he said that he was *delighted* to inform us that the first winner had been chosen. It had been hard, he asserted, to choose from *so many.* (I was sure he was lying about this, now.) But the grain was sifted, and there would be an assembly that afternoon to announce the winner. And, of course, to commemorate Kevin. "And so, I think if you'll all just applaud when she stands up, the winner is right here in this room! Alex Faustner, everyone!" Who was surprised by this? Not me! She *took a bow*. Her gleaming blue-black hair flipped up and down. I looked at Digger and Digger looked back, and no one made a sound, except for Mr. Vanderleun. "It's a thousand *dollars*, people," he said, to spur our morale and applause.

I told Digger everything at lunch. I didn't care if she answered me or not. Everything I lacked time to explain to her in Sidney Memorial. About the dogfight and the money. How the Broaduses had kept it, and how I was glad. How they *had* to be the anonymous donors. I had no idea how to feel about Alex Faustner winning the prize. Although that's what she and her ilk do: they win prizes while the wretched suffer. Right? Because they're such altruists? Digger didn't say anything, still. I talked at her for ten minutes without stopping, and she didn't say anything. She had a lot of reason to doubt my deductive capacities. But she didn't run away, either. Which I assumed meant she believed me. The crimson streak in her hair caught the light. It made her seem younger; it made her face more fragile. At least in retrospect. All I knew *then* was that it increased my serenity. I took my pear out of my lunch bag and offered it to her. That was the deal. She'd eat half and give it back. For some reason she never has pears in her house. Maybe her mother hates them. She took down about 35 percent of it in a single bite. I could just *tell* she wanted to say, *Good pear*. She did not. That's how strong her resolve is.

The festivities were set to begin at one p.m. We walked into the assembly together, into the private G&T row, and sat next to each other and waited. I wanted her knee to graze mine. We had not yet reached that phase of relations. *This is going to be good*, I thought. *Whatever else might happen, this is going to be memorable.* First we had the Singing Tigers, performing "Mary Don't You Weep." Alex didn't complain this time, that disingenuous cunt! There were three people onstage: Dr. Karlstadt, Mr. Vanderleun, and Alex. A fucked-up, über-proud family. (Where were her parents, though?) Mr. Vanderleun explained what the whole thing was about, talked about social justice, his stump wiggling with vigor, and then introduced Alex, whom he called a "very special young woman." He ran through her career at Kennedy, and the various encomia her teachers had bestowed on her. Someone from the band was playing the piano the whole time, these cheesy "stirring" chord progressions and recursions. Dr. Karlstadt talked a bit about . . . Honestly, who gives a fuck? You know how these people talk. I was clenching my fists in anticipation. Not to do violence, but just because of the unbearable tension coursing through me. Digger stared with withering skepticism at Dr. Karlstadt's flapping scarf until she ended her content-free speech. Then we had more piano music. Alex walked up to the mike, which Dr. Karlstadt had lowered, and twiddled the screw on the side of the stand. She cleared her throat. I'm not kidding: she cleared her throat.

And then the shit-show began. Alex had chosen, for some incomprehensible reason, to write about the problems of young black men. "The violence in the ghettos is often a sign of *competition*," was how she began. A statement that contains no meaning. And it went downhill from there. Her essay was full of fake energy. A dreadful imitation of intellectual activity. She just kept going on and on about violence and African Americans and African Americans and violence, as though all African Americans did was commit violence, suffer violence, think about violence, and as though "African Americans" constitute some ontologically single entity. No particularity—just violence! Now, everyone in the school knew that Alex had never set foot anywhere near these places whose spiritual condition she was bemoaning. That she had spoken to Kevin maybe twice. That she is one of the wealthiest people in school. And that she could not possibly have a single iota of experience to justify the amazing and horrifying generalities she was regurgitating.

African Americans are violent. This is not their fault, though. That was the basic theme of her lecture. *My fault, and yours, and even hers, because* . . . Why? I guess she thinks that even now black people are the slaves of whites, and that their whole existence is defined by their reactivity to whites. Saying, in essence: *Okay, guys, so, we enslaved you once and it was the most important and decisive thing that ever happened to you and now you still are our slaves in spirit, and we pity you, so here're some college admissions and Black History Month and my stupid speech and we're all good. Right? We're even now? We paid you back?* It's the ultimate fantasy of a slave owner: to own not just the body, but the soul too. Alex's outlook rests on that principle, whether or not she's aware of it. Pure November Criminality, no? Alex and Vanderleun and Karlstadt and the whole disgusting system of G&T, the whole intolerable wreck and mockery of life, created and preserved as lip service to the highest progressive principles, and dedicated in actuality to the perpetuation of hatred. Hidden, covert hatred, yes. But hatred all the same. Social justice doesn't have anything to do with Alex, or Black History Month, or Mr. Vanderleun's lost finger. It's synonymous with hatred. The way youth is synonymous with stupidity. Alex went on and on and on. Mr. Vanderleun eyeballed us, fiddling with his hair, pink tongue shoved out of the corner of his mouth. Like a fucking five-year-old. Dr. Karlstadt kept smoothing her scarf. The chorus seated facing us at the bottom of the stage rustled in their amethyst robes. Yawns, short and infrequent, riffled across the different sections of the auditorium. Alex had been speaking forever. Physical misery had crept into all my bones and veins, and was dragging me into some unbreakable condition of torpor. Nobody said anything. Everyone sitting near me squirmed and averted their eyes. Even Alex's awful friends. Tehran Wall kept rubbing the bridge of his nose, in the exact way my father does when he's too mortified to look at someone. There is some decency in the human constitution. Not mine, maybe. I mean the human constitution as a *general* proposition.

I just realized something, putting all this down. I totally forgot to tell you how Digger and I met, originally. That's a big omission. We met in ninth grade, in the second week of class. Geometry class. Taught by Mr. Street. Who is famous at Kennedy for his lacquered-looking toupee. I mean, it sits on his head like a helmet. No single strand ever moves, but sometimes it slips back or forward a bit as a whole entity. This is what introduced me to Digger: I made a loud joke about the toupee: "Looks like the whole support structure is just coming *loose* there, Bob," I intoned in the trembling bass of a newscaster watching some tragedy, as the hairpiece slid back. Prompted by one of Mr. Street's too-violent head nods in the course of a proof. He heard me, as I'd meant him to, and he got purple and furious, and asked anyone else if they thought it was funny. Digger raised her hand. So we both got detention—"custodial duty," as they call it at Kennedy. It means you have to do the work our slack-ass janitors leave undone. We spent a week picking up trash at Kennedy's property line. Taking frequent weed-smoking breaks.

I had been so *impressed* by the look she shot me when she raised her hand to answer Mr. Street, to agree that she thought my joke was funny, which it wasn't. She deadpanned, yeah. But this half-smile bowed her lips. This made the ingenuous blankness of her face all the more devastating. And you know what? When I turned to gauge her reaction to Alex's speech, she was staring at me in the same way: *I cannot believe the human species is capable of this unforgivable jackassery.* I had to act. I had no idea what to do, but I had to do something. How can you refuse Digger Zeleny's sapphire-colored imperative gaze?

Vengeance is the only fit memorial of the dead. You know who said that? This guy! Addison motherfucking Schacht. I'm not saying that the vacuity and heartlessness of Alex's speech (which, thank God, Kevin's parents were not in attendance to hear, at least that I could see) *justify* what I did next. My actions were theatrical and boorish. Shocking, I know. I bounced to my feet, muttering, "Excuse me," until I reached the center aisle. Down which I began marching. I knew what I was doing would work. Yes, I had failed up until now. I knew this new idea would work *because I had no plan, just an impulse.* I was singing a funny song I know. I learned it last year, with Digger. We'd gone to see this movie at the Camelot called *The Bridge on the River Kwai*. Which is an awesome movie. About this tough-as-shit old British soldier who loses his mind. And it has this whistled march in it called "The Colonel Bogey March." It's kind of the theme of the movie. The old soldier uses it to keep his men disciplined and cheery. After *The Bridge on the River Kwai* ended, we went to browse in Don't Shoot, and the old hippie owner heard me humming the song. "They made up words. During the war, you know," he said, one finger closed in a copy of some book called *Gravity's Rainbow*. (Retarded title, by the way.) "To the song." I was stunned and creeped out. But Digger said, "Yeah? Let's hear them, sir." So he told us. And I remembered the words now, swinging my arms and knees as I struck up my

"Colonel Bogey March" down the sloping aisle to the stage, where six human eyes goggled at my approach in consternation. The song goes:

Hitler
Has only one big ball
Göring
Has two but ver-ree small
Himmler's
got something simmler
And Joseph Go-balls
Has no balls
At all.

Pretty good, right? The owner seemed proud of it when he explained. It was a war song. A war song of the British against the Germans, from the Second World War. Pretty clever, right?

As I marched down the sloping aisle, I belted out these words in my horrible, tune-free singing voice, just *fucking up* the whole ceremony, all the piety evaporating. Mr. Vanderleun's stump waggled in boundless fury. I got in a chorus and a half before he had the presence of mind to shout me down: "Do you have something to add, Mr. Schacht?" And I did! "Hey, Alex," I screamed. "What's the difference between a Jew and a loaf of bread?" The question that started it all! The eternal recurrence of the same! "That's not *funny*, Addison," Alex admonished into the microphone, trying her best to inject maternal dismay into her voice and producing instead the tones of some *drag queen* or something, all bulky and throaty. There was a huge silence. Dr. Karlstadt got to her feet and Mr. Vanderleun started to mumble and shout. My assault was crumbling. But then from the back I heard Digger: "I don't know! What *is* the difference between a Jew and a loaf of bread?" And then she and I chanted in *disjointed stereo*, "A loaf of bread doesn't scream when you put it in the oven!" "All right, all right, all right, all right," whined Mr. Vanderleun.

Alex didn't cry. This time. She was a *prizewinning essayist*, now. And crying does not befit such eminence. She steeled herself. Tossed her inky hair. I noticed as I glanced back up the aisle, looking into the now über-uncomfortable legions of my school-mates, I noticed that the look on her face *reminded* me of some-one. Someone I'd met recently and could not summon up. But someone nonetheless infuriating. So instead of going and sitting down, I kept singing. At the top of my horrid voice. Think of a frog being sodomized. I turned back to the seated Singing Tigers and yelled, "Come on, you fuckers!" at them. I started waving my hands: *Up, up, sing!*

Nothing happened at first, except that large swaths of the audience started laughing at me. I could hear Digger howling with glee. The more people laughed the more frantically I waved, and eventually to my amazement a few Singing Tigers took up the song, and then a few more, and then they were *all* on their feet roaring along with me, with this unknown miserable boy, this child, they were singing the stirring trivial song in their mingled voices, masking my horrible screech. Dr. Karlstadt's face was now the same gull color as her scarf, and Mr. Vanderleun was on his feet, and those not singing along just *barraged* me and Alex and the whole disastrous show with whistles, yells, and catcalls. Nobody could do anything to shut us up. Their authority, their pukey authority, was for the moment suspended. I didn't know any of the Singing Tigers. I didn't know any of the people in the upper rows. I didn't know their names or their hopes or their vices. And I knew that they thought I was ridiculous, absurd, pathetic, frail. Yet we sang together, out of boredom, out of disgust with piety, out of the innate adolescent impulse to lawlessness and disorder. For three solid, rousing choruses of "The Colonel Bogey March," Hitler's Testicles edition:

Hitler
Has only one big ball
Göring
Has two but ver-ree small
Himmler's
got something simmler
And Joseph Go-balls
Has no balls
At all.

Imagine this dumb insouciance lifted up on a geyser of voices, lifted up to our auditorium ceiling, which is painted with patchy frescos, Plato and Frederick Douglass and the Marquis de Lafayette and Kennedy himself, a catastrophe of time. Stiff, self-pleased figures arranged without sense or purpose. They smirked down at me all my four years at Kennedy. Four years! The choir fucked up the words at first, but by the second chorus they'd gotten it right. Some of the Singing Tigers even clapped out a countertime. It was primordial chaos. When people lift their voices together, you don't have unity. That's a lie. You have a tremendous, inarguable cacophony. Warm, vivid cacophony. In the ranks of chairs, people sang, whispered to their friends, stood up to mock my gestures, making pinched faces. One guy in the third row did a cruel and perfect mimicry of my movements, my uncertain, spiteful movements. And we'd never spoken. Never even seen each other, that I could recall. The Singing Tigers came to a crescendo, and cut the tempo, so that "No balls at all" came out as a long, dragging flourish. Then, silence. One breath. Mr. Vanderleun was still droning away like an impotent burglar alarm. I gave two stiff middle fingers to Alex and her academic sponsors.

The applause and laudatory shouting started as the Singing Tigers bowed and danced around, out of sync now after their improvised performance. The students were NOT cheering me. I was a *distraction* from the big show, an eccentricity. Let's get that clear. I am anonymous, and I like it. This was not *Addison Schacht's Big Moment*. Those cheers were *part* of the insuppressible surge of gaiety and anger, not a response to it. They were for the Singing Tigers, our collective voice. The Tigers are much better at what they do than our mediocre sports teams. They're always winning regional contests. People *always* cheer them. And anyway it was all gestural. I know that. It accomplished nothing. I *dare* you to blame me, though. For even a millisecond. That outburst during Alex's speech was the only half-decent thing I've ever done in my life. And I know the decayed and worthless nature of my character. I'm not good for many more such acts. If any. I marched back to my seat, hoarse and singing. Digger was laughing helpless laughs. Soon my tenth disciplinary action over the course of four years at John F. Kennedy would descend. That's two-point-five offenses per year, on average. Kevin had none. Digger has two. What makes *me* so delightful to behold?

And I *did* figure out whom Alex Faustner reminded me of. It took me until I got home. After a spittle-flecked lecture from Mr. Vanderleun, with Dr. Karlstadt supervising, cooing out how *disappointed* she was in me. By chance I examined my copy of

Rage, lying on the floor next to my bed where I'd hurled it. It was Nathan Levitan, world-famous Jew and author. She reminded me of him. With his permanent, sad grimace of . . . disappointment? Complacence? Who the fuck knows. Fucking Levitan! I cackled when I realized, whooped and crowed. My father shouted down to ask what the matter was. He has a good ear. Dr. Karlstadt suspended me for eight weeks, and sentenced me to a further twelve weeks of sensitivity training at the hands of the Diversity Outreach mediators. I would be getting back to school right after Christmas break. Just in time for the start of the new millennium. I had been expecting much worse.

XIX.

Do you know about *LACRIMAE RERUM*? I said before
that Virgil was an exception to the desertlike inhumanity of Latin
writers. And *lacrimae rerum* is one of the reasons why. It's from
when Aeneas is looking at those murals I mentioned before? In
Carthage? The full lines run: *En Priamus! Sunt hic etiam sua
praemia laudi; sunt lacrimae rerum et mentem mortalia tangunt.
Solve metus, feret haec aliquam tibi fama salutem. Sic ait, atque
animum pictura pascit inani.* They mean " 'And Priam! Here, too,
his glory has its reward; here too are tears for things, and mortal
matters touch the soul. Away with fear. This renown will save,'
Aeneas said, and his spirit drew sustenance from the unreal
image." Beautiful stuff, no? Exactly what you'd expect from an
epic hero. Aeneas *seems* to be saying that, despite all the murder,
all the smoke and death, despite Neoptolemus, "glory has its
reward." Tears will be shed, life will continue, and the fame of
glorious deeds will redeem us from our sufferings. And maybe
that's true.

But you have to admit: the very last word of the scene is *inani*,
which means "unreal, insubstantial." Even "empty." Doesn't that
call everything coming before it into question? I mean, Aeneas
is crying as he says all this, weeping in front of his best friend,

Achates, and even if you take him at his word, it's still not a very comforting proposition, and if murals ratifying your glory are supposed to be so fucking great, why does Virgil then remind us that they're unreal? Just images? I'd say it's a trick on his part, a typical one, like the thing with having Aeneas return to the world of the living through the gate of ivory. I'd say (and maybe I'm wrong) this scene implies that even in calm, splendid Carthage, you can see the hideous, corrosive nature of existence. Imagine it: Aeneas has come all this way, his city is destroyed, the victorious Greeks are hurtling through its streets and laughing, his wife is dead, he's lost a huge number of men, he's overcome all these dire obstacles. Then he arrives in Carthage, and what does he find? This whole mural depicting the sack of Troy, the wreck of his own life. He can't escape from it! It confronts him, pursues him. Wherever he goes. He leaves Carthage, eventually, and Dido kills herself, like I said. But before he goes, he explains to Dido and her court what happened, which is how *we* find out. About the Trojan horse, about Sinon's treachery, about Neoptolemus. About everything.

So isn't Aeneas kind of saying these "tears" are universal? Permanent and ubiquitous? *Sunt lacrimae rerum* can be read simply as, "There are tears for things." The verb *to be* sometimes works that way in Latin. *Tears for things*: inherent in their existence, almost. You can't get away from it. All you can do is try to impose a shape on it, like Aeneas when he's telling his own sad story to the Carthaginian nobility. Probably every lasting thing created by human beings has a touch of this quality, of being infused with tears. Right? Is that crazy? It seems right to me. Eventually you have to look at the horrifying facts of your own life, of life as a general proposition; whether it was your fault or not that things went wrong, eventually everybody has to look at the shape of their life. You can't avoid it, and if you try to you'll probably end up like Mr. Vanderleun, incapable of knowing anything about anything, and filled with fucking certitude. I don't understand how in my life, which has basically been a safe and sheltered one, I could even have had these ideas. I guess you can't worry about the sources of your thinking. I've had too much time to think, recently. Which has had its usual bad consequences.

What do you want me to do, though? Life has been sort of dull since they suspended me. I knew it would; I tried to prepare myself for it. But it's still been really fucking boring. I sleep a lot. I read Virgil. I've been spending two afternoons a week at the grocery store as well. I had never gone to one under my own volition before. I mean to do like real shopping, for a household. It's mostly for me, because one morning I got absolutely enraged: there was literally no food in our house. Not a decade-old can of salmon, not pumpkin pie filling, not sourballs, fucking nothing. Not even ketchup. Why? Why was this the case? I mean, the fucking store is right around the corner. A three-minute drive. Sometimes, when the sun is out and casting stark, pale winter shadows, I even walk there, through the mild cold, my breath condensing and spiraling away.

Don't think I've gotten all sentimental or anything like that. I have literally nothing to do, and it's sociologically amazing to shop for food in the early afternoons. The store is mostly empty, but the people who *are* there are the biggest congregation of freaks I've ever seen, and I've met plenty of freaks. There's this one woman, a regular, who buys two canned hams and a carton of cigarettes every time she comes in, or at least every time I've waited behind her in line. She has a whole collection of watered-silk muumuus, with childish daisies or koi printed on them. Then there's Old Knobby, as I call him in my head, whose hands are pebbled with these brown, leathery-looking nodules, some kind of weird skin condition. From the wrist to the tips of his fingers, dun-colored lumps and protrusions. It's fucking nauseating. And remember that junkie I saw in the Tip-Top the morning Digger and I hatched our plan? He's an afternoon customer too! I rammed him with my cart. I didn't mean to. Or I only sort of meant to. He was shuffling down the produce aisle at this glacial pace, and he didn't even really respond when the front of my cart smashed into him, just grunted and kept fondling the heads of iceberg lettuce. This is my new tribe. I'm glad to say that my food purchases are more normal than theirs: regular old staples like tangerines and jarred peanuts. Although I have purchased a carton or two of cigarettes. So who am I to judge?

Lieutenant Huang came by, right after my latest exile began. He wanted to ask my father a few follow-up questions about the broken window. Neither of them had been able to find the instrument of its breakage: Lorriner's banner-wrapped brick, which I had returned to its saddening owner. So Huang was understandably puzzled, and my father was a bit afraid, but they managed to work it out between them so that neither one lost much face. They shared another awkward handshake, and Huang told me he'd read about my postering exploits. "I think you know my opinion of Arch Sexton's work as a *journalist*," he purred, "but I want to assure you that, really, we have everything under control." Fidgeting with his ring again. I guess that's why he was taking time off of heading a murder investigation to look into some stupid act of vandalism. Because he had everything under control. Then he was striding out of my house, and my father and I watched him go. Pompous, fruitless gusts of wind filled the skirts of his stone-colored trench coat. He doesn't matter. My father took almost an hour to calm down, however. Now he's put Huang's card on our fridge, with a magnet shaped like a strawberry the impossible red of welling blood. Next to it is a photo some benevolent stranger took: my father and Fatima at the Cochrane Institute party, in their absurd getups. By some miracle, they are both laughing, mouths stretched and vulnerable-looking. They're holding hands, touching fingertips, really, across an empty space on the institute's black-and-white-tiled marble floor, and hemming them is a crowd dressed in rich, clashing colors and fabrics, dominoes and monkey masks, bandages, fake fangs, capes and swords. Everything you'd expect. I wanted to hate it—the picture, I mean. I found that I could not.

I don't have much else to say. What more do *you* want to know, anyway? Factually, I mean? Still after my dick measurements, are you? You can ask Digger. That's Phoebe Anna Zeleny. With the vast resources at your disposal, you can track her down. She wants to go to MIT. I'm 99 percent certain she's going to get in. See? See how easy I make your job for you? Here're some *more* facts, free of charge. Sexton's eventual article referred to me as a "troubled young man." Which may be the one honest sentence of his career. Alex donated her prize to Planned Parenthood. My father is still seeing Fatima. She and I have started speaking to each other. It's hard, because her English is terrible and she expresses her insecurity about it as haughtiness. But whatever. I'm guilty of much worse. Also, I am *hammered*. I've been drinking wine, which I never drink. Red wine, from this bottle coated with the waxen traces of other people's handling. The label says in huge Gothic script, *Brindisi Rosso*. Red wine tastes sour. It stimulates our highest faculties. At least everyone in the ancient world makes this claim. I swiped it because I agree with them in theory, because I needed to mull something over, something difficult.

I have no weed. I haven't even smoked any since my conversation with Mr. Broadus. I guess I still need stimulation to wrangle my way through problems, though. As soon as I got even a marginal buzz, my thoughts started flowing and my heart pounded in a cerebral way. The time is now 12:56 a.m., Sunday, November 22. My house is so quiet I can hear even in my room the faint roar of the kiln, and the asphalt compressing when a car goes down my street.

Digger and I are back on speaking terms. My performance at the assembly did the trick, I think. I haven't bought or sold any drugs. And I'm actually looking forward to going back to school. My suspension will expire in about a month. I imagine things will be a lot calmer when I get back. Kevin's still dead. Noel's still fat. David Cash is still scary as fuck. I'm assuming these last two things are true. Haven't seen Noel or David for a while. How likely are they to change, though? It's been fine. Everything has been fine. So why did I take this essay up again? The deadline is almost here. Why risk it? The first draft, which was empty of truth and met all your requirements, your word limits and whatnot, was sitting on my desk in my room, under the new framed lithograph of Virgil Digger got me for my birthday. (This past Tuesday. I can finally buy cigarettes legally.) It's an illustration from the *Inferno*. Drawn by Gustave Doré. Of when Virgil first appears. Dante doubts his worthiness of such a guide, after Virgil has explained his purpose. He's tall and thin—Virgil, I mean—with the face of an exile. A wise, troubled, smooth face. Dante just looks like a muddled coward, but that's all right: he has Virgil accuse him of cowardice pretty soon after this meeting, so he probably thought he was, on some level. Although he did assign his political ene- mies to some creative and brutal tortures. So who the fuck knows.

. . .

She gave the picture to me with a little ceremony. She bought me a cupcake and stuck a candle in it, and sang. She has a good voice. Much better than mine. Though that's not hard. We were at my house. And she kissed me on the cheek. I don't know what that means. It's probably irrelevant anyway. In the light of what I'm about to explain to you. I didn't object. I'm not stupid. We had turned off all the other lights, so the candle glimmered more brightly. She laughed a low throaty laugh, and her hand caressed the back of my head, where the scar and the soft stubble of newish hair lie, and her fingers did not flinch. We heard my father come home, and the shower start up. And his warbling. He grins and sings all the time now. Who knows for how long? I think it's Fatima. No accounting for taste, right?

So what the fuck's the problem with all this? Digger's been bringing me my homework, so I don't fall behind. I've been doing college applications, too. I'm applying other places, you know. So act fast, you assholes! I have to admit that your application, despite the boring stuff on it, was the best. Also, according to your informational material you have the single biggest library building in America. Which is fucking cool. Not the biggest library system qua system (that belongs to Harvard) but the biggest *single* facility. I've been working on this essay for a long time. I didn't plan that. I wrote one version, just some nothing version, a thousand words, like what you're probably used to getting. I was planning to send it you about two weeks ago, with all the rest of the crap you demand: transcripts, recommendations. Mr. Dwight and Ms. Erlacher. I asked them through Digger, without much hope. They both agreed, to my complete surprise. I guess Ms. Erlacher doesn't hate me as much as I imagined. Maybe she fucking *misses* me or something. Or maybe they'll both write me long series of backhanded compliments. The check, fifty dollars, covering the "application fee." That's genius, ladies and gentlemen! I wish I'd thought of some similar fee in my old line of work. I could have made a fucking bundle.

All this stuff fit into a large manila envelope, addressed to you, postage affixed, the flap sealed. All I had to do was mail it. I didn't. I kind of got off on just letting it sit there, knowing all I had to do was drop it in the mail and things would change for me. I'd get to leave this striving, awful town, no more Vanderleun, no more Black History Month. I mean, maybe college is permeated with the same bullshit that high school is. I have zero experience. But I'd be fighting through it on my own, not with a fucking audience over my shoulder, my father, David, Kevin, whoever. I'd be free. Greenswards and elysian sex, all the fun you could want. And I could study the major texts of Latin literature, to say nothing of higher-level philological pursuits, all the time. Do you know how much that excites me? Not having to do classes whose subjects are hugely, impossibly vague—like World History, like English. You know, to anchor them? So they don't dissolve because of their meaninglessness? I've looked through the sample catalog. Holy fuck! *Satire and the Silver Age. The Roman Novel. Love and Death: Eros and Transformation in Ovid. The Founding of Epic Meter.* I salivated when I saw these names, because they indicate this whole world of knowledge from which I am excluded, and which I can win my way into, with luck and endurance. Right? Right? Please tell me I'm right.

Anyway, the whole deal was done. Completed. My horizon was glowing. So can you explain to me why, earlier today—or yesterday, I mean, since it's after midnight—I sat down with some paper and a pen and started writing? I mean rewriting my answer to your essay question. I couldn't stop. It *seems* to have taken forever, at this point, although not that much actual time has elapsed. Only fourteen hours. I took a short break five hours ago when I started writing about what happened after we killed the dog. I took another one about an hour ago, to go steal the wine. I thought I had finished. I drank half the bottle right away. There's a white horse on the label. My father owes me one for the weed, anyway. So it's not even really stealing. I took the breaks to clear my head. That just made it worse. Never take breaks. Constant forward momentum fends off entropy. Entropy wrecks everything. It can't be defeated. Still, though: nineteen chapters. That's a fuckload of forward momentum, if you'll permit me to use so expressive a quantity. And I'm not finished. Nineteen chapters and still not finished. Eighteen is the best number in Jewish numerology, did you know that? It's equal, if you use the weird value assignments that Hebrew letters have, to the word *life*. I don't understand how. I just know for a fact that it is. Digger told me, and she never lies. I think she gets birthday checks in units of eighteen. And seeing as I've already run one chapter over my people's lucky number, I'll try to keep this last bit brief.

My whole life is ahead of me. Even if I don't get into the University of Chicago. For classicists, which is what I want to be, graduate school matters just as much. I think. I think that's how it works. And I'm ready *not* to get in. *I* wouldn't let me in. With all this information above and beyond what's wanted or necessary I've provided. Why don't I just shut up and enjoy my good fortune at having escaped unscathed? Digger has decided I'm okay. I haven't been to see Noel and David since the night of the dogfight. Everyone's forgotten about Kevin. Except his parents, I mean. But there's the fucking problem. A huge part of the problem. Why I've spent the last hours pacing and smoking in my room, muttering to myself, starting to add to my essay and stopping. I'm late to meet Digger. We have a date, an official date. Our first. Official date, I mean. Remember? From the hospital? *The Sorrow and the Pity*, part two? We're going to take a stab at behaving like everyone else.

Digger's hand on the back of my head. The chord from the piano, when I fell. My mother's face in clay. The weight of the gun in my palm. This stack of pages. That's all I have. It's not much. It's just what happened. I can't explain it and I don't want to. Holy fuck! This is hard. Writing this is hard. It may be impossible. I'll try anyway. It's after midnight. I spent my birthday with Digger. Before she gave me my present, we didn't do anything. Just kind of wandered around smoking cigarettes. We drove past Kevin's house. The heavy, glazed-looking green curtains shone out of the front windows, and swayed a little. Other than that, no sign of activity. I love her. I don't love her in some stupid way. If it were stupid, trivial, the rest of this would be easy. It's hard and frightening, so I must love her for real. How you know, right? How else would you know? I love Digger. *What a child*, you're thinking. *Love? He's using the word* love? *What a fucking joke. He's too young to understand.* If you think that, fuck you. I don't tell lies. Not about Digger. I may be guilty of a long list of petty and secret enormities. *Not*, however, lying about loving Digger. Impossible, for me. I have no idea who any of you are, if any of you will read what I've written. I don't know anything about you. I know you as poorly as I know my classmates and my father. All this is no excuse. The stinging cramp in my hand excuses nothing. My slowed-down eyesight excuses nothing. Virgil stares with oceanic kindness down at Dante in the lithograph, surrounded by rectilinear shafts of light and mists. His face betrays the love felt by someone who regards himself as beyond love. He looks proud.

. . .

Back to *lacrimae rerum*. I've had, like I said, too much time to think. You asked me for one thousand words, ladies and gentlemen. This *has* to be more than that, and one of the reasons why is that I've had too much time to think. Too much thinking makes you nervous, makes you want to include everything, just in case. And I still haven't *said* anything, is the hilarious part. I've just gone on and on about externals, about contingent events. The most I can hope for is that the clumsiness and fear I've displayed in letting myself go on at this length help you understand the worthless sort of person I am. I guess I'm throwing myself at your feet here, and hoping that you'll see: as fragile and selfish as I am, I'm no worse than anyone else, especially the rest of the applicants you'll be dealing with. I mean, people *unlike* me, people *not* weighed down with all the vices of their era, are rare. Almost unthinkably so. I know exactly one.

I'm still avoiding the central issue here. Why add to an already overlong piece of garbage? Why extend *your* boredom? Why provoke *you* to the hatred I inspire in all authority figures? It's so fucked-up I can't even begin. I stole a bottle of wine from my father's liquor supply and have been drinking it as I sit here. I took it when I realized this horrible thing. Are you ready? I'm ready. I'm going to explain. Looked at in one light, if you take my story, just follow it from A to B or whatever, it's the story of a young man who made a number of stupid errors. Looked at in another light, though, you can derive a tremendous horror from it. I *learned* from it. I *profited* from it. November Criminality at its purest. I betray. I pervert. I can't help it. I am what those filthy proto-Nazis said. Not because I'm a Jew. Because I'm me, Addison Schacht. In metaphysical terms, I'm just as guilty as the killer. I *profited* from Kevin's death. I'm happier now. I have no right. I have less right to that than anything else. *That's* what Virgil meant, or part of it, that even in happiness there is this taste, like an undercurrent or whatever, of life being irremediably wrong.

Do you see what I mean? Everything comes at a price. Sometimes you can put the price in signs or symbols, words, an amount of money. But I can't even *tell* you what I owe. I know that it exceeds the value of my entire life, simply by geometrical principles. What the fuck, though, am I supposed to do with this debt? Can you tell me *that*, you fucking experts? I can't turn myself in to the cops. It's not a crime. I can't talk to Kevin's father. I can't *tell* anyone. If I'd thought of it before, while I was recovering, it would have been okay. People cut you slack if you're in the hospital. They get off on *indulging* you. *Now* everyone would just think I'm crazy, or trying to get attention. They'd think I was jealous of Alex getting in the paper. I'd never be able to convince anyone that this wasn't the case, that I don't give a shit about fame, that if I wanted fame I'd want *Virgil's* fame, eternal fame. The one person who might understand this is Digger. I'm not telling her. I've abused her trust enough.

I'm late to meet her. We have a firm pledge in operation to see the twelve forty-five a.m. showing of part two of *The Sorrow and the Pity*. From when I was in the hospital, remember? At the Camelot. I don't make offers like that as a joke. I was supposed to be in front of the theater ten minutes ago. What if I don't go? I won't go. I don't deserve anything. Not going would be sufficient punishment. Except it wouldn't, because it would fade, and because it would damage *her*, and I'd have contracted a new debt. I see her standing calmly on the empty street under the harplike marquee. She won't worry I'm late. Everyone is late sometimes. She has no idea what is happening inside me. I *will* go. I'll think about it. I don't know. My pen is drying up, starting to scratch the paper with that nerve-shredding sound. I'll go. I won't go. I'll go. Holy fuck. I contemplated destroying the whole thing, tossing it in the flames of my father's kiln, and offering you my original banal answer: how I love to help people, and that's my best quality, but sometimes I have trouble thinking of my own needs, and that's my worst quality. That's what I wrote, originally, before I sat down earlier today. Or yesterday, I mean. I could just send in an application no different from anyone else's in size, weight, or spiritual content. I'm so tired of this. And sorry for ever disturbing Kevin's rest. Not because of my own exhaustion. Because I recognize my guilt. Which may not make sense. To you, I mean.

But to me that's *why* it makes sense. Because it doesn't. Nothing is explicable. Not even trivial things, not even a cloud or a wave. All of those things are formed by chance. And we are too. We're just as weak, just as gone in a minute, as any of those things. I think we should find it funny that we're so transient. Every human effort expresses so much sententiousness, so much *self*. And that self is a joke, a cloud, a shadow. That's it. Then *nox est perpetua una dormienda*: "an endless night for sleeping." The poet Catullus wrote that, not Virgil. Or *vitaque cum gemitu fugit indignata sub umbras*. That's the last line of the *Aeneid*, describing the death of the Rutulian prince Turnus, Aeneas's last enemy: "and life fled with a groan, indignant, to the shades." So you don't even get the *nox perpetua*. If you're dead, by definition you can have no knowledge of eternity. It's after midnight. My hand hurts from writing. I don't know what to do. You can't exert your will over life. If there's one thing the study of Latin should teach you, it's that human beings cannot direct reality. They can do a great many things, yes, even incredible things, going down to the realm of the dead. Or founding Rome. But with permission. They have to have the blessing and assistance of a god. This is gained through loyalty. I'm not loyal. Don't mistake me for a loyal person.

I'm not even *talking* about suicide. Suicide would be too orderly and too self-respecting. I don't even deserve that. That would make me seem too important, you know? I only have one triumph: my outburst at Alex Faustner's lecture. I'm not thinking about that, though. Or about my father, and what a terrible son I've been to him, or about how I failed Digger and Kevin. What I can't get my mind off is this. Like I said, I don't think about my mother a lot. I remember her. Do you see the difference? I don't have to *think* about her, because I *remember* her. This one memory, which is always in the back of my mind. I must have been four years old. No older. It's in the morning, and I've just woken up, and she's there. Not bent over the bed or anything. Just standing quietly in the corner. I see her in my peripheral vision, but I pretend I don't for some reason, and she starts to smile, and so do I, and we both smile in silence. She's wearing a yellow sweater. Her hair is up. She has her glasses on. Rain ticks against my window. I don't want to say anything, and she doesn't speak, and all of a sudden this understanding comes over me: neither of us has to talk. It's not necessary. That's how it was with her. At least, that's how I remember it. I didn't think of it that way at the time. I was a fucking kid. That memory is basically the only thing that stands between me and (write it, you fucking coward, you fucking asshole) total oblivion.

It's after midnight. I'm writing as fast as I can, because I'm late, but not late enough to wreck my life, so this part is less legible than what's come before, I can see that. I know what I have to do. I'm going to do it. I just need a minute, five minutes. You'd think that with how fragile everything is, our whole condition and everything, it would be the same as a lie. It's not. Not at all. I don't believe *that*. I'm not a nihilist. *Death* is the consummate falsehood. Maybe that's the real meaning of the Gate of Ivory. That perfection arrives through it, which is basically the same as death. Because life—where's the perfection there? *Lacrimae rerum*, right? The sign of life. Perfection would *kill* it. Extinguish it. I'm going to leave the melted gun here while I'm out, to hold down the unruly pile of torn-out notebook paper I've been scrawling on. As proof. In case anyone finds my essay and thinks it's all fiction. Then, tomorrow, I will send it off to you. Not tomorrow. Today, I mean. It's after midnight. I won't send the gun. That would be insane. Just the document itself, which can be corroborated in all its particulars. It's after midnight, when the day begins. Isn't that fucked-up? That the day begins in darkness? I'm afraid. I don't deserve anything. But fuck you, all the same. Fuck you for thinking that all this *proves* anything. It proves *nothing*, nothing at all. A whole kingdom of nothing. You can refuse me admission. You can call the cops. You can lock me in chains or kill me. Me or anyone else. It won't prove anything. When Digger blew out my birthday candle, as she bent her head, a summer-colored moon of light rested on her face. I saw its pinpoints dance in her deep eyes. For a whole second. Then the flame went out. And we were in the dark.